WHAT COURSES THROUGH HER BLOOD

ASHLEY R. ODONOVAN

4 CHAMBER PUBLISHING

What Courses Through Her Blood

A What Lies Beyond the Realms Novel

By Ashley R. O'Donovan

Map and interior art by Kathrin- Instagram: e_kath_art

DEDICATION

To my mother. I'll always dance…even if it's only in spirit.

CLOUDRUM

THE FERAL SEA

SHIFTING FOREST

LYCAN REALM

CINDER TERRITORY

SORCERER REALM

TEMPEST MOON

BLACK FOREST

DARK LUNAR REACH

MAD TERRITORY

LAMIA REALM

MORTAL YOUNDER

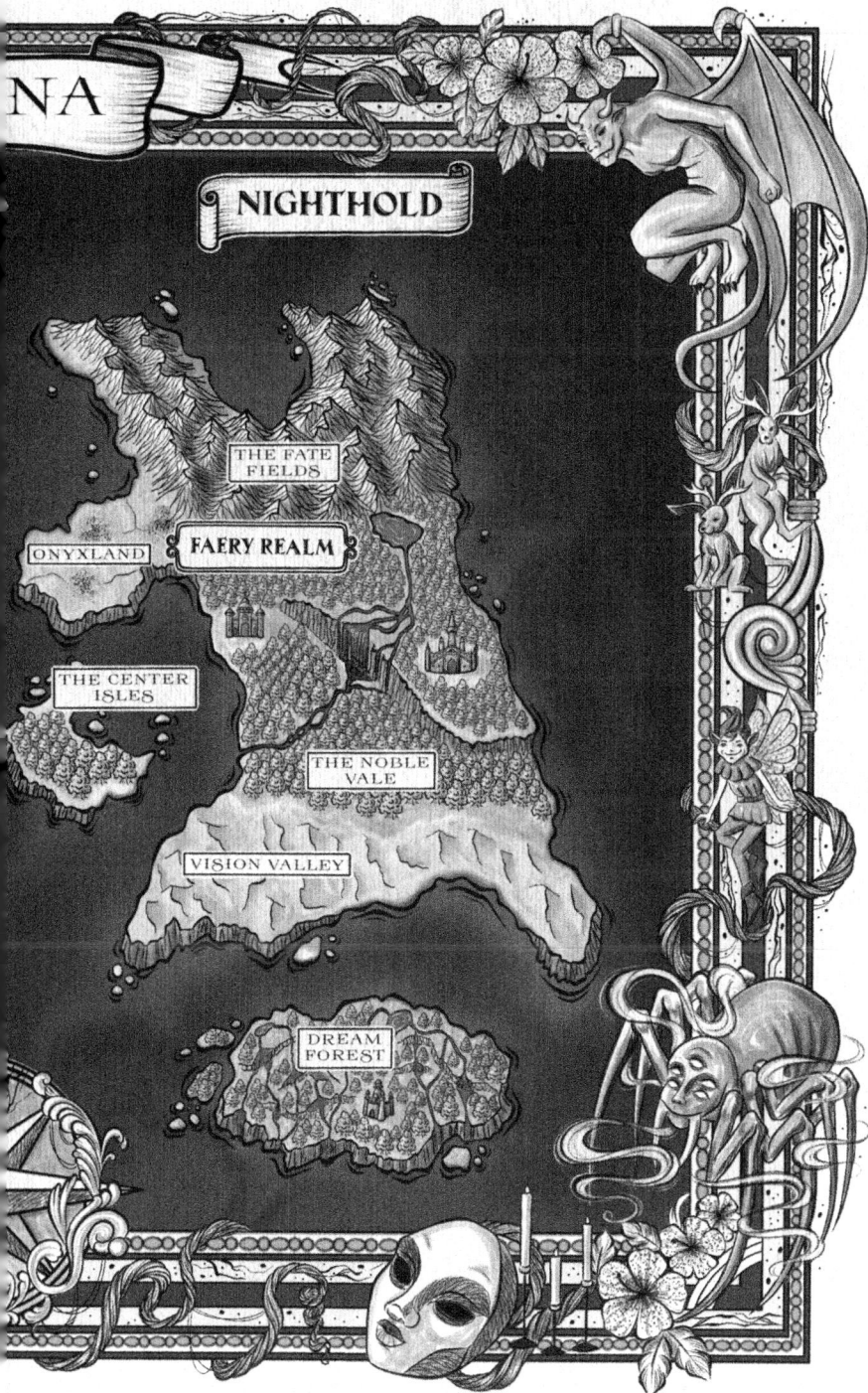

NA

NIGHTHOLD

THE FATE
FIELDS

ONYXLAND   **FAERY REALM**

THE CENTER
ISLES

THE NOBLE
VALE

VISION VALLEY

DREAM
FOREST

WHAT COURSES THROUGH HER BLOOD

Please Note: What Courses Through Her Blood is a mature fantasy novel that contains explicit content and darker elements, including mature language, sexually explicit scenes, and violence. If you would like a full content/trigger warning please visit the authors website: www.AuthorARO.com

CHAPTER 1

LYRA

SOMETHING'S HERE!

A sudden sensation catches my attention, an ominous shiver that tells me I'm not alone. Out of the corner of my eye, something flickers—a wisp of motion, almost imperceptible. At first I think I might be swooning, a feeling of light-headedness eroding the edges of my consciousness. But no, it's the world itself that shudders. A solitary pillar that I hadn't noticed before begins to tremble. The tremor is soft at first, like the whisper of a secret, then it grows, escalating into a fierce quake.

Around me, the air fills with the sounds of panic—screams and gasps echoing through what appears to be a terrace or an elevated veranda, I find myself outside where I can smell the sea and hear the waves crashing in the distance. I turn, desperate to find a grounding presence, and my fingers find Nyx's. His grip on my hands tightens, his stance firm against the chaos. His eyes, those deep pools of gray, flicker and transform, shifting from soft gentleness to hardened intensity as the light around us dims, swallowed by growing shadows.

The ground beneath us fractures, the white stone splitting

with a sharp, resounding crack, as if the earth itself is crying out. From these fissures, shadows begin to ooze silently, creeping forward with a menacing patience. I try to discern their origin, but it's impossible to tell if they emerge from within me or seep from some otherworldly place.

The crowd before me transforms as well. The faces blur together into a sea of anonymity, each figure blending into the next, their features lost to the encroaching dark. The darkness thickens, devouring the remaining light, muffling sounds until the screams taper off to mere whimpers. An icy fear grips me, rooting me to the spot. Why can't I move?

"I told you I was your light, Princess," Nyx says through the stifling silence, sharp and clear.

I glance back at him, and the sight chills me to the core. His eyes, once a soft gray, now blaze with an intense light and become almost blinding, stark against the deepening gloom. Light emanates from him, piercing the shadows, casting bright beams across the broken ground.

I gasp for air, choking as I bolt upright in bed, the sweat on my brow cold and clammy.

This dream, this haunting vision—or midnight mind— threatens to be my undoing. The same nightmare that has been stalking my sleep for months always paralyzes me, showing fragmented scenes and shifting the person standing beside me from Colton to Nyx. I'm left wondering whether these dreams are harbingers of what is to come or simply the chaos of a subconscious torn between my mind and my heart, struggling with indecision.

I release a slow breath and summon my shadows back to me. In recent months, not only have my dreams become more vivid, but my shadows have also started to exhibit a will of their own when I sleep—or at least when I dream. I wake to find them sprawled across the room, pressed against the windows and doors, as if their presence might offer some form of protection in my slumber, a dark sentinel standing guard.

The first time it happened, I know it unnerved Colton—though whether it scared him or intrigued him, I can't say. It might have been a bit of both. I woke to find my shadows had ensnared him, binding his limbs to the bed with wispy tendrils and sealing his mouth with an inky veil. I was mortified at the time, but now the memory makes me giggle.

Oh gods, I hope I'm making the right choice. I'm confident it's the right choice for my heart, but whether it will be right for my people, for the realms, only the gods know. Soon enough, I'll find out. I have a good feeling though, a feeling of peace, like all the pieces are finally falling into place and I am exactly where I am supposed to be in this moment.

Glancing at the clock, I see it's 3 a.m. Ironically, it's officially my nineteenth birthday—a day I've always believed would be of great significance. It was supposed to be the day I awakened my magic, discovering whether it was dark or light. This day, which I anticipated and dreaded in equal measure for so many years, is finally here, yet it holds significance for an entirely different reason.

I already possess all the magic I could ever desire, and I've mostly come to terms with my dark magic. But I could never have predicted this turn of events. A couple of years ago, if someone had told me I'd be facing this on my nineteenth birthday, I would have laughed in their face.

Yet here I am, officially a woman in the eyes of my people, and only hours away from the bridal binding, the twining of souls, the final bonding ceremony. They all signify the same thing—my wedding day, the culmination of all ceremonies.

Today, I will bond my soul with the man I've chosen, my beacon of light in the darkness.

SIX MONTHS EARLIER

I whirl around.

Without thinking, I slam the gates shut. A wave of relief washes over me as I hear them click and lock back into place. But there was a flash of something—so fleeting that I almost believe I imagined it. Yet when my fingers brushed against the cool metal, an image seared into my mind. An image of the gods...I think. I can't be certain, but I swear I saw Ryella, the Goddess of Darkness and Shadows, with her head bowed.

Nyx moves next to me and grabs the gate, rattling it vigorously. Small pieces of ensnared branches crumble under his touch and fall from the metal bars. "It doesn't open for me," he says, turning to look at Colton.

"I imagine that's a good thing," Colton replies, eyeing me as if I'm a puzzle he's yet to solve.

"I want to know what purpose these gates serve, but we have more pressing matters to deal with first," I say, extending both my hands.

Nyx instantly takes my hand, stepping in close to me. Colton takes my other hand, but I can't help noticing the slight hesitation in his touch, which sends a pang through my heart. I focus, channeling us back to the heart of Eguina.

The beating takes root in my mind, a chilling prelude even before we materialize in the cavern at the center of the tunnels. As our feet touch down, I feel the crunch of decayed roots underfoot, and a shiver runs up my spine. The sight before me is something I doubt I'll ever grow accustomed to. In fact, I yearn for the day when I needn't witness it again, once healed.

The heart continues to thud, a dismal echo of its former vitality—now more black than red. The glistening sheen that once covered its surface has turned lackluster, and the vessels branching out across the chambers appear almost dried up in places, especially since Euric drained my magic from it, leaving it more ghastly than before. With each beat, a gush of dark, viscous liquid spurts from its apex, trickling down the gnarled roots before dripping onto the floor.

"What the fuck is that?" Nyx exclaims.

I turn to him, reminded that they are unaware of its significance. Colton, releasing my hand, steps closer to the heart, his gaze intense and investigative.

"Is this the beating you mentioned hearing before? I hear it now," Colton remarks in awe.

"Yes, it was beckoning me. I suspect I was the only one who could hear it, because I'm the one intended to save it."

Releasing Nyx's hand, I move closer for a better view.

"It's dying," Colton murmurs, and I lightly brush his shoulder in agreement.

"Is this another of Euric's secrets?" Nyx asks, impatient.

Meanwhile, Colton and I remain captivated by the heart. Despite its eerie presence, its beauty and power are undeniable.

"This," I begin, "is the heart of Eguina. Drew was accurate in saying that the heart of all magic is here in Zomea, though I doubt she meant it so literally. This heart specifically is the nexus of all life and magic in Eguina, and Euric has been leeching its magic," I explain.

"This is why magic has been weakening in Eguina," Colton says, his gaze shifting to me. His emerald eyes are glowing bright, a stark contrast to his disheveled sandy-blond hair. I nod in agreement, and he lets out a breath, running a hand through his hair, twisted strands falling lightly over his shoulders.

I catch eyes with Nyx, who adds, "So this is why magic was fading and the monstrous creatures were spreading. It wasn't you. Euric was meddling with things he shouldn't, disrupting the balance. What was happening here had immediate effects in Eguina."

"Yeah, I think so," I confirm. "It was never about Gholioth blood needing to be returned to Zomea. It was always about my father getting what he wanted regardless of the consequences."

"And why exactly was he siphoning power from this heart? And you mentioned 'this heart.' Are you saying there's more than one?" Colton inquires.

I fill them in on everything that transpired before their arrival at the gates, where they found me confronting Euric.

"So there are other continents, similar to Eguina, and that's what the portal we discovered in the tunnels leads to?" Colton asks.

"Yes," I reply sorrowfully. "He showed it to me to convince me of his truth. The land was ravaged, desolate as far as the eye could see."

Nyx's tone hardens. "I always knew Euric was power-hungry. That's precisely why my father exiled him from Nighthold and why I ended him the first time."

Colton steps closer, his hand gently brushing my cheek. "Hey, regardless of his motives, I know this must be tough for you," he says.

I swallow hard, not wanting to dwell on all of this here in

the tunnels.

"I'll tell you the rest later. Right now, I need to touch the heart again and let it absorb some of my dark magic. It's the only force potent enough to heal it."

I step forward, feeling the pull as I raise my hands.

"Wait," Nyx says, concern etched on his face. "You've already touched it once, and you said it weakened you. What if you're not ready for more contact? What if you've already given too much?"

"I can do this. I need to," I assert firmly, facing Nyx. "Step back."

I glance at Colton, and my look has them both giving me the space I need.

Guided by instinct, my hands press against the wet surface of the heart. As I do, my head falls back, and time seems to warp around me. I feel as if I'm merging with the heart's fluid coursing through its chambers. My mind is inundated with images, sweeping me through a torrent of visions: lands I don't recognize, scenes flashing by too swiftly to grasp. Then an intense cold grips me.

I sense hands on my shoulders, pulling me back against a warm body, and I sink to the ground, my strength ebbing away. My eyelids are heavy, and I blink several times, struggling to clear my vision. As I do, I notice the heart beginning to transform, its color growing more vibrant, its form fuller, its beats strengthening.

Next thing I know, Nyx squats before me, still worried. Warm arms encircling my waist, and I must be sitting in Colton's lap, my back resting against his chest. I'm too weak to move, barely able to speak. Something did happen.

"I'm alright," I whisper. "This is how I felt before. It won't last long."

Nyx stands, starting to pace, a visible tension in his movements. "I don't like this," he mutters, or at least I think he does. I'm too exhausted to dwell on it, succumbing to the weariness that envelops me.

"I've got you," Colton murmurs in my ear, his arms tightening around me. The urge to succumb to sleep tugs at me, but I resist, leaning into the warmth of his embrace. Being here with him, I realize how much I've missed this closeness. Since awakening my dark magic, a distance had crept in between us, but now in his arms, I feel a profound sense of rightness.

I attempt to reach out through our tether, seeking to gauge his feelings, but my strength falters, and his shielding is too effective.

"We need to get out of here. The heart is stable now. Let's take her back to the bridge," Nyx suggests, his voice carrying from a few feet away where he paces restlessly.

"No." I muster the energy to object, feeling a gradual return of my strength. It's not enough to stand but sufficient to hold a conversation. "I want to go to the palace. I need to find Athalda and rest before facing everyone again."

Nyx halts, turning toward us. "Palace?" he questions. His lack of knowledge about my time here with Colton is evident.

"Where Euric and Athalda were staying," Colton explains. "With Euric gone and Lyra embracing her dark and scary side, it should be safe."

I resist the urge to elbow him, instead retorting playfully, "Hey, I'm not scary."

His laughter echoes through the tunnel, a sound that has been absent for far too long, warming my heart.

"Speak for yourself, my shadow," he whispers, teasing, and I can't help the smile that begins to curve my lips.

But then a sharp pain pierces my chest, as if I've been stabbed by an icicle. My smile falters, and an icy chill starts to spread throughout my body.

CHAPTER 2
COLTON

SHE'S OUT OF REACH, our bond stretched thin. I don't let on to Nyx, who's got a flair for drama that I can do without. His constant presence is like a chokehold—unnecessary and grating.

I watch over Lyra in bed, the rise and fall of her chest under my palm the only thing steadying me.

Since she blacked out in the tunnels, dragging her back to this place felt like a march through purgatory. It's too quiet, the kind of quiet that screams, and I'm close to regretting not listening to Nyx about using the bridge. Close.

"We should be tracking down Athalda, make her bow to Lyra or...end her," Nyx says, looming over Lyra's other side.

"As tempting as that is, Lyra's got first dibs on the witch, and that's non-negotiable," I say, my hold on her unyielding. "I'm not going anywhere. She stays with me."

"I'm here, aren't I? She'll have me until she wakes," Nyx shoots back.

I can't help but laugh. "That's supposed to make me feel better?"

"Get over yourself, Colton. When are you going to come clean about your own tales? Can't wait to see her face when she hears about our lineage," Nyx says with a smirk that I want to wipe off his face.

"You're afraid that I might be the light she needs," I say, keeping my voice even. "But at least I'm not drowning in a sea of lies. I never once plotted against her, not like you."

Nyx's smirk doesn't waver. "Afraid? Please. You're the one playing the dutiful guard dog. But it suits you, brother. Keep barking at shadows while I deal with the real threats."

I match his smirk with a cold one of my own. "Guard dog? That makes you the court jester, always dancing around the truth. We both know who Lyra can count on when danger comes knocking. Don't forget I was there to help put back the pieces after you broke her."

He leans back, his eyes hardening. "She'll need more than muscle and pretty words, Colton. When the time comes, it's my power that'll save her. It's a king she needs."

"You think power is enough?" I retort, my grip on Lyra tightening, a silent promise to shield her with more than brute strength. "It's not merely about power. It's about trust, something you know nothing about."

Nyx stands, a storm brewing in his gaze. "Trust is earned in blood and battle, not whispered sweet nothings. I've seen the way you look at her since her dark magic awakened, the hesitation in your eyes. Don't think for a second she hasn't noticed it too. When she wakes, we'll see whose side she's on."

"She's not a trophy to be won," I snap, rising to meet him eye to eye. "She's her own person. But when she wakes, she'll see through your illusions. The only reason she's been keeping you around is your father's crazy prophecy about your light saving her. Soon she'll know the truth."

Our stares lock, two immovable forces bound by blood but

divided by our secrets. The tension could spark a war, yet we're both unyielding, protectors and pursuers of the one we claim to love.

"Don't you mean our father? May the best brother win," Nyx says quietly, turning away with a shadow of a grin, leaving the words hanging like a guillotine's blade between us.

And as the silence settles over us, I can't shake the feeling that the real battle for Lyra's heart is beginning.

My Lyra... I take a seat at the foot of the bed, paying no mind to Nyx as he ambles over to gaze out the window. She seems unchanged, yet there's something distinctly different about her from the last time we found ourselves here. Those initial nights were fraught with her restlessness, her heart torn by the turmoil with Nyx, Aidan, and Samael. It's undeniable—she's endured far too much for her young age.

Her hair, a bit longer now, retains its vibrancy, the white-blonde waves spilling around her like a luminous frame. In sleep, she appears almost serene, a big contrast to the exhaustion I know has claimed her. Drained from funneling too much power into the heart, she might succumb to this deep sleep for days, a luxury we can ill afford.

The uncertainty outside these walls, including the unknown whereabouts of Athalda, weighs heavily on me. Lyra's resolve to face Athalda herself is clear, but the security of our surroundings cannot wait.

I'm torn between the desire to remain by her side and the necessity of ensuring the palace's safety. I thought maybe with her newfound strength she would have awakened by now, but the connection between us feels fragile, her vitality diminished.

"Can I trust you to stay here with her?" I ask, rising to my feet. Nyx's attention snaps from the window to me.

"Where are you going?" he demands.

"Can I trust you?" I repeat, holding his stare firmly.

"You'd know if I moved her. We're bound by this tether until someone can undo it," he says with resignation as he kicks off his boots and moves closer to the bed.

I let out a heavy sigh. Deep down, I know Nyx will look after her. I think he might actually love her, which is something new for him. But the thought of him touching her, being close to her, is unsettling. I pull the door open, and before stepping out I cast one last look back. Nyx is tucking Lyra into his side, pulling her close on the bed. I shake my head and slam the door behind me to drown out the image, to prevent myself from doing something I'll regret.

The possibility of Lyra choosing Nyx is something I have to face, and it's a thought that's hard to swallow. Running a hand through my hair, I push that worry aside. I can't dwell on it now. My immediate task is to figure out why this palace feels so deserted and find out where Athalda and Anika are.

I decide to methodically search the palace, starting with the halls closest to Lyra and gradually working my way toward the more decrepit side. I sweep through every room and corridor, the lava channels carved into the walls illuminating my path.

As I approach the side of the palace that's rotting, the once sparkling walls darken, and the rugs underfoot become dilapidated. This is Athalda's domain, her dark spells seeping into the very stones, decaying the walls themselves.

"I wondered when we would meet again, although I can't say I expected you to come alone." Athalda's voice reaches me before my hand even touches her door. Her old, raspy tone more than unsettles me—it ignites a deep-seated loathing.

The door swings open, and I step into the dimly lit room, finding the old woman with tangled hair ensconced in a wooden chair in the far corner, rocking gently.

"You're lucky I'm alone. After what Lyra did to Euric, I can't say she'd be as... accommodating," I say, my voice steady as I close the distance between us, until those pitch-black eyes snap into focus on me.

"So it's true then. Lyra has killed her father? I felt his death but wasn't certain who delivered the final blow," she says, her tone eerily nonchalant, as if the outcome was something she had foreseen.

"You knew this would happen?" I challenge, noting how she absently taps her long nails against the wooden armrest.

"Euric was becoming restless. I warned him that Lyra wasn't prepared. The dark magic needed more time to corrupt her essence, but his arrogance clouded his judgment," she reveals with a dismissive wave of her hand.

"Corrupt her essence? What are you talking about?" I ask.

Lyra had confided that Euric sought greater power, expecting her to accept the demise of Eguina, to let its heart—and with it, everyone—perish. But Lyra, even touched by darkness, would never entertain such madness. Euric's faith in this was sheer delusion.

"The shadows within her grow, already reshaping her. You've felt it, though denial seems to cloud your sight. A boy blinded by love," she taunts, her laughter grating on my nerves.

A low growl forms at the back of my throat, the urge to end Athalda feeling nearly overwhelming as I recall how she exploited Lyra, shaping her into a tool for Euric's ambition. It revolts me.

"Easy, boy, did I strike a nerve?" she adds, her expression flickering with what looks like concern for a fleeting moment. And that's when the air shifts, when I sense her presence.

The door bursts open, torn from its hinges, as Lyra steps into the room. Her gaze finds mine. "Colton," she breathes, and the sound of my name on her lips unravels me.

She wraps her arms around my neck, holding me as if we've been apart for ages. I inhale her familiar scent, trying to ignore Nyx's disapproving glance as he saunters in behind her, leaning casually against the wall with his arms crossed.

"You were supposed to look after her," I accuse Nyx, unable to hide my irritation.

"She insisted on coming," he retorts with an eye roll. "Said she felt you were in distress."

It seems I wasn't as adept at masking my emotions or controlling our connection as I thought. Despite knowing she was resting, I hadn't sensed her awakening, nor her approach, until her magic brushed against mine. She's honing her ability to shield herself from me, a development that leaves me unsettled.

She releases me too soon and turns to face Athalda, who's masked her expression again with that typical indifferent facade.

"You," Lyra says, pointing at the old hag, her voice carrying a mix of accusation and defiance.

"Don't you point your finger at me, girl," Athalda retorts, her nails beginning that infuriating tap again.

I'm overwhelmed with the urge to step in front of Lyra, to whisk her away from this venomous presence, to shield her from the woman before us. Every so-called family member Lyra has ever known has used her and abused her, but I swear it ends today.

"This isn't going to go how it usually does," Lyra says, her voice dropping an octave, heavy with something dark and powerful. I steal a glance at her and notice wisps of shadows threading through the whites of her eyes—a sight that I may never get used to seeing.

Before I can fully grasp the situation, the wooden rocker beneath Athalda splinters, collapses, and darkens. Something like spilt ink pours from Lyra. Shadowy tendrils, like branches in a twisted forest, wrap around Athalda, pinning her against the wall.

"To think, I once shed a tear for you when Samael killed you," Lyra says with a laugh, but the sound is chilling, foreign to the warm laughter I know. I glance at Nyx, who hasn't moved and is leaning casually against the wall, seemingly unbothered by the transformation unfolding in Lyra, by the dark magic coursing through her.

"Do you remember the last time we were in this room practicing magic and you slapped me for asking too many questions?"

Lyra steps closer, her presence dominating the room. When Athalda remains silent, Lyra strikes her across the face. The impact forces the old witch to wince, especially on the side marred by scars, closing her bad eye momentarily.

"What a fool I was, thinking you actually wanted to help me, to make me stronger for my sake and that of my people. But you've always been his lackey, haven't you? Always dancing to my father's tune like a loyal puppet," Lyra accuses, her voice dripping with contempt as she starts pacing before Athalda, trapped and helpless.

"He saw great potential in you, a chance for you to rise to divinity alongside him. Your actions not only destroyed his ambitions but also obliterated any hope of transcending the mortal coil," Athalda retorts through gritted teeth, defiant even in a compromised position.

"I did more than shatter his ambitions. I tore out his heart," Lyra counters with a cold, mocking laugh, the sound echoing off the walls as she moves. "And as for becoming a god, I wield more power now than I could have ever imagined. In your eyes, I might as well be a deity. I don't need whatever lies beyond those gates."

Nyx and I share a look of unease, a silent acknowledgement of the dangerous path she treads.

"Mind your words, child. Mock the gods, and you may find yourself facing oblivion, as your father did," Athalda snaps back in a raspy whisper as the shadows constricting her tighten cruelly, eliciting a choked gasp before Lyra eases her grip.

"I have questions for you, and since my father is gone and you've got no one left to hide behind, I suggest sticking to the truth. If I sense even a hint of deceit, it'll be the last lie you ever tell. Do you understand?" Lyra leans in close to Athalda's face, the threat unmistakable.

After a moment's pause, Athalda clears her throat. "I understand." Her compliance surprises me slightly. I half-expected a snide comeback, but given her precarious situation, her usual combativeness seems to have deserted her.

"I know I saw Luke in the burning forest. He was here in Zomea. I've seen him multiple times through my midnight mind. My mother too—I've heard her voice. Where are they now? Why is it that we hardly ever see another soul in Zomea?" Lyra's inquiry is earnest, her eyes searching Athalda's for any flicker of dishonesty.

I find myself leaning in, equally eager for the truth. The scarcity of faces in Zomea has been a puzzle to me as well. Aside from Anika, encounters with others have been rare, mostly during my ventures far from the palace in search of Aidan.

"Zomea is vast, and your midnight mind isn't always reliable—" Athalda begins, only to stop abruptly when Lyra's dark tendrils tighten around her throat.

"I'm tired of the lies, the same ones my father peddled. I refuse to believe that not a single soul I've known has made it into Zomea. You're as delusional as he was if you expect me to accept that," Lyra counters, her resolve steeling in the face of Athalda's evasions.

Her fierceness, though slightly terrifying, fills me with pride. She's standing her ground, challenging the untruths that've been fed to her.

"Everyone from your past who entered Zomea was hunted down and eliminated. Is that clear enough for you? Your father wouldn't risk leaving anyone alive, not with the threat they could pose to his plans. Any face you recognized with your midnight mind was before they met their final end, either by Euric's hand or mine," Athalda reveals, her voice cold and matter-of-fact.

For a moment, I brace for Lyra's wrath to erupt, for the shadows to do their worst. But instead she takes a deep, measured breath, and when I dare to look into her eyes, I find them not fully consumed by the darkness—still flecked with warmth. It's a reassurance that she remains in control of herself, despite the swirling tempest of power at her beck and call.

"What about Nyx's parents?" Lyra probes.

My heart clenches, hoping nothing slips that could unveil our shared lineage. It's a revelation I'm not ready for Lyra to hear, not until I can explain it myself in my own way.

"That, I truly do not know. Zomea's expanse dwarfs all the realms of Eguina combined. And the scarcity of souls near this palace? Partly because it's nestled within an active volcano, and partly because Euric's reputation precedes him even here. He was both respected and feared. His desire for solitude was well known. Those who ignored it quickly regretted their curiosity," Athalda explains, and something in her tone convinces me she's speaking the truth this time.

The mention of my biological father, Callum, stirs a whirl-wind of thoughts. If he's somewhere in Zomea, he might hold the keys to the many unanswered questions that haunt us—the nature of the prophecy, the identity of the light, and how it all intertwines with our fates.

"What lives behind the gates?" Lyra halts her pacing to fix Athalda with a questioning look.

"What makes you think anything lives there?" Athalda counters tersely.

"Don't deflect my question with another question," Lyra insists, drawing in a deep breath. I sense her struggle for composure, yet I stay silent, a mere observer to this exchange.

"Your father was of the belief that it's the dwelling place of the gods," Athalda finally concedes, prompting a flicker of disappointment across Lyra's features.

"Doesn't it strike you as peculiar? A random gate in the eeriest part of Zomea, unopened yet purportedly home to all the gods?" Lyra muses, almost to herself. Her skepticism mirrors my own thoughts. The gates do possess an unsettling aura, one I'm not eager to delve into further.

"Where are all the Gholioths? Why haven't I seen one? Do they still bear resemblance to their Fae origins? This all spiraled from your lie about Gholioth blood," Lyra presses on, her frustration evident, though it's unclear if she's seeking answers from Athalda or simply voicing her thoughts aloud.

"Their appearance varies with the observer. They might reveal themselves to you, should they find you worthy," Athalda replies, her answer eliciting an involuntary eye roll from me.

"I'm tired of your riddles. Why can't you provide a straight-forward answer?" Lyra howls, her anger surfacing as shadows writhe and stretch, causing Athalda to cry out in pain.

Glancing at Nyx, I catch him smirking, and there's a troubling glint of amusement in Lyra's eyes. This cruelty, this delight in another's torment, is uncharacteristic of the Lyra I know. The influence they exert on each other is toxic. They're drawing out the worst in one another.

As I'm about to intervene, Athalda, amidst coughs, manages to choke out, "Are you certain Samael is merely your step-brother? You might find you share more with him than you realize."

"He's a monster. He tortured the innocent. Do you think you're innocent?" Lyra challenges, her voice hard, but then unexpectedly she withdraws her shadows, allowing Athalda a moment's reprieve. The old witch collapses to the wooden floor, her knees hitting with a thud that echoes through the room. Looking up at Lyra, there's a fleeting moment where I feel a pang of sympathy for Athalda. Perhaps, in some twisted way, she and Lyra aren't so different—both manipulated by Euric, both deceived and used for his ambitions. Yet this common ground doesn't excuse Athalda's actions.

"What are you doing? Do you want me to finish her off for you?" Nyx offers, but the suggestion seems off, especially coming from someone who claims to be the light against the darkness.

"No, I'm not a monster. And your power... It's nothing compared to mine," Lyra asserts, her authority undisputed in the dim light of the room, as she turns back to Athalda. "You claim Zomea's vast? Then I banish you from this palace. Find a new corner of misery for your existence. Perhaps away from my father's influence, you might find redemption. Or not. Either way, if our paths cross again, I may not hold back. I may be a monster."

Without responding, Athalda disappears from the room, perhaps wisely choosing silence over a parting jab. The air feels cleaner, somehow lighter, though Nyx's quick move to embrace Lyra sets a knot in my stomach. I turn away, unable to watch their display of unity.

"Let's move away from here, please," I mutter as I head toward the main sitting room.

The weight of what she said weighs heavily on my mind. "I may be a monster." The possibility of her embracing that darkness fully is a thought I don't want to entertain.

CHAPTER 3
LYRA

"Do you think Drew will welcome me back into her home after what happened?" I ask and draw near Colton, who has paused by the fireplace. It's the same fireplace where my father and I shared countless conversations during my last visit here.

"You mean after you annihilated half of the Luminary Council—practically vaporized them?" Nyx chimes in from behind, causing a wave of nausea to wash over me. I feel an urgent need to escape.

"Shut up, Nyx," Colton snaps then turns to me with a softer expression. "Drew will definitely welcome you back. She's with us. After what you did, the rest of the council scattered. My parents have even retreated to Nighthold by now."

It's a relief to hear that.

"We need to go back then. Now," I declare, ready to use my magic to transport us to the bridge.

"Wait, aren't we going to discuss what happened here?" Nyx interjects, but I'm not in the state to delve into that conversation.

"I need some time...alone," I say, my gaze shifting between Nyx's frustrated look and Colton's concerned one. They both nod, albeit reluctantly, understanding my plea for a moment's solitude.

The journey back to the hive is uneventful, a small mercy for which I'm grateful. Once back, Nyx and Colton leave me to my thoughts after I assure them I'll manage on my own. My room feels both comforting and isolating as I close the door behind them.

I find myself yearning for Chepi's company, his presence a calming force amidst the storm of my emotions. Lili's care for him eases one of my many worries, but it's a small comfort against the tide of fear and uncertainty that threatens to drown me.

The dread of wielding my dark magic again, of the potential harm I could cause, knots my stomach. The control I managed over it with Athalda was only due to my weakened state, a temporary leash on a power that's both exhilarating and horrifying.

Seeking some semblance of normalcy, I head to the bathroom to wash away the physical reminders of the day's events. Stripping off my blood-stained clothes, I confront my reflection in the mirror, relieved to find my eyes a swirling mix of blue and green, untainted by the black veins of corruption. The sight offers a momentary respite, but it's short lived. As I wash, the sight of dried blood under my fingernails—my father's blood—overwhelms me, sending me reeling to the toilet where I'm gripped by dry heaves.

The tears that follow are not for him but for the pain he caused, the pain I've inflicted, and the inevitable suffering yet to come. The thought of losing control again, of the darkness within me breaking free and taking over, is a weight too heavy to bear right now. I try to tell myself the council members deserved to die, that Euric deserved to die, but that doesn't make it any easier to swallow.

Eventually, I find the strength to rise, wash my face, and don the black nightgown Drew provided. I'm thankful she keeps this room stocked with clean clothes. Crawling into bed, I'm enveloped by the soft linens, a cocoon against the chaos of my thoughts and the world outside. Here, in the quiet darkness, I allow myself a moment to breathe, to mourn, and to steel myself for what lies ahead.

I might have been asleep for mere minutes or entire days for all I know when I'm roused by a soft knock on my door. Silently cursing the disturber, I hop out of bed.

Opening the door, I discover Colton in a pair of shorts, his hair tousled, and his impressive abs on display. Whether he's just woken up or finished working out, I can't ascertain.

"You were in pain. I felt it. Another nightmare?" he asks. Strangely, I can't recall if I was dreaming, which is unusual. I must still be weak, too exhausted to even dream properly.

"I'm not sure," I respond, tucking my hair behind my ears and gesturing for him to come inside.

"I need to talk to you about something," he says, but the thought of discussing anything is overwhelming at the moment.

"Can it wait until tomorrow? I'm... My brain feels like mush," I plead.

He smirks, a glimmer of understanding in his eyes, "Mush, huh? Sure, we can talk tomorrow, Princess," he concedes, turning to leave. Yet the thought of him leaving fills me with a sudden sense of urgency. My moments with Colton are precious, especially with the uncertainty surrounding Nyx's role in all this.

"Stay. Come to bed with me, please," I say, offering a small smile.

"You never have to beg, my shadow," Colton reassures me

as he climbs into bed, pausing to kiss me on top of my head. He pulls me close, enveloping me in warmth and safety. Resting my head on his chest, I let out a sigh of relief, feeling his fingers gently massaging my scalp, playing with my hair, soothing both my mind and body almost instantly.

As I trace my fingers across his chest and down over the contours of his muscled stomach, a different sensation begins to replace my worry, transforming it into desire. "Colton," I whisper, tilting my head back to lock onto his emerald eyes, which glow in the darkness.

"Yes?" he responds, his voice a soft hum. In that moment, I decide to lower my defenses, to open up entirely and let him feel the depth of my emotions. I lower my mental barriers, and I can tell the exact instant he senses the change—his lips find mine with an urgency that mirrors the sudden intensity of our connection.

Gods, how I want him—not merely as a distraction, but from a deep sense of longing. I've missed him, missed us together. He positions himself above me, and as I reach up, yearning for another kiss, he threads his fingers through my hair, gently tilting my head back while his other hand softly clasps my throat. He kisses me with an intensity that feels like both a discovery and a claim. His tongue moves with a familiarity that's exploratory yet possessive, leaving me gasping for air and reveling in the sensation.

Each kiss feels like he's marking me as his all over again.

"Fuck, Lyra," he gasps as I pull away, desperate for air. When I face him again, he brings his forehead to mine, and our eyes lock. He lowers his shields, baring his soul to me. The torrent of emotions that floods me is staggering—not merely lust and desire but a genuine care and a profound yearning... Could it be love?

Though Colton has never uttered the words, this surge of

emotion that washes over me, warming me from within, can only be described as such. My heart expands in response, soaking in the momentary connection until his defenses rise again, and I exhale a breath I hadn't realized I was holding.

The sudden, overwhelming need for more of him courses through me, the mere thought of ever losing him igniting a sharp fear in my chest. In response, I reach up, my hand finding the back of his neck, gently coaxing him down until his lips meet mine once more. His lips, soft and yielding, draw me in, and I savor them—licking, nibbling, exploring each contour with a growing hunger. With my free hand, I tug at his shorts, a silent plea for closeness, until he complies, effortlessly shedding them with a swift kick.

He then lifts me slightly, enough to slide my nightgown upward, and our kiss breaks for a mere moment—long enough for him to remove my garment entirely.

His hand traces a path down the center of my body, and as he introduces a finger inside me, a moan escapes, blending into our kiss. The evidence of my desire for him is undeniable. He hums into the kiss, a sound laden with satisfaction, as he deepens the exploration with two fingers, skillfully moving within me.

"I want to feel you wrapped around my cock like this," he whispers, voice thick, and my entire being yearns in response.

"Yes," I breathe out, my hands seeking him out, confirming his readiness.

A soft plea escapes me, encouraging him closer, and when he positions himself at my entrance, I bite down on my lip in anticipation. The need for him to fill me, the need for more of him— all of him—is so strong in this moment.

The door bursts open, and I let out an embarrassing scream of surprise. "We're under attack. Get dressed and get to the surface," Nyx commands.

The intense fury in his eyes as they sweep over us before he slams the door sends a chill through me. Colton springs into action, quickly pulling on his shorts and tossing my clothes to me. I hastily pull on my nightgown and grab a black sweater from the closet to throw over it. As I step into my boots, Colton is already reaching for my hand, leaving me no time to process the chaos unfolding around us.

Colton pauses, looking down at me. He clasps my face with both hands and kisses me hard.

"We will continue this later," he promises, and all I can do is nod, the intimate moment we shared already feeling like a distant memory. The haunting image of Nyx's fiery gaze lingers in my mind. "Stay close and stay in control. I don't know what's out there, but try not to let your dark magic take over. If it does, know that I'm here and will guide you back, always."

Taking my hand again, he tugs me out into the hallway.

Nyx is nowhere in sight, and the hallway is deserted, which isn't unusual for this part of the hive. I hardly ever see anyone here. We go to the center of the hive, where staircases spiral up and down as far as the eye can see—yet there's nothing. For a moment, I wonder if Nyx was playing some kind of joke, perhaps knowing we were in bed together and wanting to separate us. But then Colton pulls me into his side, and the familiar, comforting scent of him surrounds me as a gust of wind picks up around us, and we channel to the surface of the hive.

Nothing could have prepared me for the sight unfolding before us.

CHAPTER 4

NYX

As if drawn by my subconscious, I glance up the hillside as Lyra and Colton emerge at the surface. The urge to rush to her is overwhelming, but I'm too furious, still seething from finding them together. Darkness descends around us, the scene quickly becoming an ominous shroud. I tilt my head back, my gaze piercing through the gloom, fuck. Countless Sarrols swoop down from the sky, their dark forms blotting out the moonlight.

Where are these creatures coming from, and why? If it's still a matter of the bridge being unlocked, then sealing it must become our top priority—before any more of these fiends infiltrate and spread to Nighthold. The last thing I need during my absence is my kingdom under siege. I trust Bim to manage, but it shouldn't have to come to that. I'm not leaving until I can take Lyra with me—alone.

Her presence is distracting. A Sarrol descends upon me and nearly knocks me over. I duck under its wing and stab it through the chest. Its frothing mouth drips black sludge onto my arm, and I look down at the creature, repulsed. Sarrols truly are among the ugliest monsters ever to set foot in the realms—deformed, goblin-like creatures with pointed noses and sharp fangs.

I shake my head and turn to face another two that landed behind me. I swing my blade, slicing the wing off one and kicking the other in the chest, my leg barely escaping its claws. Then I send a burst of fire into the face of the creature, burning it to ash in seconds.

There are so many of them. I want to check on Lyra, but every time I turn, more are dropping in. The Lamia are enraged, and their realm is under attack. I don't think I've ever seen the Lamia fight like this before.

I make eye contact with Drew across the field as she sweeps across the terrain so swiftly it looks like she's levitating. She bites into the throat of a Sarrol, tearing it out with her fangs and spitting chunks of dark flesh onto the ground. Black blood flows freely down her chin and onto her chest. I can't look away as she repeats the gruesome act and then winks at me. She truly is terrifying—no wonder so many fear her.

The descending Sarrols finally give way to the moonlight, and the battlefield before me reveals a harrowing sight. It's a maelstrom of chaos where hundreds of these wretched creatures dart across the dark sky, their grotesque forms casting fleeting shadows over the ground.

Below, only a few dozen of us stand, vastly outnumbered but resolute against this infernal onslaught. My mind races to Lyra, whose dark magic is desperately needed to turn the tide. With this thought fueling my urgency, I push up the hillside. I suspect Lyra and Colton might have headed down the other side toward Blood Lake, perhaps seeking a strategic advantage or a momentary refuge.

I draw my second sword, feeling its familiar weight bolster

my resolve. Each time the image of Colton entangled with Lyra flashes through my mind, I channel my fury into the battle, decapitating another Sarrol with a swift, clean stroke. My fire magic follows, incinerating the fallen creatures, scorching a path through the mountainside that leads me closer to her.

But the Sarrols are relentless. One audacious beast dares to claw at my back, its talons sinking deep into my shoulder blade. With a grunt of pain mixed with anger, I twist around, my blades dancing a deadly arc through the air, severing its head in a smooth motion. It falls, its body not yet realizing its fatal separation.

In disgust and frustration, I tear off my tunic, now a ragged piece of cloth soiled by the battle's grime and the creatures' vile blood. Reaching the crest of the hill, I pause to survey the scene below on the other side. There, in a grim tableau, are Lyra, Soren, Adira, and Colton, their backs pressed together in a tight circle. They move with desperate precision, each strike and parry a testament to their training and desperation as they fend off the relentless waves of Sarrols. Despite their skill, they are clearly getting overwhelmed—their numbers too few, the enemy too many.

From my vantage point, I see the rest of the Lamia engaged in fierce combat near the town, too far to be of immediate help. A surge of frustration washes over me. Why isn't Lyra tapping into her dark magic? The power she holds could sway this battle, could scatter these demons back to the shadows from whence they came.

Neither Lyra nor Colton holds a weapon—no surprise given the rather compromising situation I interrupted. I grunt, shoving a beast aside and leaping onto its back, driving my blade deep through its hide. Black froth sprays from its mouth with its final breath. Despite my efforts to reach them, the Sarrols swarm relentlessly.

Colton skillfully entangles them with roots, freezing them in place, while Lyra delivers the killing blows with her fire magic. Nearby, Adira, one of Drew's fiercest fighters, wields a sword with deadly grace and uses her teeth in a savage display of Lamia ferocity.

Shaking my head at the madness, I glance at Soren, one of the few mortals brave enough to join the fray. Armed only with a single sword, he fights valiantly, but his human limits are painfully obvious.

A beast lunges at him, seizing his leg and hoisting him into the air. Its claws and fangs tear into his thigh. Adira reacts fast, soaring through the air and driving her blade through the creature's skull. However, their tight defensive circle begins to falter.

I channel to Soren's side to fend off more attackers. As I reach him, our eyes meet, and I see his pained face. I touch his wound, and he cries out—an involuntary reaction to the searing pain. Blood is everywhere. The situation is dire.

Lyra drops to her knees opposite me, cradling Soren's head.

"Soren, you're going to be okay," she murmurs, trying to steady him. When her gaze meets mine again, tears brim in her eyes, but as they begin to fall, they transform—shifting from liquid to shadow, dark veins creeping across her skin. "Get him out of here."

I look up to find Colton nodding in agreement. Despite our mutual disdain, I trust him to watch her back. Lifting Soren, I channel back to the castle, stealing one last glance at Lyra. But she's no longer herself. The darkness within has taken hold, leaving only black voids staring back at me as I duck into the hive.

"Take me to the infirmary," Soren gasps between heavy breaths, his blood staining the front of my clothes.

"Where's the infirmary?" I ask, not knowing the layout of this hive.

"Eighteenth floor," he manages to say, and I silently thank the gods for the ability to channel. I glance down the hive and quickly count the staircases until I reach eighteen then channel to the floor. If only I had been to the infirmary before, I could have channeled directly inside.

"Where now?" I ask as we arrive, and he points to the second left down the hall. Reaching the door, I kick it open and am surprised to find the room already filled with several people.

"Put him down here," instructs one of the human males, wearing gloves, pointing to a gurney. I gently lay Soren down and watch as they inject a long needle into his wound. It looks painful, but he seems to relax slightly, likely due to some numbing effect.

"I can help. I have some healing magic, though it's not very strong, and I'm not accustomed to healing humans," I offer halfheartedly, not wanting to cause further harm.

"It's not necessary. We know what we're doing," another man replies, pressing gauze against the wound. Feeling out of place, I step back, ready to check on Lyra.

"Wait," Soren calls out weakly. I turn back to see his face growing paler from blood loss. "I was on guard tonight, and those things didn't come from the bridge. They didn't come from Zomea."

Intrigued and concerned, I step closer, my eyebrows furrowing. "Where did they come from then?"

"I don't know, but every time we've seen them before, they came out of the bridge. Tonight, they started descending from the sky, appearing out of nowhere," he rasps.

I nod, absorbing this alarming information then channeling back to the surface, my mind racing.

I find Lyra immediately in the midst of the chaos, her dark

magic unleashed. She's casting shadows around her, ensnaring the creatures and yanking them from the sky. With a mere gesture, she hurls them to the ground and obliterates them into pieces. She's systematically taking them out, one by one. I glance at Colton, who is still diligently watching her back, but these damned creatures are everywhere.

As I'm about to channel my energy to join them, the creatures swarm me again. Deciding enough is enough, I sheath my blades and resort to using only my magic. We need to end this onslaught before we suffer any casualties, though some may have already fallen.

With clenched fists, I unleash my magic, turning these monsters inside out. Their insides are as grotesque as their exteriors, rotting organs emitting a vile stench. Amidst the chaos, I hear a shriek—a sound that cuts through the battlefield. It's Lyra. My eyes snap to the base of the hill where I last saw her in time to see two Sarrols seizing her by the shoulders, lifting her into the air.

The sight ignites a fury within me. I gather my power, preparing to intervene. I don't bother channeling. Instead, I let my own wings materialize and take to the sky. I dive toward the Sarrol that's gripping her right shoulder and wrench it off her. We start spiraling through the air, it snapping its jaws at me, trying to latch on with its fangs. I jab my fist into its mouth and channel my magic to rip its jaw in half, then I drop its lifeless body into the lake below. Once it submerges, a school of shadow fish instantly set upon it.

Fuck the fish—I scan the sky for Lyra. She's still battling the other Sarrol. Oddly, it doesn't seem to be trying to kill her, and a troubling thought crosses my mind: what if the heart of Eguina had nothing to do with these creatures? What if, unbeknownst to her, Lyra herself is the catalyst, her dark powers attracting these beings like a beacon?

She emits a burst of light, and they both plummet into Blood Lake. I dive after her, but before I reach the water's surface, her body catapults out, propelled by her shadows to the shore. She lands hard on the dirt. I channel to her side immediately, but by the time I get there, Colton is already kneeling beside her, his concern palpable as he assesses her condition.

She has little bite marks all over her bare legs where the fish had started to latch onto her. I watch, fascinated and horrified, as the darkness she was emitting slowly gets reabsorbed into her body through the tiny red puncture wounds, sealing them. It's like nothing I've ever seen, and I can't look away until Colton's frantic voice breaks my concentration.

"Hey, are you alright, Lyra? Look at me," he urges.

I glance over as she blinks up at Colton, the inky black slowly fading from her eyes. Noticing the back of her head is bleeding, I can't tell how much of it is her blood versus the stain from the viscous red water of the lake.

"It looks like she hit the back of her head on a rock when she landed," I inform Colton, trying to piece together the sequence of events.

He stands, lifting Lyra gently into his arms, but she protests. "I'm alright, Colton. It's me."

Her hand reaching up to touch his face. I swallow my disgust and look away, only to notice that the creatures have vanished.

"They've retreated," I announce in disbelief, my eyes shifting back to Lyra and Colton.

"Good. I'm taking Lyra inside to assess her wounds. Tell Drew we'll find her after," Colton says firmly and disappears with Lyra into the safety of the hive.

I bristle at his tone — when did he start giving orders to me? I'm only his fucking king. I run my hand through my hair and let out a long breath. It's been a long night, so I swallow my pride. In this moment, he is better equipped to care for her than I am. He's always been adept with healing magic. With a heavy heart, I trudge through the carnage strewn across the forest floor, the decay of the battle lingering in the air, as I go in search of Drew.

CHAPTER 5
LYRA

"Colton, I'm fine, really," I insist as he fusses over me, spreading his healing magic across my skin to be sure.

With a casual wave of his hand, he dries me off instantly, for which I'm grateful. Falling into that lake was the last thing I needed, especially considering what lurks beneath its surface. The memory of the shadow fish that Soren once showed me flashes through my mind, its teeth making me shiver. Then I remember—Soren!

"Did Nyx take Soren to the infirmary?" I ask, turning to face Colton, whose lips flatten at the mention of his name.

"He went to find Drew," he replies.

"Well, where is Soren? I need to make sure he's alright. He's the one you should be fussing over right now and using your healing magic on," I exclaim, already heading toward the door to search for him. But before I reach it, the door swings open, and Drew walks in, clad in black leather pants and a dark-red bodice that matches the color of her long hair. She always looks so put together, even after a battle.

In contrast, I look down at my own appearance, my hair a

tangled mess of clumpy waves. I shake my head—this isn't important, yet how does she always manage to look so elegant?

"Drew," I say, coming to a stop.

"We need to talk. Alone," she states then glances at Colton, nodding toward the door for him to leave. I smile and wave him off, reassuring him as he reluctantly exits the room.

"I don't need any prying ears hearing what I have to say. Follow me to my chambers," Drew says as we step out into the hall, where unsurprisingly Colton and Nyx are both waiting. I have to pinch my lips together to keep from laughing at their not-so-subtle eavesdropping. I follow Drew to the staircase, casting a disapproving glance back at them.

Nyx is still coated in black blood from the battle, shirtless, his broad chest catching my eye for a moment before I look over at Colton, who's even larger. *Gods, what am I going to do with these men in my life?* I think to myself as I turn down the staircase, noticing that neither of them makes a move to follow us.

Once alone in Drew's room, she gestures for me to take a seat. I walk past her bed, eyeing the horrific creatures carved into the bedposts and wondering who carved them and how many other monsters exist like the Monstrauths and Sarrols.

"Is Soren alright?" I ask as I settle into one of the chairs, crossing my feet.

"He will be okay. We lost a few tonight, but none who you've met. They were all from the town," she replies, sinking gracefully into the chair beside me.

"I'm sorry for your loss," I tell her, looking into my lap, unsure of what else to say. So much has happened since we last spoke, and though it wasn't long ago, it feels like a whirlwind, my mind still racing to catch up. "The Luminary Council—"

Drew cuts me off. "The council members were idiots. They attacked you, they didn't listen to reason, and I'm done trying to appease a council that's been hanging on by a thread for years.

You need to fill me in on what happened in Zomea. What did Euric say? And before you begin, I already know he's dead. Nyx mentioned that," she states, unfazed as usual, calm and collected.

I do my best to recount everything that transpired after I fled the council meeting for Zomea. I explain about the heart and Euric's plan to ascend to godhood, the gates, the other continents that exist, and the other hearts, including one already destroyed by Euric. Drew's red eyes stay locked on me, giving a quiet "hmm," every now and then to prompt me to continue, but none of this information seems to shock her. I'm left wondering how much Drew actually knows, considering all of this was quite a revelation to me.

Breathless by the time I finish recounting the events, Drew finally speaks up. "Do you know what's beyond the gate?" she asks.

"No, and I'm not sure I want to find out. Maybe my midnight mind will take me there like my father said, or maybe it won't, but I get the strong feeling that maybe I should leave it alone for now. Find a way to close the bridge and pretend Zomea doesn't exist and get on with my life," I tell her a bit more frantically than I'd like.

"Pretending something doesn't exist doesn't make it go away. Have you made a decision about which one of these men you're going to commit to?" Drew says, shifting the conversation in a direction I hadn't expected. After all I had told her, she brings it back to my tangled love life.

"No, I haven't," I reply, taken aback by her question. "But if there's any truth to this prophecy, and if Nyx is indeed my light, then...I'm not sure."

My thoughts drift to Colton, to how my heart aches for him even while my mind tells me that my destiny might be inexorably linked with Nyx.

"The reason I ask is because if you healed this magical heart and things in Zomea seem stable, the only other thing I can think of that is causing this destruction in Eguina is you," Drew says matter-of-factly. I swallow hard, not wanting to hear this. Anxiety grips me, and I start chewing on the inside of my cheek, feeling sick to my stomach as I ponder what to say, what to do.

"I don't mean for this to be harsh, but Colton and Nyx are fools, fools in love, and they are not going to give it to you straight. And I think that's what you need right now," she continues, and I nod, agreeing but bracing myself for what she's going to say next. "Those creatures tonight didn't come out of the bridge. They were already here. I fear they may be drawn to you, to your dark magic. I can't help but wonder if these prophecies that say you will destroy everything if Callum's son's light doesn't save you don't mean what we originally thought. I don't think you physically will go mad and destroy the realms with your dark powers."

Drew crosses her legs and collects her thoughts.

"But I do fear that with so much darkness in the realms, we have started a shift, which is causing these evil creatures to multiply and emerge from the depths they once hid in. I think they may be drawn to your darkness, and in turn we may be overrun by all this madness. The shift we are on the brink of might be too far gone if we don't act soon."

"What are you saying?" I ask, wiping the sweat off my palms on my nightgown.

"I'm saying pick a brother, and soon. Pick the right brother and commit to him. Make your final vow in a bonding cere-mony, and if there's any truth to this prophecy, then this one simple act could end the destruction in Eguina. At the very least, it will give us an answer," Drew insists.

I shake my head, my eyebrows knitting in confusion. "Brothers? What are you talking about?" I ask, bewildered.

Drew curses under her breath. "Of course, neither of them has said anything to you yet. King Onyx and Colton are half-brothers. They share the same father—Callum," she says.

"I'm sorry, what?" I exclaim, struggling to process this new information.

"Yes, I'm afraid I've known for some time, but it wasn't my place to tell you. Onyx didn't know, and after you left the council meeting, Colton made it public knowledge to everyone. I assumed one of them would have told you by now," she explains further, and I'm still struggling to catch up.

"Colton knew and never told me," I murmur more to myself than to her.

"Colton had his reasons for not telling you, and Nyx presumably chose not to tell you out of his own selfish reasons, wanting you to choose him because you thought he was the only right choice," she continues.

I uncross my feet, feeling the need to stand, to pace. This revelation throws everything I thought I knew into disarray. The weight of the decision before me feels even heavier now, tangled with betrayal and hidden truths. How could I make such a choice under these circumstances? The very foundation of my relationships with both Colton and Nyx has been shaken, and now with Eguina teetering on the brink of collapse, the pressure to make the right choice is too much.

"And if I choose neither of them?" I say, my anger bubbling over. They both knew how much I've struggled to make the right decision, and yet they kept this from me.

"Choose neither, and we will find out if your darkness really will destroy us all," Drew responds coolly.

I turn back to face her. "Aren't you worried?" I ask, my tone edged with annoyance at her nonchalant attitude.

"I don't want more of my people to die, if that's what you're asking, but I also don't know the right answer here. Only you can make this decision. I have a feeling many more things will come to light before you do," she replies, calm yet enigmatic.

I let out a breath of frustration, temporarily pushing the deception by those boys to the back of my mind. "What would you do if you were me?" I ask, meeting her steady gaze.

"I would choose the one I love and damn the realms, if that's what the outcome is," she states frankly, a response I hadn't anticipated.

"Choose the one I love even if I don't know who the light is?" I press, seeking clarity.

"I don't think you will truly know who the light is until you make a choice, so you might as well choose the one you love, assuming you don't love them both," she says, a smirk curling her lips for the first time since we started talking, one fang gleaming slightly.

"And if I do love them both?" I let the words slip, regretting them almost instantly.

"That is more complicated. Trust yourself, and don't get me wrong. You do have some time. I don't think the realms will be overrun tomorrow, if that's what you're afraid of," she answers, her tone light.

"Reassuring," I say, the sarcasm thinly veiled.

"If it helps, you can use my echosphere. Remember, it only shows possible futures, and the future is forever evolving," she offers, and I curse myself for not considering it sooner.

"Yes, I'd like to use it again," I tell her, though a knot forms in my stomach at the memory of the last time I accidentally came across it and it showed me a version of myself I was afraid to face then.

"Very well, it has been a long night. If you'd like to get cleaned up and think about all this for a bit, you can. I trust you'll find the echosphere when you're ready, if that's what you choose," Drew says, and I can't help but notice the cryptic undertone in her voice, but I simply nod. I assume it's back in the same place it was last time I touched it.

"Don't you have any other questions?" I ask her, still feeling frustrated by the entire conversation.

"What questions would you like me to ask?" she responds, and I inhale long and slow.

"For starters, why didn't you seem fazed by the news of these other continents and the heart of all magic for Eguina being in Zomea?"

"I'm the one who told you I believed all the magic was held in Zomea," she replies, not defensively.

"I know, I... I didn't think you meant it so literally," I say, and she gives a slight shrug. "What about the other continents? Why don't you want to find out more?"

"Lyra, did you know I was once in love, a great many years ago?" she starts, and again I have no idea where she's going with this.

"No, I didn't. I always assumed you and Soren had something going on," I admit.

"Yes, Soren," she says, her gaze drifting across the room as if looking out a window that doesn't exist, as if she can see beyond the hive and recall a memory from the past. "Soren is young and human. I may care for him, yes, but love is something else entirely."

"I thought all Lamia only mated with humans. There are no male Lamia," I say, voicing the common knowledge of our realms.

"That is true, but what if I told you I came from another time, another continent long ago where I wasn't called a Lamia at all." She still gazes into the distance.

"I'd say, have you been drinking tonight?" I joke, incredulous.

She flashes a fang again with a smirk. "You see, I'm not surprised to hear about these other portals to places in Zomea, because I come from one of those very places. A place where men and women alike could feed off blood to survive and have extraordinary strength, could live together forever. We were called vampires, and I used to go by Cilla," she explains, and suddenly a lot of things make sense.

Drew is thousands of years old, no one knowing exactly how old, and she oddly knows things about, well, everything, and very little is known about Lamia. "Vampires...Cilla," I repeat, absorbing it all.

"Yes, my full name is Drewcilla. Once I had to leave that life behind, I dropped the end and started anew here as Drew," she says, revealing a past shrouded in mystery and a life far more complex than I had ever imagined.

"Why did you come here? And is that how my father knew of these other places? Does anyone else know? I thought you had never been to Zomea before?" I fire off a barrage of questions, my curiosity peaking as I try to absorb her revelations.

"So many questions, but my story is a tale for another time. What's important right now is you and the future of this continent," Drew says, her voice calm yet commanding. "I tell you this because I want you to know that you will know the right choice to make when it's time. When you love someone, not only who but that you are truly in love, you'll know."

She stands and moves closer to me. I fight the instinct to step back as she extends her hand and places it gently on my chest. "You will know in here," she says, her touch firm yet reassuring. "Use the echosphere, take your time, do what you need to do to come to terms with your decision. But in here..." She taps my chest lightly. "...the decision has already been made."

She moves her hand to the side of my head. "It's everything up here that's getting in the way. Now go get cleaned up. You have a long road ahead of you and some choices I don't envy. We'll speak again, in time," she concludes, offering me a smile and a dismissive wave.

I want to continue the conversation, to delve deeper into her past and extract more answers, but I realize the moment for questions has passed. I take my leave without another word

CHAPTER 6
LYRA

IT MUST BE close to morning now, and given the scant sleep I've managed over the last few days, it's a wonder I can still walk, let alone think straight. I don't channel back to my room. Instead, I take my time walking through the quiet halls. Through the tether, I can sense Colton is in his bedchamber. As I pass by, the urge to see him, to confront him is strong, but I stifle it.

He's been hiding the fact that he and Nyx are brothers from me all this time. He knew about my internal struggles, understood that my hesitation stemmed from not knowing if Nyx was the one I was destined to be with—the one destined to save me from myself. How could he keep this from me?

I want to confront him, to hear his explanation, but the pain is too sharp, the betrayal too deep. After everything we've been through, after all the nights he held me while I cried over Nyx's lies, to discover he harbored his own secrets cuts deeply. My heart aches with the realization.

I pass by Nyx's room next, and although I'm furious with him too, part of me is curious about how he's handling these revelations about his father, considering Colton has been deceiving him as much as me. My pace quickens, fueled by a mix of anger and a desperate need for answers.

I need to see whatever the echosphere is going to show me. If I wait and think about it for too long, I might have second thoughts. I head down the staircase to the ancient library, where a familiar red glow hums through the room, confirming the orb's presence. I follow the light source and find the echosphere sitting on one of the dusty bookshelves in the back of the room. Its inner light pulses slightly, and I feel the urge to touch it.

I think about the last time I was here and what the orb showed me—my dark eyes and shadow magic that I wasn't ready to accept then. I check my shields and completely block Colton out. He doesn't need to know what I'm doing or what I'm feeling when I touch this thing. I don't need him to save me from the orb this time.

I extend my hand toward the crimson glow and swear the room darkens in anticipation of my touch. This time, I don't bother grazing my fingers against it and eagerly grasp the orb with both hands. As the chill spreads up my arms and everything goes black, I let it take me.

I feel myself dissolving into the void, enveloped by an abyss so deep and dark it consumes me entirely, leaving nothing but the sound of my own heart thundering in my chest. I command my racing heart to steady as the darkness shifts, morphing into a scene of...beauty. I find myself—or rather, a spectral version of myself—standing on a grand terrace that seems woven from the stuff of dreams.

The terrace stretches vast and splendid before me, lined with towering marble pillars that gleam under a celestial sky. Below, the relentless sea crashes against jagged cliffs, sending sprays of white foam into the air, as if applauding the scene above. All around me, a crowd of figures clad in exquisite garments of velvet and silk, their faces indistinct and blurred as though veiled by mist, sit in rapt attention.

As I drift closer, the focus sharpens on me and Nyx at the center of the terrace on a stage. We are in the midst of completing our bonding ceremony. The air is thick with the scent of salt and blooming nightflowers, mingling with the subtle perfume of incense. I observe our expressions—there's genuine joy, a radiant happiness that lights up Nyx's features and mirrors my own. But my spirit feels restless, my eyes roving over the sea of faces for a glimpse of Colton, seeking any touchstone of familiarity in the blur. My search is futile. The figures remain elusive, their features shifting so I can't make anyone out.

Suddenly, the earth trembles beneath my feet—a low, menacing rumble that escalates into a deafening roar. A pillar beside us fractures with a sharp crack, its fragments tumbling toward the ground in slow motion. As I panic, the scene shifts abruptly.

Now, I'm transported inside what appears to be Nyx's home, altered subtly to reflect our joint existence. I follow the sound of a lullaby to the balcony where I find myself humming, gazing out over a serene, starlit jungle. Nyx's arms encircle me from behind, his hands gently resting on my swollen belly—oh gods. We are a picture of peace, yet an unnerving silence pervades, and I find myself wondering where Chepi is.

The tranquility shatters without warning. I'm thrust back to the terrace, now a scene of chaos. Guests scream and scatter as shadows, like ink spilled across parchment, spread and twist around the pillars. The ground under us convulses violently. I search for Nyx amidst my panic. Our eyes meet, his usually soft gray eyes now blazing an intense, almost supernatural white.

The vision disintegrates, and I am expelled from the echosphere's embrace. I tumble backward, landing hard on the cold library floor. My senses reel, the tang of the sea and the cries of terror still ringing in my ears as I blink against the dim light of the library, struggling to piece together the fragmented visions of a possible future.

I scramble to my feet, battling the urge to grab and hurl the echosphere across the room. Instead, I unleash my frustration on it. "Why does everything have to be so fucking vexing? Can't anything be straightforward? I'm fucking tired of these endless prophecies, secrets, and cryptic messages."

I clench my fists, taking a deep breath to calm myself as I feel my agitation simmering, my magic stirring restlessly beneath the surface.

Nyx is my light, the one I am meant to be with, and that vision must have been our wedding day. I can only assume his white eyes signified that he is the light and that we defeated the darkness on that day, going on to start a family. That's the conclusion my logical mind reaches from the vision.

But then I start to wonder—where was Colton during all of this? Why couldn't I make out anyone's face in the crowd? Where was Chepi, and why did something feel off about Nyx's home?

Perhaps my reluctance stems from the fact that I'm in love with Colton. My feelings for him are undeniable, and when Drew revealed the truth about their brotherhood, my heart surged at the thought that Colton could be the one destined for me. Yet the vision I witnessed challenges this hope, suggesting that Nyx might be the key to saving the realms. If aligning with Nyx could safeguard my people, then despite my feelings for Colton, I might need to consider the greater good.

While life with Nyx wouldn't be undesirable—I genuinely care for him and respect most of his qualities as a king—the thought of not following my heart doesn't sit well with me.

With a heavy sigh, I decide to put these considerations aside and retreat to my room for a change of attire. I braid my hair neatly, letting it fall over my shoulder, and choose an ensemble fit for stealth and mobility: black tights paired with a dark top accentuated by a leather bodice.

Before I depart, I pen a brief note on a piece of parchment, "I need some time. Don't come looking for me." I leave it prominently on my bed. With the note placed, I take a deep breath, fortifying my resolve. It's time to clear my head and get Chepi back.

Being on my own will also give me the space to contemplate my next steps without the immediate pressure of choosing between Nyx and Colton.

I pull a cloak from the closet, drape it over my shoulders, and tug the hood up over my head, securing the tie at the front. After how the meeting with the Luminary Council went, I'm uncertain about the reception I'll receive from Kaine and Sybil in the Sorcerer Realm. Kaine, taking his role as regent far too seriously, didn't even defend me during the meeting, even though I am supposed to be his future queen. Both he and his wife seem nothing more than power-hungry, which infuriates me, especially given that they now reside in my childhood home—a place that, though not particularly warm toward the end, still holds significance for me. It's painfully clear he's not on my side and was even looking for ways to strip me of my dark magic.

My shadows begin to stir, slithering within me, and I forcefully shake off the unsettling sensation. Right now, all I want is to retrieve Chepi, speak with Lili, and find out what transpired after Kaine cowardly fled the meeting. Even if I'm not ready to be queen, I still want to make sure my people are alright. They've suffered enough at the hands of power hungry rulers already.

THE SORCERER REALM is breathtakingly beautiful in spring. The morning air is crisp, filled with the harmonious singing of birds and the mingled scents of fresh pine and wildflowers carried by a cool, damp breeze. I pause for a moment, closing my eyes to savor the freshness, letting the serene environment wash over me.

Having chosen to channel outside the castle, near Lili's quarters, I avoid a potential encounter with Kaine—I'm not in the mood to deal with his machinations. It's better to remain unseen. I soak up the warmth of the sun on my face for a minute longer, basking in the peace of the early morning.

Then, with a thought, I channel directly into Lili's room. It's early, but she's already up, as usual, dressed in one of her simple yet elegant gowns, meticulously making her bed. The sight of her, so composed and serene, brings a smile to my face.

"Lyra," she practically squeals, her voice filled with delight. At the same time, Chepi leaps into my arms. His wet nose nudges against my neck as he showers me with affectionate licks and excited yips.

I settle onto the edge of Lili's bed, gently placing Chepi down beside me. Intrigued by the new changes in his appearance, I examine him closely. "What are these?" I inquire, eyeing the peculiar little horns made of a dark, smoky substance that seems much like my own shadows. They seem to ebb and flow with a life of their own.

"They simply appeared," Lili explains with a note of bewilderment in her voice. "One minute he was normal, and the next he had these horns."

That confirms what Ryella mentioned about Chepi sharing some of my gifts. This unexpected development makes me curious about what other powers he might have acquired. "Do you like your new horns, squish?" I ask him playfully, but Chepi flops onto his back in response, his tongue lolling out happily. I chuckle and indulge him with a belly rub.

Lili walks over, locks her door, and then draws the blinds closed, creating a private sanctuary within the room. She sits down on the bed beside me and pulls me into a tight hug, the warmth of her embrace reminiscent of days long past.

"Now, tell me everything," she says, her voice comforting me.

I don't dive into the minute details but provide her with a rundown of everything that has transpired since we last met. She listens intently, nodding occasionally and pursing her lips in thought.

I decide to omit the details about the existence of other realms within Zomea. Some things, I feel, are better left unknown, especially when they could only add to her worries. However, I do share the troubling events surrounding the Luminary Council—how they wanted to either kill me or strip me of all my power. I recount how the meeting ended with me unleashing my darkness, resulting in the death of half the council members.

As I divulge these events, Lili's eyes widen in response to the gravity of the situation, but her expression remains compassionate and understanding. There's no hint of judgment in her gaze, only concern and a deep-seated empathy that reminds me why I have always felt safe confiding in her.

"That explains a lot," Lili says, her voice carrying a hint of understanding that piques my curiosity.

"What do you mean?"

Lili rises from the bed and moves to her desk, where she begins rifling through various papers and documents. After a moment, she retrieves a piece of parchment and brings it over to me. "Kaine had these made, put up, and handed out all across the Sorcerer Realm right after he got back from the meeting you speak of," she explains.

I take the parchment from her, my hands slightly trembling as I unfold it to see what Kaine had distributed.

The flyer is stark, its message as chilling as it is clear. At the top, in large bold letters, it declares, "BEWARE THE SHADOW QUEEN!" Below is an ominous warning.

"Protect our realms from the dark enchantress, Lyra Lewis. Do not be deceived by her guise of nobility. Underneath lies a heart governed by dark magic that seeks to dominate and destroy. She has already unleashed her terrifying power upon the Luminary Council, proving her willingness to slaughter those who stand in her way. We must act now to preserve our heritage and safeguard our future. Stand united against the tyranny of dark magic. Reject Lyra Lewis as queen. Protect our realm, protect our traditions!"

Beneath the inflammatory text, there's a detailed sketch of my face wreathed in shadows, the borders traced to make the image appear even more menacing. My hand trembles uncontrollably as I take deep breaths, trying to calm the magic stirring within me, urging me to find Kaine and unleash my wrath upon him.

"What the fuck?" I utter as I read the flyer again, my gaze fixating on the sketch.

Given that few know what I look like due to my years secluded in the castle, Kaine's actions aren't merely inciting an uprising. He's ensuring that everyone can identify me on sight.

BEWARE
THE SHADOW QUEEN !

Protect our realms from the dark enchantress, Lyra Lewis. Do not be deceived by her guise of nobility. Underneath lies a heart governed by dark magic that seeks to dominate and destroy. She has already unleashed her terrifying power upon the Luminary Council, proving her willingness to slaughter those who stand in her way. We must act now to preserve our heritage and safeguard our future. Stand united against the tyranny of dark magic.

Reject Lyra Lewis as queen.

Protect our realm, protect our traditions!

Lili reaches out to steady my shaking hand with her own. When our eyes meet, she gasps, "Your eyes." I close them quickly, praying to the gods for strength to maintain control. After a few tense moments, I open them again. Seeing Lili's face relax, I know the black tendrils have retreated and my eyes have returned to normal.

"What is he thinking? He wants to stay regent forever? Become king of Cloudrum?" I say through gritted teeth.

"I'm afraid it's worse than that," Lili says, her tone grave, pulling me back from the brink of my own turbulent thoughts.

I search her face, anxiety pricking at the edges of my mind. "What could be worse?" I ask, my voice barely concealing the tempest within, ready to channel out of this place if I lose control of my magic.

"Are you sure this is the best time to talk about this? Where's Colton or King Onyx? Maybe we should discuss this with them present," Lili suggests, her concern palpable as she reaches over to squeeze my hand gently.

That ignites a different kind of fire in me—the frustration of being perceived as unable to control myself. "I don't need a man here to make sure I don't get out of line. I can handle it," I snap sharply. Immediately, I regret my harshness, but the sentiment remains. I'm weary of being underestimated, tired of the assumption that I can't handle things on my own.

Taking a deep breath, I try to temper my frustration, focusing on Lili's intent rather than my own irritation. "Please, tell me," I add, softening my tone, urging her to continue. My eyes hold hers, pleading for the truth, no matter how dire it might be.

"I think Kaine knows he wouldn't be accepted as a permanent placement on the throne. That's why he's seeking other options," Lili explains with concern. She pauses, appraising me.

"Other options?" I prompt, eager for clarity, my gaze drilling into hers for answers.

"You know, all of us here—we hear things and see things around the castle, and we're supposed to keep it to ourselves, but people gossip, even the guards," Lili confesses, her hands twisting nervously in her lap. My impatience mounts, ready to coax every detail out of her.

"What gossip have you heard?" I press, needing to know more.

"Kaine and his men have taken that girl out of the basement, Citlali, and they are enlisting her to help them find...Samael."

CHAPTER 7
LYRA

I BLINK AT HER, my mind overwhelmed with thoughts swirling so fast I can barely catch them. "Samael," I manage to echo back slowly, the name heavy on my tongue.

"Kaine believes, as vile as Samael may be, that he is a better alternative than you. At least with Samael the people know what they're getting. I think he believes the realm will back him regaining control as king, while you're a wildcard and not many know you. And now, with these flyers and the rumors spreading…"

My fists clench so tightly that I can feel my nails digging into my palms, the sharp pain a minor distraction from the surge of anger and betrayal swelling within me. I need to get out of here before I do something I'm going to regret. Quickly, I rise to my feet, and Chepi's wings materialize as he flies into the air beside me.

"What are you doing?" Lili asks as she jumps to her feet.

"I'm sorry, Lili. I need to get away from here. I need some air," I say, my voice strained. I scoop Chepi into my arms and pull my hood back up over my head.

"Wait, I'll come with you. We can go for a walk around the back. The forest is rarely patrolled these days, and I doubt we'll run into anyone," she suggests with a hopeful tone.

Her offer tempts me. The promise of calm in the forest is appealing, but I can't trust myself not to unravel further, especially not in her company. "No, I need to go alone and don't think it's a good idea for me to roam the castle grounds right now. But I'll visit again soon," I promise, though the words feel hollow, my mind already racing ahead to the problems that await.

"Alright then. Be careful," she says with resignation, pulling me and Chepi into a tight hug. I return her embrace, savoring the familiar scent of lavender that clings to her, a brief respite that makes me wish I could linger.

"Thank you for looking after Chepi," I murmur, grateful for her support. As I begin to summon my powers to channel us away, a dark wind starts to swirl around us, the energy crackling with my rising emotions.

"Of course, anytime," Lili responds with a warm smile as Chepi and I disappear.

I channel us to the Nocturn Willow grove in the Black Forest, the only place I could think of where I was certain we wouldn't encounter anyone. The sun is high overhead, casting a brilliant light over the scene, which is a stark contrast to the usual veil of night when I've seen this place. Colton was the one who brought me here before, under a blanket of darkness where the shimmering black leaves mimicked a sky full of stars.

In daylight, these trees possess a different kind of beauty. The sunlight filters through the long, sweeping branches of the willows, and the typically dark leaves catch the rays, sparkling in response. This play of light creates a visual effect similar to water cascading through the branches.

I walk slowly, taking in the sights and trying to process

everything. Chepi dashes ahead of me, pausing intermittently to investigate intriguing scents before trotting off again. "Don't go too far," I call out to him, his quick yip in response barely reaching my ears. The Black Forest isn't safe, which is partly why I chose it for solitude—it's unlikely anyone would venture here casually.

As I walk, the weight of Kaine's actions presses on my mind. I can't believe he's attempting to bring Samael back to power, and that flyer...spreading fear and distrust about me. How can I convince my people that I mean to do right by them when I struggle to control my own dark magic? I want to use it for good, but each time I do, I fear the increasing risk of losing myself to it. Losing control when anger strikes is a dangerous gamble. I don't want to harm anyone, despite the council deserving their fate plotting my death right in front of me.

I sigh, my boots kicking up dust as I meander along the path. Perhaps the answer lies in confronting this directly—maybe I need to stop listening to the fears of others and start embracing my dark magic more openly. With more usage, perhaps I can achieve finer control over it. The thought of unleashing it right now is dangerously enticing. The power is intoxicating, seductive.

I can almost feel the dark energy pulsing, eager to be called upon. It's a part of me, after all. Harnessing it fully could either be my salvation or my downfall, but shying away from it hasn't helped. Maybe it's time to let the darkness show me the way.

I MUST HAVE BEEN WALKING for hours now, and it's somewhat surprising that neither Nyx nor Colton has appeared to shepherd me back home. Perhaps they saw my note and decided to grant me the space I requested—shocking, really.

Chepi freezes ahead, and I halt instinctively, tuning my senses to match his alertness. Faintly, the sound of voices drifts over the murmur of running water. Gods, we have ventured all the way to the river that travels the outskirts of the Black Forest, and across it lies Alchem Hollow.

I shiver as I recall my first visit here, and the haunting words from the goddess of darkness and shadows that the seer relayed to me still echo in my mind. "Choose wisely, and you'll harness the darkness in unprecedented ways. Yet a wrong choice will lead the darkness to consume you—and doom all." The memory still bothers me. Thanks, Ryella. How am I supposed to know what the right choices are?

Visiting the seer isn't on my agenda today, but the thought of a drink to ease the tension sounds appealing. "Let's pay a visit to The Crystal Chalice, Chepi," I say, and he darts back toward me and leaps into my arms with his typical enthusiasm.

I channel us to outside the town across the river, emerging near the familiar cobblestone streets that lead to the tavern. Chepi trots contentedly beside me as we weave through the vibrant village. The streets are bustling with life, and the path is illuminated by colorful lanterns floating overhead, leading us like beacons through the familiar marketplace. The air is fragrant with the aroma of burning incense and herbs, a scent that evokes a nostalgic comfort. Despite the shit that has shadowed my recent days, the Sorcerer Realm holds an irreplaceable spot in my heart.

I imagine it always will, no matter where I end up.

As we stroll, I can't help but pause to peer into the windows of the shops we pass. Each display of books, potions, and mystical artifacts calls to a part of me that yearns for the days when I could indulge in such simple pleasures for the sheer joy of it. Fun—something that seems like a distant memory amid the chaos of my current life. Although I'm not sure I've ever had very much fun ever. My mother would never have let me come to this village as a child.

Before long, the familiar façade of The Crystal Chalice looms ahead. Its large sign is a welcome sight, and I read the words written beneath it aloud to Chepi, who looks up with perked ears. "Known for our magical performances and drinks that play tricks on the senses." I chuckle softly, glancing down at him. "That sounds exactly like what we need, doesn't it, boy?"

The promise of a momentary escape into the world of magical illusions and sensory delights feels right. As we approach the entrance, the sound of laughter and music spills out into the street, pulling us into the warm embrace of the tavern.

As I glance around, a live band plays energetically, setting the rhythm for people dancing amidst a cascade of different-colored lights. The smoke hangs thick and heavy like fog on the ground, adding a delightful, otherworldly touch to the tavern's ambiance. I make my way through the crowd to the bar and choose a seat toward the quieter end, away from the direct bustle of the stage. Chepi hops onto a stool next to me and sits.

As Chepi and I settle into our seats, a bartender with striking blue spiky hair approaches us immediately. "What can I get you?" he asks, his tone friendly yet brisk.

I stutter, momentarily unsure of the menu options. "Anything strong will do for me, and could you get water for my pet? Also, do you have any snacks he might like?" I inquire, hoping to treat Chepi as well.

"Honestly, the only thing we have to eat here that won't alter your senses are the meat pies," he replies.

"Perfect. One meat pie as well, please," I say, relieved to have something simple for Chepi.

The bartender nods and walks to the end of the bar, where

he speaks through a small window that I assume leads into the kitchen. I watch him skillfully combine several bottles into a mixer and vigorously shake the contents before pouring it into a tall glass and adding a few ice cubes that glow pink.

Returning to us, he sets down a meat pie and a bowl of water for Chepi, who perks up immediately at the sight of his treat. He then places the tall pink drink in front of me with a grin. "This is called Blind Punch," he announces.

"Why is it called that?" I ask, wary of the name.

"Because it's so strong you won't be seeing much for long after you drink it," he laughs then moves off to assist another customer.

As I take a cautious sip of the Blind Punch, the potent flavors hit me instantly. It's delicious and fruity, but I can tell it's dangerous because I can't really taste the alcohol.

Chepi starts munching on his pie, and I sip on my drink, allowing the rhythm of the music to sway me gently. Before I realize it, I'm on my third drink, and a sense of ease begins to wash over me. I feel freer than I have in a long time—warm, relaxed, and somewhat detached from the usual burdens that weigh me down. This drink is like magic, exactly what I need.

My stomach rumbles, reminding me that it's been a while since I last ate. I order another meat pie, savoring the crust and potatoes, and share the meaty chunks with Chepi, who seems equally grateful for more food. As I eat, I become aware of the time slipping past. It's already past three in the afternoon, and I haven't yet figured out where I'm going to spend the night. The tavern, with its dim lighting and cozy ambiance, makes it easy to forget the passage of time.

Returning to Drew's hive is not an option I'm willing to consider right now, and the castle in Tempest Moon is off limits for obvious reasons. Lost in thought, I'm startled when a hand clamps onto my shoulder, turning me around in my chair.

"Hey, I recognize you," a man says, his face uncomfortably close to mine.

The sudden contact snaps me back to reality, and I tense up, my mind racing with possible scenarios. Who is this man? Does he know me from the flyers Kaine has distributed, or is there another reason for his recognition? I need to tread carefully, especially here in a place where I thought I could blend in unnoticed.

"I don't think so," I reply swiftly, my eyes darting over the man's features to gauge any hint of his intentions. He's definitely a sorcerer—tall and lanky with a neatly trimmed beard and unusually bushy eyebrows. My gaze fixates on those eyebrows a moment too long, which seems to tighten his grip on my shoulder.

"Lyra Lewis, destined to be queen. Well, not if I have anything to say about it," he declares, his tone harsh as he yanks me off the stool. My feet hit the floor, and I wobble unsteadily, a clear sign I've indulged too much in the tavern's potent offerings.

Focus, Lyra.

Chepi growls protectively beside me as several more people crowd around, eager to catch a glimpse or join in the confrontation.

Realizing the situation is quickly escalating, I try to summon my composure along with a hint of my dark magic—enough to ensure I can protect myself and Chepi if things take a turn. My head swims slightly with the effects of the Blind Punch, but the imminent threat sharpens my senses, readying me for whatever comes next. I need to handle this carefully. Any rash actions could have far-reaching consequences now that I'm so exposed.

"Wow, a rebellion leader in the making. Should I get you a crown?" I quip, flashing him a cheeky smile. I hope my sarcasm might defuse the tension. But as the man clenches his fist and raises his hand—whether to point, cast a spell, or strike, I'm not sure—I brace myself for whatever may come.

In a sudden shift, Chepi's head dips, and from his horns erupts a dark burst of pure power. The force of it sends the man flying back into the crowd that has gathered behind him. The band falls silent, and the murmuring commotion of the onlookers swells.

Seizing the moment of stunned surprise, I wrap my arm protectively around Chepi and channel away.

CHAPTER 8

LYRA

WE TOUCH down in the only place I could think of, given my inebriated state and current lack of friends—the Lycan Realm. As soon as we arrive, the familiar sight of the midnight trees greets me, their branches heavy with spectacular shades of blue. Everything here is in full bloom for spring, and the lush, vibrant colors are probably the only thing I miss from this realm. Well, that and Rhett.

This realm is where everything started. It's where Aidan stole my innocence and where Athalda orchestrated the first ceremony. As much as I may truly hate this realm, I've owed my old friend Rhett a visit, and considering everything that's happened, I fear he won't be pleased to see me.

I remember Luke pointing out Rhett's house to me during my first visit here, but it's hard to say if he still lives there or how he'll react to seeing me again. Gods, I haven't seen him since before Nyx killed Aidan, and so much has changed since then. Now, after the council meeting where I killed Larc—their new leader and Rhett's former pack leader and friend—I'm anxious.

My steps grow heavier as I draw closer to Rhett's house. The memories of my last visit, mixed with the recent violent events, churn a storm of nerves within me. Despite the dread that tightens my chest, I know I need to see Rhett. I need to ensure he's okay and need to know if I can call him an ally in the coming days. Especially if Kaine is starting an uprising against me and seeking Samaels help...avoiding the Lycans forever isn't an option.

The village is eerily silent as I walk, the sun having long begun its descent from the sky. I glance over at Chepi, who's staying close by my side, opting to fly rather than walk. "Neat trick you did back there with your new horns," I say, and he swoops in close to lick my cheek.

I wonder what other magic Ryella gifted him. He doesn't seem to change at all when he uses his new magic. Still my same sweet boy, no black eyes or anything.

I think I need to stop being so afraid of my dark magic and start using it more, giving into it and embracing it. I don't care what anyone else thinks. They don't know how I feel, and if I'm going to truly master this new magic, I need to practice using it.

It's probably a good thing I didn't go all black-eyed and release my shadows back at the tavern. That would have only helped to solidify their fears, making me appear like the monster Kaine is painting me to be. Who was that guy anyway? I can't believe he recognized me and grabbed me like that.

I run a hand over my face, feeling the weight of the day's events. All I want right now is another drink and to curl up in a warm bed. The temptation to channel back to Drew's and retreat to my room is strong. But I know I need to face this, to talk to Rhett alone. It's important and needs to be done without any more delays or distractions.

As I pass through another farm field, I turn down the trail

that leads to Rhett's cabin. I can already see it in the distance, and the plume of smoke curling from the chimney assures me someone is home. My pace quickens with anticipation, but as I draw nearer, I spot him sitting on the steps as if he's been waiting for me. Rhett, with his jet-black hair and tan skin, those piercing baby-blue eyes cutting through the dimming light—it hasn't been that long since we last met, but he looks even more imposing now. He rises, his figure looming larger as he takes a few steps toward me.

I muster a smile, though his face remains stoic, unreadable. Swallowing the nervous lump in my throat, I brace myself. "Hi," I manage to say cheerfully, my voice tinged with a silly, buzzed lilt. The simplicity of the greeting hangs awkwardly in the air as I approach.

"What are you doing here, Lyra?" Rhett asks as I come to a stop in front of him. His tone is guarded, not the warm greeting I had hoped for, but at least he's not shifting into a wolf and attacking me.

"Can we talk?" I ask, managing a small smile in an attempt to lighten the mood. He regards me with a scrutinizing look, his arms crossed, taking a moment to weigh his options or decide how much to let his guard down.

"Come inside," he finally says, turning back toward the cabin and gesturing for me to follow. I exchange a nervous glance with Chepi, who seems to sense the tension, and then I follow after Rhett.

Once inside, I quickly take in the cabin's interior, relieved to see he appears to be alone. The space is charming in its rustic simplicity. A small stone fireplace sits in the corner of the main sitting room, surrounded by a couch and a few lounge chairs that, though worn, look invitingly cozy. A giant fur rug sprawls across the floor in front of the fire.

"Do you mind if I sit?" I ask awkwardly, still standing near the front door.

"Be my guest," Rhett replies with a hint of irritation. I move to the fur rug and sit cross-legged, grateful for the warmth of the fire, and Chepi sprawls out next to me. I clear my throat, preparing to explain everything, but Rhett sits down across from me, leaning back against a chair and stretching his legs toward the fire. This gesture feels like a good sign. He doesn't hate me if he's inviting me in and sitting close.

"What's happened to you, Lyra?" he asks, locking eyes with me.

"What do you mean?" I respond, puzzled by his question.

"Last I saw you, you're with King Onyx looking for some old sorceress, then rumors spread that your Fae king is responsible for killing Aidan." He runs a hand through his tousled black hair, looking genuinely confused and concerned. "Fuck, good riddance really, none of us cared for Aidan. But then you disappear for months, and all the realms are going to shit, being overrun by attacks. Then I hear Larc has to attend a meeting to discuss you and some new dark magic you've gotten into."

He pauses, allowing the weight of what he's saying to sink in, and I unconsciously start to chew on the inside of my cheek.

"And then he ends up dead, and according to Kaine, it was at your hand. I didn't want to believe it—to believe all the things I've been hearing about you. I mean, what the fuck is going on with you, Lyra?"

His barrage of questions hits me harder than I anticipated, each one a reminder of the chaotic spiral my life has become. I realize I need to be transparent with Rhett, to explain the complexities and pressures that have driven my actions, hoping he can understand.

"First of all, I haven't 'gotten into' dark magic," I begin, trying to keep my voice steady. "You say it like I went seeking out trouble. I inherited my magic, which is dark magic, and it wasn't by choice." I pause, taking a deep breath to steady myself for the explanation that needs to come next.

"Larc was called to meet as part of this council, the Luminary Council, which has been around forever, I guess. They are responsible for ridding our world of dark magic, for getting rid of the last dark sorcerer to wield it," I explain, hoping to clarify the gravity of the situation.

Before I can continue, Rhett interrupts harshly, "You say it like it's a bad thing. We don't need dark magic in Eguina. There's already enough darkness here."

I try to remain calm, not wanting to escalate the tension. "Rhett, you have to understand, the council was attacking me. They wanted to kill me or find a way to strip me of my magic. I had no choice..." The memory of that night's desperation surfaces.

"Say it. I want to hear you say it. He was like a father to me. He was good to you when you visited here. He was a good man, and you killed him," he presses, his tone hardening.

I swallow the lump in my throat. "I killed him," I admit, the weight of the confession heavy on my tongue. I want to continue, to defend my actions, but Rhett doesn't give me the chance.

"You killed him, and from what I hear, he wasn't the only one. You killed half the people in that room that night because they were trying to protect Eguina from your dark magic. You killed innocent people. Now tell me, how does that make you any better than Aidan himself, or Samael for that matter?"

Hurt, I feel my magic stir, a dangerous boiling beneath my skin.

My shadows yearn to break free, to respond to his accusations with the fury they demand. Yet I know that yielding to that impulse would only prove his point. It's a struggle to keep them contained, to avoid letting the darkness define me as it has defined so many before me. I clench my fists, fighting to keep control, to find a way that can explain and bridge the gulf of misunderstanding and hurt between us.

"Rhett, he may have been good to you, but that night I was cornered. I was provoked," I say, my voice heavy with the burden of that memory. "I do regret that lives were lost—not because they didn't force my hand but because it hurt you." My plea hangs in the air, but Rhett's shake of his head tells me he's not ready to accept it.

"You don't regret what you did. You think it was justified," he challenges.

I pause, absorbing the accusation, feeling its weight. I have no idea how this escalated so fast, but I need to diffuse things. "Perhaps I don't regret it, Rhett, because I'm exhausted. I'm exhausted from being a pawn, from being used and tormented. Everything has been stripped from me, and I refuse to let them take my magic too. I will not bow to those elders who parade as sages yet understand nothing of my struggle or my power." My voice grows firmer, fueled by a mix of defiance and raw honesty.

"That night, I was surrounded by the fearful and the power-hungry, by the cruel and the ignorant, and I defended myself," I assert. "I defended my very essence."

I let out a heavy sigh, the air filled with tension and unspoken thoughts. Rhett looks down at his hands in his lap. Seeing his contemplation, I reach over and place my hand atop his.

"I'm sorry," I whisper softly. He doesn't pull his hand away, which I take as a sign to continue. "I'm sorry my actions hurt you. I'm sorry you lost someone you cared about. I'm sorry things have been so bad lately."

I give his hand a gentle squeeze, hoping to convey my sincerity and my desire to mend what has been broken between us.

But when Rhett finally looks up, his eyes are filled with fury. "I don't accept your apology. I can't have you here right now. I thought I could, but I can't," he says sharply, knocking my hand away and rising to his feet.

"Rhett, please, I thought we were friends. Can't we talk for a bit longer?" I plead, standing to face him.

"I'm the new leader of the packs now, and having you here looks bad. It looks like a betrayal to my packs, to my people," he growls.

A flurry of thoughts swirls through my mind—I want to ask who he fought to become the leader and what kind of moon ceremony happened. I also want to give him a hug, knowing the Lycan Realm could benefit from a leader with a good heart. But he's already walking to the door, and the reality that he's ejecting me from his life hits hard. I bend over and pick up Chepi, who had fallen asleep in front of the fire.

"At least tell me this," I say, stopping in front of the door. "Do you want Kaine to remain regent over Cloudrum? You know he's actively looking for Samael in hopes he will reclaim the throne. Is that really better than me?"

He runs a hand through his hair, a gesture of frustration, and sighs. "I can't promise I'll be your ally, Lyra, if that's what you're asking. But I'll try to keep the packs out of it," he replies.

"What does that mean?"

"It means I can't be your ally, but I won't stand against you either. Now go before someone spots you and decides to do something stupid," he says, opening the door.

I step outside, pausing to turn back, and catch Rhett's gaze one last time. "Goodbye, Rhett," I say. He nods once, his expression unwavering. But as he begins to close the door, I catch a fleeting softness in his eyes—an echo of past closeness.

The door closes with a gentle thud, and I'm left with the lingering sense of what once was and what might have been.

CHAPTER 9
LYRA

I CHANNEL us away from the village and then continue on foot through Cinder Territory. The forests here are predominantly pine, interspersed with the occasional farmland, but it's too dark to make out much under the night's cloak. The moon is obscured by a thick fog, and the forest is silent, save for the occasional hoot of an owl. Chepi is exhausted, so I carry him, allowing him to rest while I search for a place for us to stay the night.

The only place that comes to mind is Nyx's old bunker, where we once stayed while searching for Aidan.

I wish my conversation with Rhett had gone differently, but even if he can no longer be my friend, I still believe he's a good man. I think he will do well by the Lycans, and perhaps one day I'll be able to regain his trust.

I resolve not to feel guilty any longer about what I did. The council deserved it, and dwelling on regrets is futile. There's no point in getting worked up over the past when it's beyond my power to change. Instead, I focus on navigating the silent, fog-shrouded path ahead.

I recall Nyx's advice that I should be able to sense the hidden bunker entrance using my fae magic. Focusing intently, I search for any subtle pull on my essence, any faint signal that might guide me to our covert refuge. Despite my efforts, I don't feel anything. It seems I'm not close enough yet, or perhaps my senses are dulled from the day's emotional toll—or the alcohol. But I think my conversation with Rhett pretty much sobered me up.

I continue my trek toward the coast, keeping my senses heightened and attuned to any hint of the hidden bunker. The day has stretched long and wearisome, filled with too many events, too many emotional upheavals. The thought of finding the bunker, of finally being able to crawl into bed and escape the weight of the day, is my sole motivation now.

Chepi begins to stir restlessly in my arms, pawing at me as if eager to be let go. I pause, puzzled. "What is it, boy?" I ask, loosening my grip. His wings materialize instantly, and he takes to the air, fluttering anxiously next to me on high alert.

I strain my senses, trying to detect what has alarmed him. Suddenly, I feel a soft rumble under my feet, too subtle at first then unmistakably growing stronger. Before I can fully process the danger, the ground beneath us bursts open.

A colossal serpent rises, its massive body cloaked in glistening black scales that shimmer with a sinister, oily sheen. My eyes trail up its elongated body until I'm met with a pair of glowing emerald orbs. The serpent's bright green eyes pierce the night with an eerie intelligence that has me frozen in place.

I barely have a moment to react as the creature starts to wrap its massive body around my legs, its scales cold and sharp. As it moves, the air fills with the sound of its scales scraping together, a harsh, rasping noise that chills my blood. The serpent's strength is overwhelming, pulling me down as I struggle to keep my balance and find a way to escape its tightening grasp.

Chepi's growl escalates, and I glance up to see several Monstrauths approaching in the distance. "Fuck," I mutter under my breath. In desperation, I reach for the sword Colton gifted me. As my hand grasps the hilt, the blade extends with a swift click. I swing at the serpent, aiming for a weak spot, but the blade merely glances off its armored scales without making a dent.

The serpent tightens its grip, dragging me backward toward the hole it emerged from, intent on pulling me into the depths. Realizing the futility of my sword against such armor, I sheathe it quickly, my heart pounding as panic starts to set in. I have no choice but to tap into the dark magic that courses through me—magic I've been wary of unleashing.

I close my eyes for a brief moment, gathering my focus. The dark power within me stirs, eager and waiting for my command. When I open my eyes, I release it all in a surge of shadowy energy. The magic bursts forth, enveloping my body in a shroud of darkness. Tendrils of shadow whip out from around me, targeting the serpent with precision and force.

The shadows seethe with power, searching for any crack in the serpent's armor, any vulnerability. As they wrap around the beast, they begin to squeeze and constrict, countering the serpent's own deadly embrace. The struggle intensifies, the outcome hanging in the balance as I pour more of my will into the shadows, determined to break free from the creature's lethal hold.

As I wrestle with the serpent's grip, a horrifying realization dawns on me: my dark magic isn't as effective because this creature might be wrought from dark magic itself. I've never encountered such a serpent before, and its sudden emergence is as mysterious as it is terrifying. But where is it from?

As I feel the creature's hold begin to loosen, another serpent bursts from the ground. This one targets my arm, coiling swiftly up toward my neck. I come face-to-face with it, its eyes a swirl of emerald and obsidian. Bracing for a bite, I flinch, but instead it merely tightens its grip, intent on dragging me into its lair. The thought of being taken to its home to be devoured sends a shiver down my spine. "Not today," I mutter through gritted teeth.

Closing my eyes, I withdraw my shadows then gather every ounce of my power. With a focused burst of dark energy, I channel it directly into the serpents. I visualize them turning inside out, their bodies igniting into flames from the inside. A rush of euphoric magic surges through me, the thrill of control and power washing over me as the creatures writhe in agony. When I open my eyes, a satisfied smile plays across my lips.

"That's more like it."

Scrambling to my feet, I survey the scene. Chepi is keeping the Monstrauths at bay. He flaps his wings vigorously, generating a powerful gust of dark wind that the approaching creatures struggle against. I see he has more powers than I thought.

I extend my hands, and inky black smoke pours from my pores, seeping into the air around us. My shadows slither across the forest floor, reaching the first couple of Monstrauths. They wrap around the creatures' rotting skeletal bodies, climbing all the way up their long, twisted horns. I completely envelop them in darkness while my shadows consume them, feasting on their flesh until there's nothing left.

As my shadows continue their relentless work, I turn my attention to the three other Monstrauths to my right. The one in the front lunges toward me, its giant mouth agape, revealing sharp, frothing teeth. The high-pitched screech they emit echoes through the forest, piercing the silent night air. Swiftly, I draw my blade and slice its head clean off, silencing the dreadful sound instantly. The body collapses in a heap, the threat abruptly ended.

For the remaining two, I decide to employ a different tactic. Focusing intently, I channel my power directly with my mind. I watch, a cold smile spreading across my face, as they disintegrate before my eyes, turning into nothing more than powdery bone and a few chunks of rotted flesh. The ease with which I dismantle these monsters fills me with a dark satisfaction.

"Come on, boy. There'll be more coming," I warn Chepi. We quicken our pace in search of the damn bunker. The high-pitched scream of the Monstrauth was unmistakable—it was a call, likely summoning more demons to our location.

A sudden crunch of a branch causes me to jerk my head around. Peering through the thickening fog, I discern the shapes of at least a dozen more Monstrauths beginning to emerge from the encroaching darkness of the forest.

Chepi, sensing the immediate threat, springs into action. He dips his head, and from his horns, a beam of dark energy erupts, striking with precision. The force of his attack knocks two of the Monstrauths off their feet, sending them sprawling into the underbrush.

I steel a quick moment to reflect on all that Ryella taught me when she awakened my magic, all the abilities harnessed by dark Sorcerers before me. With a burgeoning curiosity about the limits of my own power, I decide it's time to experiment, to truly test the breadth of my capabilities without fear. I concentrate, summoning a spear made of pure, condensed darkness. It feels cold and heavy and dangerous in my grasp.

With a fluid motion, I hurl the dark spear at one of the encroaching demons. It strikes square in the chest, and upon impact the spear bursts into a swarm of shadow wisps. These tendrils of darkness branch out, voraciously attacking anything within their reach. I watch in awe of myself as everything the tendrils touch starts to boil and disintegrate, as if my spear burst into acid. It's a neat trick, devastating in its simplicity and effectiveness.

I can't help but smile, imagining how to demonstrate this new technique to Colton. Yes, he'll definitely be impressed. As I ready myself for the next assault, I store this new trick in my mind, a powerful addition to my growing arsenal of dark magic.

The Monstrauths can't even get close to us. Chepi continues knocking them down with dark beams and impeding their approach with the magical winds generated by his wings. As I consider which dark magic technique to practice next on these creatures, I can't help but almost laugh at the ease of it all. To think these demons almost killed me once, and now they can't even touch me with their rotting, bony hands.

Feeling bold, I decide to take the challenge directly to the monsters. I charge toward them, then at the last second I duck and sweep my hand across the ground, encircling two of them in a swift, fluid motion. Instantly, a dimensional rift forms beneath them. The ground vanishes, swallowing the demons whole before the rift seals shut and the earth reappears as if nothing had happened.

"Holy shit," I whisper to myself, astonished. I had no idea I could conjure such a thing, and I certainly have no clue where I sent those demons, but the thrill of it is exhilarating.

As I unleash more dark magic, waves of almost orgasmic energy surge through me. My body tingles, infused with an unstoppable force. However, a thunderous sound in the distance snaps my attention to the skies. The flapping of dozens of wings fills the night air—Sarrols are diving toward us. My heart tightens for Chepi, but he adeptly dodges and fends them off. Yet the numbers are overwhelming—serpents, Monstrauths, and now Sarrols, all converging here in the desolate Cinder Territory.

Suddenly, I'm knocked to the ground as one of the flying demons crashes into me. I react instinctively, blasting it with my power, flipping over and leaping to my feet. But they're relentless, attacking from all directions. A real fear pierces through me, the first genuine terror I've felt in this encounter. I consider opening my tether to Colton for backup, but I decide against it, determined to handle this myself.

Two Sarrols swoop down, knocking me to the ground again. Their talons dig painfully into my shoulders as I hiss in pain. The situation worsens as I hear Chepi yelp, seeing him slammed against a tree by another Sarrol. That's the final straw. Closing my eyes, I surrender fully to the dark energy swirling within me.

For a moment, all I hear is the chaotic symphony of wings and collisions. Then in the next breath there's utter silence. I unleash my magic in a cataclysmic burst, radiating outward in all directions, obliterating everything it touches. When I reopen my eyes and draw a breath, the scene before me is eerily calm. Not a single creature remains. Everything has been disintegrated into nothingness. The forest floor is clear, as if the ferocious battle never occurred.

Chepi, unharmed, scurries over and nuzzles against my leg. I scoop him up, stroking his head as I set my sights on finding the bunker.

"Let's get out of here," I murmur, sending out my magic until I finally feel a tug.

ONCE INSIDE THE BUNKER, I wash up as best I can then rifle through some of the boxes stored here until I find one of Nyx's t-shirts. To my relief, it's clean. After changing, I scavenge a bit more and come across a bag of nuts and some dried meat. I share some with Chepi before we both crawl into bed. Summoning my orb of light back into my palm, I let the room return to complete darkness.

Despite the day's chaos, I feel safe here, a sense of ease settling over me. Tonight, I didn't lose control of my dark magic. True, there was no one around to get hurt, but I managed to rein it back in, feeling entirely myself afterward—a definite win.

Chepi begins to snore softly beside me, and I can't help but smile, relieved he can find sleep so quickly. The bed still carries the scent of Nyx, which stirs a complex mix of feelings within me. This very bed was where Nyx and I first had sex, and now, as I try to open myself to the possibility of bonding with him, marrying him, and letting go of Colton, I'm conflicted.

The darkness within me lingers beneath the surface, whispering temptations to claim them both as mine. I forcefully shake off the invasive thoughts. Using my dark magic always ignites a craving for more—more power, more pleasure, more of everything. It's a voracious hunger, similar to what other dark Sorcerers must have succumbed to. There's a perpetual dissatisfaction that festers within me, my shadows pulsing, eager for release.

A reckless part of me, buried deep, yearns to summon these men here and surrender to my desires right now. The very idea makes me blush—my magic seems to possess a will of its own, pushing against the boundaries of my restraint. I blow out a breath and push the temptations aside.

The echosphere hinted that Nyx might indeed be my fated mate. But as sleep begins to claim me, a persistent ache tugs at my heart—an ache for Colton. Despite everything, my heart yearns for him, and this undeniable feeling lingers, a silent whisper in the back of my mind as I drift into sleep.

"SOMETHING'S HERE!"

A sharp shudder ripples through the earth beneath my feet. I'm on a stage, and Colton stands before me. His expression is eerily calm, stark against the chaos erupting around us. The ground quakes violently, threatening to tear everything apart. He grips my hands firmly but doesn't move.

"What's happening?" I cry out, panic rising in my voice. Colton only stares back, his eyes deep wells of silence. A pillar next to us fissures with a deafening crack, and I feel a dark, oppressive force pressing down on my chest. Darkness erupts from the fissure, swallowing the entire ceremony space in an impenetrable black void. My heart races. My breath quickens.

Frantically, I scan the darkness, but visibility is zero. *Is this my bonding ceremony to Colton?* The thought blurs with fear and confusion. He remains statue-like, an unmoving figure in the consuming shadow. Then the sensation changes—it's no longer pressing on me. It's pulling me downward. I gasp as Colton vanishes before my eyes, and the stage beneath me disappears. I'm falling, tumbling through nothingness, until suddenly my feet hit solid ground.

I whirl around and find myself standing before the gates— massive, imposing metal barriers entwined with thorn-laden branches. The atmosphere is thick with an eerie silence. I'm utterly alone, no sign of Colton or any familiar face. As I stand there, transfixed, the gates creak ominously, beginning to swing open on their own. The slow, grating screech of metal echoes through the silence, and I hold my breath, heart pounding in my chest.

I don't dare move or breathe deeply as the gates open wider, inviting or perhaps beckoning me into the unknown beyond. The anticipation, the fear, it all melds into a moment suspended in time, when every possibility seems terrifying and inevitable.

"Lyra, wake up."

The sudden sound of my name and the sensation of two strong arms shaking me jolt me from sleep. Gasping, I sit up, instinctively casting out my orb to flood the room with light as Nyx comes into view beside me on the bed. My eyes blink rapidly, struggling to adjust.

"Am I still dreaming?" I stammer, the line between reality and my nightmare blurring.

He chuckles softly. "No, Princess, you were having a nightmare, and I woke you. Are you alright?" His voice is gentle, concerned.

I search his face, still trying to anchor myself back in reality from the vivid terror of my dream. "What are you doing here?" I finally manage, my voice steadier.

"Did you really think you could enter my bunker and I wouldn't feel your presence?" he says.

I glance around, realizing I hadn't considered that. I'd blocked out Colton's tether so he couldn't locate me, but it hadn't occurred to me to worry about Nyx finding me. "I guess I thought I could," I admit, my voice heavy with exhaustion.

"Scoot over. It's late. I'll help you sleep," he says casually, and without a second thought I make room for him. He kicks off his boots and slides into bed beside me. When I turn onto my side, he wraps his arms around me, pulling me close to his chest. This time, I don't pull away or protest. Instead, I let myself breathe in his familiar scent, finding an unexpected comfort in his embrace.

As I drift back to sleep, Nyx runs his fingers gently through my hair, his voice a soothing whisper in the darkness. "I've got you. I've always got you." He wraps around me like a warm blanket, and I surrender to the feeling of safety, letting the remnants of my nightmare fade into the night.

CHAPTER 10

LYRA

I WAKE to the sound of steady breathing in my ear, and the realization hits me—last night wasn't a dream. Nyx really did show up here and is still sleeping beside me. Carefully, I flip over to face him. His eyes snap open, and a slow smile curves his lips.

"Good morning, Princess," he murmurs.

"Does Colton know you're here?" I ask before I can consider their impact. I almost regret asking as I watch his expression change. His smile disappears, replaced by a sudden seriousness as he rolls onto his back to stare at the ceiling.

"No," he answers after a heavy pause. His voice is flat, a stark contrast to the warmth of just a moment ago.

"I'm glad you came," I say, attempting to ease the tension. Perhaps this is a sign that I should spend time with Nyx without lingering on Colton, to genuinely explore the possibility of a future with him. I do care for him, and if he's truly who I'm destined to be with, accepting that might be the next step.

He turns back to face me, skepticism shadowing his

features. "Don't play with me," he says softly, his hand reaching out to stroke my arm gently, a hint of caution in his touch.

"I'm not," I assure him sincerely, my voice steady. "I am glad you came. I..." My words falter as I search for the right way to express my tangled feelings without hurting him further.

"You wish it had been him instead," he says sharply, full of hurt and accusation.

I shake my head. "That's not what I was going to say," I insist, meeting his gaze directly. "I'm trying to figure things out, Nyx. It's complicated, and I'm torn. But right now, I'm here with you, and I'm honestly glad for your company." My voice softens, hoping to convey my genuine feelings and the complexity of the emotions I'm wrestling with.

"You know Colton doesn't appreciate your dark magic. Ever since you first unleashed it, he looks at you as if you unsettle him. Haven't you noticed?"

I can't help but frown. Indeed, I've observed Colton growing distant, his cautiousness apparent whenever I wield my powers. But we were finally having a good moment together before the attack in the Lamia Realm. He let his shields down, and I felt his feelings for me.

"He's being protective and doesn't want me to lose control again," I defend, trying to rationalize his concerns.

"I would never look at you the way he does. To me, you're incredibly beautiful and sexy, especially when you're embracing your dark magic," Nyx counters smoothly, his tone dropping to a soothing murmur as he reaches out to tuck a lock of hair behind my ear. "Lyra, I've felt a shift between us even before the council meeting. That kiss... I know you felt its power too. We are destined, you and I. Together, we can govern Eguina, and I will stand by you as your beacon, ensuring you never succumb to the darkness fully. I'll support your growth in dark magic, encourage its use under your reign, and you'll always be safe because you'll have me by your side."

I look down at his chest, grappling with the emotions that his declaration stirs within me. The room is heavy with silence, hanging thick between us, until finally he breaks it.

"I love you, Lyra. I will die loving you," he confesses, his voice a fervent whisper that fills the space around us. "You are the only one I see, the only one I yearn for. My heart is irrevocably yours, whether you choose to claim it or not." The intensity in his voice is palpable, and it presses against the walls of my heart with an almost physical force.

His hand gently lifts my chin, compelling me to meet his stare. His eyes, fiercely glowing gray, hold mine in a gaze so intense that the world around us seems to fade. "You're mine, and I will fight for you through all eternity because we are fated you and I," he says with an unshakeable conviction.

He leans in close, his presence gentle yet commanding, and places a tender kiss on my forehead. Then he raises a hand to cup my face, his touch careful and filled with emotion. As his lips meet mine, the kiss is soft and gentle.

But when I kiss him back, returning his passion with my own, something shifts. He seems to lose control of his restraint. The kiss deepens, intensifying as if a dam has been broken, unleashing a torrent of pent-up emotions. His hands, firm, pull me closer, and I can feel the urgency and desire pouring from him.

He presses me back, rolling on top of me as the intensity escalates. Breaking the kiss, he cups my face, looking down at me with an expression that mixes desire with something deeper. "Fuck, you have no idea how long I've thought about this, about being inside you again," he murmurs hoarsely then claims my mouth again with fervor.

His kiss is rough, filled with longing and urgency. He tugs

at my shirt, pulling it up to grasp my breast. I gasp into his mouth as he squeezes my nipple, sending a sharp pulse of sensation through me.

He undoes his pants, and as I feel the firm press of him against my thigh. The shadows within me stir, purring with a dark pleasure, urging him to claim me here and now. A whimper escapes me into his kiss as he presses closer, pinning me beneath him. I feel the press of his cock at my entrance, but he pauses there, a part of me yearning for him to fuck me, while another, the more rational part, is seized by a sudden panic.

My heart thunders in my chest, but not from excitement— fear grips me. The realization hits hard: I'm terrified of making a monumental mistake, because deep down I love Colton. I thought I could bury those feelings, thought I could make it work with Nyx, but it doesn't feel right. This feels so wrong.

As Nyx's hand trails down my body, I catch it with my own, stopping him before he can go further. He pauses, his eyes searching mine, and I sense he feels the tension in my body stiffen.

"What's wrong?" he asks.

"Nyx...I don't think I can do this. I'm sorry," I manage to breathe out, the words thick with emotion.

In an instant, he's off the bed, pulling his pants up and pacing the room, a hardened expression on his face. I pull my shirt down and quickly get to my feet, attempting to bridge the sudden gulf between us. "Nyx—"

"Don't speak, you fucking tease," Nyx hisses, stopping in front of the wall and slamming his palm against it as he leans forward, his back to me.

The thud echoes in the suddenly cold room. I freeze, words failing me as the gravity of my actions hits hard. I've screwed things up so badly. I wanted a world where I could have them both—Colton's love and Nyx's friendship. Then I believed I was destined to be with Nyx, but now after learning they are brothers, a future with Colton seems possible again. Fuck, none of that matters because, as Drew said, deep down, I already know.

I've always known but have been trying everything possible to justify it. I love Colton, and he's the one I want to be with, even if it could damn us all.

Nyx breaks into my spiraling thoughts. "It's because of him, isn't it?" he asks, his voice cutting through the tension.

"Yes," I admit after a painful pause, my voice barely a whisper. "I'm in love with him. And Nyx, I love you too, but it's not the same. I love you as a friend, and I want you to be happy."

He starts to laugh, but it's bitter and hollow, sending a chill down my spine. "Friends. You love me too and want to be friends. You're both fucking dead to me," he spits out, the venom in his words stinging.

I take a step toward him, my heart pounding. "Nyx, please. You said you would love me until you die. Can't we talk about this?" I plead, desperate to salvage at least some part of what we had.

In an instant, his movements blur with speed, and suddenly my back is pressed against the wall. One of his hands is anchored above my head, firm against the cool surface, while the other grips my hip, holding me securely in place. His gaze narrows on me, intense and searching, and as he leans in close, I instinctively close my eyes.

Uncertainty swirls within me. His lips are so near I can feel his breath over them. I'm unsure if he's going to try to kiss me again, then he shifts slightly, his breath warm against my ear, and he whispers, "Well, we both already know I'm a liar."

By the time I open my eyes, he's gone in a whirl of darkness as he channels.

Tears stream down my face uncontrollably as Chepi pokes

his head out from under the covers at the edge of the bed. I try to lighten the mood with a tease, "Oh, nice of you to come out now." But my laughter is hollow, drowned out by the flow of tears. In a moment of vulnerability, I drop my shields and let my longing for Colton surge through the tether that connects us. I need to see him—to feel him. I need to make things right.

Almost instantly, a stir of wind kicks up, carrying the familiar citrus scent of Colton. He materializes beside me in the bunker, one hand cupping my cheek and the other resting gently on my shoulder. His presence envelops me, providing the instant comfort I desperately need.

"Why are you crying? What's wrong?" he asks, conjuring a small orb of light, and his eyes scan the bunker before settling on me with a deep frown. "Did Nyx hurt you?" His voice lowers to a growl, filled with protective fury.

"Gods, no. He didn't do anything," I rush to explain to prevent Colton from any rash actions.

"Then tell me what happened? Why are you crying?" Colton asks, reaching up to brush a tear from my cheek.

"Can we get out of here first? I want to talk, but not here," I say, sniffling and struggling to control my emotions. I need a change of scenery, somewhere I can think clearly.

"Take me wherever you want, enchantress. You're the powerful one now." He smirks, stepping closer to me, his warmth enveloping me in reassurance. His light-hearted comment is meant to lift my spirits, and it brings a small, grateful smile to my face despite how I'm feeling about hurting Nyx.

I scoop Chepi up from the bed and let Colton wrap his arms around me. Feeling secure in his embrace, I breathe in his sweet citrus scent, focus my thoughts, and channel us away from the bunker...away from the last place I may ever see Nyx.

We touch down in Colton's living room, and the sudden

brightness from the sun streaming through the massive windows forces me to squint—the darkness of the bunker really does skew your senses. Chepi, invigorated by the familiar surroundings, leaps from my arms and scampers down the hall, his small paws echoing slightly.

The villa remains unchanged since my last visit, and I take a moment to admire the expansive glass dome overhead. The view beyond is still breathtaking, with towering cliffs and a distant waterfall framed by trees in hues of green and lavender. The bark of the trees seems to sparkle even from here.

I make my way to the large sofa in front of the flagstone fireplace, sinking into its comfy cushions. The soothing sound of water flowing through the indoor pond on the ground floor fills the room, easing the tension from my body. The beauty of this place is already soothing my soul.

Colton joins me on the sofa, turning to face me with an intent look, giving me his full attention.

"Come on, my shadow, cheer up. Talk to me," Colton says gently, and I take a deep breath, searching for the right thing to say.

"Do you mind if I use your shower and change my clothes first?" I ask, craving a few moments alone to collect my thoughts. Honestly, I feel grimy, and after so long with only baths, a shower sounds heavenly.

"Do you want me to join you?" Colton asks, one side of his lips quirking up in a playful smirk.

I shake my head, smiling despite myself. "No, but thanks."

"Alright, take as long as you need. I'll be here when you're ready," he responds.

Grateful for the space, I head up to his bathing chamber, ready to wash away the remnants of the last couple of days.

As the warm water washes over me, I try to come to terms with the possibility that Nyx may truly be out of my life for good. The accusation of being a tease haunts me. I never intended to toy with their feelings. While I do care for Nyx, the realization settles deep within my bones: I am in love with Colton, and it's him I want to be with.

All this time, my emotions have been a tangled mess, misled by the notion that Nyx was my destined partner. But as Drew pointed out, the choice is ultimately mine, and now knowing they are brothers, Colton could very well be the light the prophecy speaks of. His nature, always bent on saving creatures and striving to do what's right, coupled with the white glow of his healing magic, makes him seem like a beacon of light in contrast to Nyx's often darker demeanor.

No definitive answer will reveal which brother is the light foretold by the prophecy, so I must follow my heart, which unequivocally yearns for Colton. It pains me to think of Nyx hurting, but I hold onto the hope that someday he will understand, and perhaps in time we could even be friends...but knowing Nyx it's probably a reach. I hate the way he looked at me in those last moments in the bunker. He didn't seem himself, understandably so, I guess.

I rinse off the last of the soap, my tears with it. By the time I shut off the water, I feel a little better.

CHAPTER 11
COLTON

I PACE AROUND THE KITCHEN, my thoughts racing as I wait for Lyra to come back downstairs. Each second feels like an eternity, gnawing at me with the image of Nyx being there with her.

How long were they together in that bunker? Did they spend the whole night together? Did he touch her...or worse? The mere thought twists my gut with a mix of rage and nausea. She was wearing one of his shirts. I could hunt him down, unleash my fury—but I grit my teeth and run a hand through my hair, opting to pace instead.

I had told Lyra she needed to make her own choices, assured her I wouldn't get mad, hoping she'd realize on her own that I'm the one she should be with. But the possibility that it might take her sleeping with Nyx to see that cuts deeper than I want to admit. Imagining his hands on her skin...

I'm probably jumping to conclusions. Maybe nothing happened. But finding her in tears, wearing his damn t-shirt, in a room that reeked of him—it's hard to believe it's all innocent.

Chepi strolls into the kitchen, lying down with a yawn, seemingly oblivious to my frustrations.

"I don't suppose you want to fill me in on what happened?" I ask him half-jokingly. He looks up with those innocent eyes, offering no clues.

After getting him some water, I hear the shower stop and head back to the living room.

I continue pacing in front of the fireplace, summoning a blaze with a wave of my hand, knowing how much Lyra loves the warmth and light of a fire. As I await her return, a ripple of anxiousness pulses through me. When she finally appears, descending the staircase in a pink dress that clings softly to her frame, my breath catches. The dress's delicate straps and the way her damp hair cascades in waves over her shoulders, I can't look away.

She approaches with her shields up, the faintest hint of her emotions trickling through to me, tinged with anxiety. Without a word, she wraps her arms around my waist and rests her head against my chest, her gaze fixed on the flickering flames. I encircle her in my arms, relishing the contact, content to stand here in silence, holding her forever if that's what she wants. The fire crackles, filling the room with a comforting, familiar sound.

After a moment, she looks up at me, her eyes reflecting the firelight. "Do you want to sit down?" she asks softly.

"After you," I reply.

Reluctantly, I let her slip from my embrace, feeling the loss of her body against mine immediately. I follow her to the sofa, sensing the weight of the conversation ahead. We settle next to each other, close but not touching, a respectful distance that seems necessary for the serious dialogue she's poised to initiate. I steal a glance at her, wishing I could simply pull her into my lap and forget the world outside but knowing she needs this moment to speak her mind.

"I'm sorry, Colton. I'm sorry for being so indecisive and for letting Nyx get into my head," she starts, her voice faltering slightly. "When I believed Nyx was the key to the prophecy— the one destined to save me—I thought I might have to be with him. If being with him could save the realms, save me from my own darkness, I was willing to try," she confesses.

I remain silent, giving her space to continue, although hearing her say she was willing to try with Nyx feels like a dagger to my heart.

"I admit I had unresolved feelings for him, and I do care about him. I want him to be okay, happy," she continues. I clench my jaw, bracing for what she might say next.

"He came to the bunker and woke me in the middle of the night. He told me he loves me and that he'll love me until the day he dies. He told me my dark magic unsettles you, and..." She pauses, but I cut in before she can continue, my temper flaring.

"Nothing about you could ever unsettle me, Lyra," I assure her, the intensity of my feelings pushing me to speak. I remind myself to let Nyx have it the next time I see him.

"He kissed me," she whispers, her voice quivering as her eyes meet mine. "He got on top of me, and I...I kissed him back." She swallows hard, her expression troubled. "But it felt wrong, like a betrayal, because my heart belongs to you." She pauses, her gaze searching mine, bracing for a wave of anger or judgment. Instead, I'm filled with a sudden relief that she halted things before they went any further. "I told Nyx I couldn't continue with him and that it's you I want, Colton. It's always been you, if you'll still have me."

I feel a wave of fear from her and I realize it must be fear of rejection.

"I thought I would never have you," I confess, letting my frustrations and fears surface. "When I found your note, and Drew told me she had revealed the truth about Nyx and me being brothers, I was afraid you'd never forgive me for keeping that from you." I pause, running a hand through my hair, trying to find the words to explain the chaos that followed the council meeting, how my parents stormed out, likely grappling with the fallout of secrets long buried. "I wanted to tell you, Lyra. So many times, I nearly did, but something always got in the way. And now with everything out in the open, my mother must be livid. After the council meeting, she and my father... I don't even know if they'll stay together. Granger found out she cheated on him years ago, kept this secret about me not being his biological son."

She narrows her eyes, the hurt evident. "Why did you keep it from me for so long?" she probes, and I know I need to be honest.

Looking into her eyes, filled with a mix of hurt and the need for truth, I realize any justification might sound hollow. "I tried to find the right moment, but fear always held me back. We shared so much in Zomea, where you opened up about everything. And there I was, holding back the one thing that might change everything between us. I'm sorry, Lyra. I should have trusted you more." My voice is thick with regret, understanding the weight of my withheld truth and how it might have shaped her struggles.

"If you can forgive my consideration of being with Nyx, then I can forgive you for keeping this secret," she says, and my heart swells with relief.

I admit, if she had chosen Nyx, I would have found a way to forgive her, eventually. We weren't committed to each other, and under the weight of that prophecy, it's hard to fault her for considering every possibility.

"No more secrets," I promise. Her smile lights up the space between us, and it's all the permission I need. I pull her into my lap, tipping her back slightly as I capture her lips with mine. The soft squeak of surprise that escapes her fuels my desire, deepening the kiss, reveling in the feel of her in my arms.

She pulls away, breathless. "Take me somewhere," she says.

"Tell me where you want to go," I murmur as I trail kisses down her neck, the taste of her skin igniting a deep hunger within me.

"Out there," she breathes, pointing up through the glass dome. I rise to my feet, keeping her close in my arms. Her delighted squeal makes me smile as I channel us away.

In an instant, we're at the top of the highest waterfall in the Dream Forest, a place clearly visible from the villa. Setting her down gently, I watch her expression transform in awe—she's breathtaking under the sunlight filtering through the trees.

She turns slowly, absorbing the view of the river winding through lush greenery. Magic crackles softly overhead with the breeze, making the leaves shimmer. Her eyes light up, reflecting the enchantment of this secluded spot.

When she looks back at me, there's a fierce hunger in her gaze that matches the intensity of my own. I close the distance between us, drawn irresistibly to her.

The sweet aroma of spring water mingles with the scent of fresh leaves as the wind swirls around us, showering down green and lavender foliage. Lyra looks up, her smile radiant under the cascade of leaves. I reach up, gently removing a leaf tangled in her hair, then slide my fingers through the silky strands to clasp the back of her neck, drawing her closer.

As she meets my gaze again, the mesmerizing swirl of cobalt and emerald in her glowing eyes captivates me. I'm lost in the depths of her look, enraptured by the enchanting allure, until I lean in, reconnecting our lips in a kiss deepened by the magic of the forest around us.

I hoist her into my arms, and she wraps her legs around my waist, clinging to me as I devour her. There's no room for soft and gentle kisses; my need is too urgent, too demanding. Clutching her tightly, I press her against me, my arousal undeniable against her stomach. Impatience gets the better of me, and with a snap of my fingers, our clothes vanish, becoming a pile on the forest floor. She breaks our kiss with a giggle, glancing at our discarded garments.

"Someone's in a hurry," she teases.

I lean close, whispering into her ear, "Oh, my shadow, I plan to savor every moment once I'm inside you." I nibble at her earlobe then carry her toward the water's edge. Her grip tightens as we approach the top of the waterfall, her excitement palpable. "Hang on tight."

I leap off the ledge.

Her scream pierces the air, a thrilling sound that makes me chuckle as my wings unfurl, gliding us smoothly through the cool mist of the falls. We plunge into the warm waters of the swimming hole below. As Lyra tips her head back to look up at the cascading water, I take advantage of her distraction. I capture one of her breasts, teasing her nipple with my mouth, eliciting moans as she begins to grind against me.

I release her breasts and grasp her hips, lifting her until my swollen cock aches at her entrance. The need to be inside her is almost overwhelming. She brushes my damp hair out of my face and reaches down between us, grabbing my cock and giving it a firm stroke, her teeth tugging at her bottom lip with anticipation. I press into her a bit, testing, and the warm clench of her pussy nearly undoes me.

Her arms wrap around my neck, and our eyes lock—intense, fiery. With a firm grip on her hips, I slowly lower her onto me. Her breath catches, a soft whimper escaping her lips as she takes me in, inch by inch. The sensation is excruciatingly perfect, and I resist the urge to fuck her hard, letting her adjust to me.

I lift her up slowly, setting a rhythm that has her meeting my thrusts instinctively. She runs her hands through my hair, gripping my shoulders for leverage, her nails digging in slightly, spurring me to pull her tighter against me. When her lips find mine again, she devours me with a desperation, as if I'm the only water in a desert she's been lost in. Her tongue explores my mouth with urgent hunger, and I'm lost in the ferocity of her need.

My hand stays wrapped tightly around her, while my other hand wanders between us, pressing against her clit. At my touch, she moans into my mouth, a sound so raw it nearly drives me over the edge. I circle her clit with my thumb, coaxing another moan that vibrates between us, fueling my arousal further.

Moving us to the edge of the water, I press her back against the cool, wet rocks, lifting one of her thighs to deepen my thrusts. She breaks away from my kiss, her head falling back as she gasps, "Colton, oh gods."

The sound of my name on her lips intensifies my movements. I want to hear more, need more from her. "I want to hear you say that you're mine," I demand, pausing with my cock teasingly pulled back. "Mine and only mine," I clarify, before driving back into her hard, claiming her with every thrust. I want her to remember the feel of my cock for days to come.

"I'm yours, only yours," she says, her breath ragged as she locks eyes with me. "Now and forever," she adds, her voice a whisper of commitment against the rush of the waterfall around us. I thrust into her relentlessly, driven by the affirmation of her words, until she is screaming my name, her body convulsing around me in a powerful release. Her climax triggers my own, and I surrender to the sensation, spilling into her as waves of pleasure crash through me.

As her body relaxes, spent from the intensity, she leans heavily against me for support. Carefully, I maneuver us to a nearby ledge and sit down, keeping her in my lap, my cock still pressed inside her. She rests her head on my shoulder, her breaths evening out.

Gently, I brush wet strands of hair from her face and plant a tender kiss on her forehead. Around us, her hair floats in the water like a blanket of white silk, framing her face in the soft light filtering through the water.

She slips off my lap to sit beside me, leaving a void where her warmth had been. Even submerged in the water up to her neck, her form shimmers invitingly through the crystal-clear depths.

"What are you smiling like that for?" she teases, catching my admiring glance.

"I think you know exactly why, enchantress," I reply, my voice a low rumble. Her laughter rings through the air, beautiful and carefree, and she playfully splashes water at me. I catch her hand mid-splash, pulling her back to me with a gentle tug. She willingly wraps her legs around my waist again, her hands threading through my hair.

Leaning in, she kisses me—her lips soft, her touch tender. Her tongue traces my bottom lip tantalizingly before she pulls back slightly, her eyes sparkling with emotion. As she lowers her shields, her intense feelings flood into me, leaving me nearly breathless.

"I love you, Colton," she whispers, her voice laden with sincerity. Hearing those words—ones I've longed to hear and have held within my heart—stirs something profound in me.

"I know. I can feel it," I respond, surprising her slightly with my response. Before she can retort, I let my own shields drop, revealing the depth of my feelings. She inhales sharply, overwhelmed by the raw emotions now laid bare between us.

"I am so madly in love with you, my shadow," I confess, my voice thick with emotion. "It would take more than any prophecy, more than the gods themselves, to keep me away from you. You're mine now, and I'm never letting you go."

Her smile, sweet and filled with love, draws me back to her lips. I kiss her again, sealing my vow with the taste of her mouth.

"Lyra Lewis, marry me. Let's complete the ultimate bonding ceremony and intertwine our souls forever," I say, holding her gaze, feeling the ripple of surprise through her open shields. It quickly warms into excitement and love, confirming she's not just agreeing out of obligation.

"Yes," she breathes out, her smile widening.

She kisses me again, and the kiss turns desperate, both of us needing to be closer, to become one. She reaches for me, her hand wrapping around my hard cock, a satisfied sigh escaping her as she feels me ready for her. I lift her from the water, positioning her on the edge of the rock at the perfect height for me. As I enter her, she clings to me, her need mirroring my own. I thrust into her deeply, giving her all of me, over and over.

LATER, as we manage to pull ourselves away from each other, we dry off and get dressed. Lyra suggests walking back home instead of channeling. Despite my warning about the distance, she insists, eager to take in more of the Dream Forest. Hand in hand, we walk through the forest, the day nearly spent. The sun hangs low, casting long shadows, and the evening chorus of frogs begins to fill the air, echoing around us as dusk settles in.

"Today has been utterly perfect," Lyra says beside me.

I nod but can't help adding, "Even with the rough start." I immediately regret mentioning Nyx. The last thing I want is to sour the mood.

"Yes, because now I get to spend the rest of my life loving you," she counters, stirring a fierce desire within me.

"If you keep talking like that, we'll never make it back home," I warn her, giving her hand a gentle squeeze, but she just laughs, her joy infectious.

"Colton!" A high-pitched voice cuts through the air, and I turn my head around in time to see one of the small Pixies dart out from the underbrush. I extend my hand, offering her as a landing spot, which she takes immediately.

"Hollie, what brings you so far from home?" I ask, knowing the Pixies rarely venture this deep into the Dream Forest.

"Haven't you two heard? It's dangerous to be out here in the evening. There have been Sarrol attacks in Nighthold and even a few here in the Dream Forest. The last one even occurred in daylight," she warns us.

I frown, disturbed by the news of the increasing attacks but careful not to alarm Lyra. "We can handle ourselves. It's you I'm worried about," I reassure Hollie.

"I'm tiny enough to hide. If I even get wind of one of those smelly creatures, I'll fly up into a tree hole where they'll never find me," Hollie declares, her light-blue eyes sparkling with a mix of defiance and bravery.

"Oh, Hollie, this is Lyra." I realize Lyra has been eager to meet one of the Pixies. "Lyra, this is Hollie."

"So nice to meet you," Lyra says, beaming at her.

"It's wonderful to meet you too," Hollie replies, her voice chirping with curiosity. "So what brings you two out here this evening?" She taps her foot impatiently on my palm, her tiny white dress and flowing pink hair rustling in the breeze.

"We were swimming at Ruby Falls and have just gotten engaged. Lyra here is going to be bonded to me for life," I announce, drawing her close with my arm around her shoulders.

Hollie's eyes light up with excitement. "I love weddings! Oh, you two are going to have the most beautiful babies!" she exclaims. I feel Lyra tense beside me. We've never really discussed a future involving children.

"Thank you," Lyra manages, her voice tinged with a mix of surprise and uncertainty.

"And where will the ceremony be? When is it?" Hollie buzzes with curiosity, twirling around on my palm.

"We still have a few details to work out, but you'll be the first to know," I assure her, trying to ease the sudden pressure of the moment. Hollie's shimmering translucent wings flutter as she prepares to leave.

"I should head home before it gets dark, but it was such a pleasure to meet you, Lyra," Hollie says, beginning to fly away into the deepening shadows of the forest.

"You too," Lyra calls after her warmly.

"Don't forget my wedding invite!" Hollie's voice drifts back to us as she disappears among the trees.

"I can't believe I finally got to meet a Pixie! Do they all have pastel-pink hair like that?" Lyra's excitement is palpable as we resume our walk through the forest.

"No, they all have different colors—some are blue or purple. I've even seen green. But it's always soft pastel shades," I explain, avoiding the sudden jump into discussions about children.

"Are you worried about the Sarrol attacks?" she shifts the topic, her tone more serious.

"Yes, it's concerning. I need to organize some patrols to ensure the Dream Forest is secure, and coordinate with others to get a clearer picture of what's been happening," I say, my mind already racing through logistics.

"You know who could help," she suggests tentatively.

I sigh, knowing exactly who she's referring to. "Yeah, I might have to pay Nikki boy a visit soon too. He's likely got more detailed information," I concede, and she nods in agreement, understanding the necessity despite the recent tensions with Nyx.

CHAPTER 12
LYRA

ONCE UPSTAIRS, I sift through the wardrobe full of clothes Colton had brought for me here, finally settling on a pale-blue nightgown. Its fabric is super soft, adorned with intricate lace designs across the top.

Downstairs, I hear Colton moving around in the kitchen, the clatter of dishes and the sizzle of something cooking—his promise of making us dinner tonight sparks a blend of anticipation and warmth in me. I can't help but smile at the thought of him cooking me dinner.

I settle next to Chepi on the rug in front of the fireplace, stroking his fur as he rolls onto his back, tongue lolling out happily. "It's finally happening, squish," I murmur, a smile spreading across my face. "I'm going to bond with Colton. We're going to have a ceremony and everything."

Chepi responds with a couple of yips, his tail wagging excitedly.

As I stand and head into the kitchen, Chepi follows. Colton is there by the stove, apron tied tight around his waist. "Would you like wine, whiskey, or water?" he asks.

"Hmm, wine, please," I answer, drifting toward the pantry to find something for Chepi, only to see Colton already placing a bowl in front of him, which Chepi attacks with gusto. "I see you're winning him over more and more by the day."

Colton hands me a glass of red wine, his emerald eyes glowing slightly. "I know the way to your heart," he retorts, clinking his glass against mine. The wine is sweet and warms me from the inside out.

"If you want to go sit at the table in the next room, I'll bring our food in. It's about ready," Colton says, and I nod, my heart swelling with affection for him.

I take my wine to the table, settling into a chair with a content sigh. As I sip my wine, the reality of my decisions, the contentment of being with Colton, washes over me. I'm finally making the right choices. Gods, do I love him.

"I hope you're hungry," Colton says as he places a plate of pasta in front of me, along with some sliced baguette between us.

"I'm starving, and thank you," I respond, taking my first bite. The pasta is tossed with fresh tomatoes, basil, garlic, and olive oil. It's light and delicious, and notably meat-free. I usually prefer vegetarian options, and I appreciate that Colton has noticed.

"Do you like it?" he asks from across the table, his own fork paused in mid-air.

"I'm very impressed," I say, giving him a quick smile before picking up a piece of bread to soak up some of the sauce.

"I don't have much experience cooking, but I'd love to try and make something for you sometime. Maybe Rix or Rune could help me," I suggest, taking a bite of the bread.

"I'm sure they'd be thrilled if you really wanted to learn a few tricks in the kitchen," Colton replies, pausing to take a sip of his wine. "Tell me about yesterday. What did you do after you left the Lamia Realm? Clearly, you went to get Chepi. Did you see Lili?"

His question brings back a flood of the previous day's events, and I nearly wish I could forget all the drama, content to play house with Colton forever.

"Yeah, we do have some stuff to talk about... Kaine is trying to stir up an uprising against me. It's working too. A man grabbed me at that tavern we all went to together. He had seen these flyers Kaine sent out to the entire Sorcerer Realm, talking about my dark magic and how I need to be stopped," I explain, watching Colton's jaw clench.

"A man grabbed you? What happened after that?" he asks, his tone sharpening.

"Chepi used one of his new tricks. We made it out of there without anyone getting hurt, but I don't like what Kaine is doing. Lili told me he's looking for Samael and actively trying to get him to take the throne back," I continue, and Colton's expression darkens further.

"I knew we should have killed that fucker when we had the chance. Drew warned things would get bad after the Luminary Council incident, so I was ready for some backlash, but Kaine acted fast," he says, frustration evident in his voice.

"I also visited Rhett. It's complicated. We're not exactly allies anymore, especially after Larc's death. He was close to him, and..." I pause, struggling to articulate the mix of personal and political fallout.

Colton reaches across the table to touch my hand, his voice soothing. "You don't have to explain if you don't want to. I understand," he says gently.

I nod, feeling a bit relieved but still compelled to share more. "It's okay. I hope I can mend things with him eventually. He's taken over Larc's position as leader of the packs now."

"So Rhett is the new Aidan," Colton remarks.

"Yes, but Rhett is a much better man than Aidan ever was. I believe he'll be good for the packs, even if he does hate me now," I admit, feeling a pang of sadness at the lost friendship.

"I'm sure he doesn't hate you. He knows things are complicated," Colton reassures me despite no knowing how I was forced out. "You had quite the day. How did you end up at the bunker?"

"I needed somewhere to be alone after it became clear staying with Rhett wasn't an option. I was attacked again on my way there too. I managed to use my dark magic and stayed in control the entire time," I say with pride.

But Colton grows concerned. "You were attacked, and I didn't feel anything through the tether? Who attacked you?"

"I guess I'm getting better at blocking you out. I didn't want to worry you—I had it under control. But I am concerned about the increasing attacks. It seems like these evil creatures are still multiplying across the realms," I explain, taking another bite of my pasta.

"Tomorrow, I'll speak with Bim and Dorian to see what they know about what's been happening while we were away," Colton says thoughtfully.

"And you'll talk to Nyx too?" I probe, knowing that despite everything Nyx would have valuable insights.

Colton sighs. "I suppose I might visit him too, if we can manage to be civil long enough to exchange information. I'm sure he's not thrilled with me right now," he admits, his tone dry.

I wish there was something I could do to ease the tension between them. "He's your half-brother. You should try to maintain some relationship with him, even if he despises me."

Colton gives me a stern look, his jaw setting. "We both know he doesn't despise you. I've known about our relation for a while, and I never wanted a relationship with him before.

Nothing's changed. I'll visit him because we need to under-stand what's happening, but we won't be leaving as friends."

"Will Rix and Rune be returning anytime soon?" I ask, trying to steer the conversation toward something lighter.

"Yeah, I'll send word we're back tomorrow, and I'm sure they'll come to restock the kitchen at the very least," Colton replies, though his tone suggests his mind is still on the recent troubles.

"Are you tired?" I ask after finishing the last of my food, noticing the slight furrow in his brow.

"I am. It's been a long time since I've had a full night's rest, and I'm sure you're feeling the same. Tonight, with you in my arms, back in our home, I plan to sleep deeply," he declares, a warm smile replacing his earlier concern.

I chuckle. "Let's go to bed then." The idea of curling up beside him and shutting out the rest of the world, even for a few hours, feels like exactly what we need.

We clear the table together and then head upstairs. I pause to give Chepi a quick pet. He's already curled up in his favorite spot by the fireplace, deep in sleep. As we enter the bedroom, Colton turns to me with a questioning look. "Interested in taking a shower before bed?" he asks.

"Only if you're the one washing me," I reply with a mischievous smile, teasing him.

He laughs, a deep, genuine sound that fills the room. "Deal, but only if you return the favor," he says, winking.

CHAPTER 13

LYRA

COLTON WOKE EARLY THIS MORNING, bustling with tasks he wanted to accomplish today. He offered for me to join him, but I was more content with the idea of sleeping in and having the day to myself. Besides, I doubted his conversation with Nyx would go smoothly with me there. The thought of seeing Nyx again so soon still twists my heart. I hope he finds happiness...without me.

Eventually, Chepi's persistent yips coax me out of bed, clearly eager for breakfast. I throw on some tights and a shirt then head downstairs to feed him and grab a slice of toast with jam for myself. While Colton didn't ask about my plans for the day, I'm sure he trusts that I can handle myself. The freedom to do what I want, when I want, without having to answer to anyone, still feels strange—unfamiliar but thrilling.

Now that I'm engaged, there's only one person in all of Nighthold who I think will genuinely be happy for me. After finishing my breakfast, I slip on a pair of boots and scoop up Chepi. "Come on, boy. Let's go find Flora," I say, eager to see my friend.

It's been too long since our last meeting, which had ended awkwardly at Colton's parents' house when I had asked her to lie to Nyx about running into me.

I channel us to Bim's house, knowing Flora often stays there, but when no one answers my knocks, I let us inside and send Chepi to scout upstairs. "No one's here?" I query as Chepi returns alone, jumping into my arms with a lick on my cheek.

The only other place I can think to look is Colton's parents' library in the Elders' Palace. I certainly don't want to venture into Nyx's castle, and I'm not keen on running into Elspeth or Granger either, especially after the council meeting. But I believe I'm now powerful enough to channel directly into the library without being noticed.

Once there, I spot Emmalina, the librarian, on the top floor of the library and immediately channel us down to the next level. I'd rather avoid alerting Colton's parents of my presence here and am not sure if Emmalina would tell them, but better safe than sorry.

"Is Flora here, boy?" I ask as I let Chepi down, and he darts off. I hurry after him, weaving through rows of towering bookshelves, the rich smell of old parchment filling the air. We descend two more levels before I spot her—Flora's unmistakable dark-red wings and curly red hair visible from behind. Chepi reaches her first, and she turns around, her face lighting up with excitement.

"Chepi!" she exclaims, lifting him into her arms to lavish him with affection as he licks her face happily. "Oh gosh, you have horns now," she muses, petting his head carefully around his new additions. When her chocolate eyes meet mine, they soften, and she pulls me into a warm, tight hug.

Flora pulls me over to a cozy corner scattered with plush, oversized pillows in a secluded reading nook. We sink into the softness as I begin to unpack the recent whirlwind of events in my life. She listens intently, nodding along without much surprise—likely Nyx had already briefed her. After I finish, she leans forward, concerned.

"How are you really handling all this?" she probes gently.

I pause, weighing the tumult of emotions that have become my constant companions—stress and anxiety from the looming threats and the political unrest and malevolent attacks, yet a deep-seated contentment from my decision to marry Colton.

"I think I'm managing okay," I respond, feeling more reassuring than I expect.

Flora purses her lips, her gaze piercing as if she's trying to read the deeper currents of my turmoil, but she doesn't press further. Instead, she shifts the topic to something that makes my heart skip a beat.

"And you're certain about Colton? You truly believe he's the light of the prophecy?"

My smile widens as I think of Colton, of us together, united not only by fate but by choice. "Yes, I believe he is. But even if he weren't, I know in my heart, in every bone in my body, that choosing him is right."

The memory of our intimate moments last night warms me.

Flora's face lights up with a mischievous gleam. "Well, I must do what any good friend would do," she declares, pulling me to my feet with a surprising strength.

"What's that?" I ask, curiosity piqued.

"Dress shopping," she announces with a flourish. "We must find you something spectacular for the ceremony day. Given Colton's status and his parents' prominence, your wedding will be a major event. Everyone who's anyone will be there."

Her excitement is infectious, but a flutter of nervousness tickles my stomach at the thought of the intense scrutiny such a high-profile ceremony will invite. Nevertheless, the prospect of celebrating our commitment with an exquisite dress sends a thrill through me, and I can't help but return her smile, swept up in the joy of the moment.

FLORA TUGS ME into a village shop in Onyxland.

"You need something original, something befitting a queen. I know just the person to make the most fitting dress for you," she exclaims.

The shop is nestled on the bustling coastline, it's architecture is beautiful appearing to be made entirely of driftwood. The air carries a light scent of salt mingled with exotic perfumes. Sunlight streams through teal-colored stained glass windows, casting colorful patters that resemble the sea across the wooden floor. This place is filled with some of the most glamorous dresses I've ever seen. Nothing like this would ever be worn back in Cloudrum. But then again, the Fae have always had unique taste, far from the traditional styles of the Sorcerer Realm. Everywhere I look there's something sparkly or sheer or fur-lined.

"I've never seen so many fancy dresses in my life," I muse as Chepi and I follow Flora to the back of the shop. She pushes on the back wall, revealing a hidden door that opens up, leading us down a small staircase. We reach the hidden room below, which is adorned with even more extravagant fabrics and jewelry, clearly a workshop where the dresses are crafted.

"Flora!" A young woman looks up from where she's sewing something with magic and comes around to give Flora a hug. She's unmistakably Fae, with a short white bob haircut and bright silver and white wings neatly tucked behind her back.

Gods, she's wearing a spectacular dress too, as if she's headed to a palace party, and I can't imagine dressing like that every day. She's even wearing the most uncomfortable-looking high, strappy shoes. "What brings you in today?" she asks, releasing Flora and looking over at me and Chepi with a sweet smile on her face.

"This is Lyra," Flora introduces me with a wide grin, gesturing grandly in my direction. "She's about to have the most-talked-about bonding ceremony in all of Nighthold, and we need something that truly stands out."

The young woman's eyes light up as she looks me over, her gaze sharp and assessing. "It's a pleasure to meet you, Lyra. I'm Seraphina, and I'd be honored to design your ceremony attire," she says, her voice melodious, matching her ethereal appearance. She extends a hand, which I take, feeling a slight tingle of magic at her touch—her energy vibrant and lively.

Seraphina leads us deeper into her hidden studio, where rolls of fabric in hues I've never seen before line the walls—colors that shimmer and change as you look at them, some seeming to glow softly from within.

"We'll need something unique, something that encapsulates your strength and beauty, perhaps with elements that reflect your dark magic in a subtle, enchanting way," she muses aloud, pulling down swatches of fabric that catch the light and seem to dance with color.

How does she know I have dark magic? I wonder, and Flora turns back to me, sensing my train of thought.

"It's one of her gifts. She can get a good feel for people and design things especially for them. It's why she took your hand."

I run my fingers over a piece of deep-black fabric that shifts to a translucent white and back again as I move it. "I love this," I confess, watching the colors change.

"Perfect." Seraphina claps her hands, clearly pleased. "If it's the color change you like, I can use that as the base and perhaps add accents of silver to represent the moonlight.

Maybe even a hint of shadow magic could be woven into the train, delicate thread that only reveals its patterns under the right conditions."

Her ideas flow like a wellspring, each one more enchanting than the last. Flora watches, her eyes twinkling with approval and excitement. "And don't forget some dramatic elements, perhaps a cascading cape or a subtle glow from within the gown itself that lights up with your emotions."

Seraphina nods enthusiastically. "I can integrate tiny enchanted crystals throughout the bodice and along the cape, which will softly illuminate based on your heartbeat—subtle but effective, especially for the evening ceremony."

The thought of such a dress, one that not only embodies my essence but also reacts to my feelings, sends a thrill through me. "That sounds incredible," I breathe, my heart already enamored with the concept.

"Leave everything to me," Seraphina assures us, sketching rapidly as ideas crystallize. "This will be a dress worthy of your love story and the magic it represents."

Flora squeezes my hand, giving me an encouraging smile. "See, I told you she was the best for the job." As we discuss more details, the excitement builds within me—for the dress and my future with Colton. By the time we leave the shop, I'm confident I will absolutely love whatever Seraphina creates for me. I can't quite imagine what the final look will be with all of her extravagant ideas, but I'm excited.

We settle into a quaint café, and they serve us a delightful tray adorned with neatly cut sandwiches and fresh fruit. We each pour a glass of sweet white wine, and I start nibbling on a cucumber and soft cheese sandwich.

Between bites, I express my gratitude, "Thank you for bringing me out today, Flora. I can't imagine what I would have ended up wearing without your guidance."

"You're welcome, darling. I can't wait to see what she creates for you. It's going to be spectacular. Colton will be breathless when he sees you," Flora replies, her eyes sparkling as she sips her wine. "So have you two set a date yet? Where will it be?"

I pause, my food halfway to my mouth, "Oh, we haven't really discussed the details yet."

Flora's enthusiasm doesn't wane. "You know, Colton's parents own a property on the coast of Onyxland. It's not as grand as the Elders' Palace, but it's absolutely beautiful and overlooks the water. The terrace there would be a perfect spot for your ceremony."

I hesitate, unsure how Colton's parents will receive the news of our engagement, given everything that's happened. Opting not to dwell on potential complications, I steer the conversation back to more pleasant topics. "That does sound amazing," I say, smiling genuinely.

Flora beams at me, her joy infectious. I grab a tomato sandwich and offer it to Chepi, who's perched on the window ledge next to our table, watching the people pass by.

We continue our meal in silence for a few minutes, allowing me to gather my thoughts. I've been wanting to ask about Nyx, so I finally break the silence. "How is Nyx doing? Have you seen him since he got back?" I ask, trying to sound casual.

Flora's brown eyes study me carefully, as if deciding how much to tell me. "He's alright, his usual broody self. Don't let him ruin your happiness, Lyra. He will be okay," she reassures me, but I sense she's holding back. I nod, accepting her vague response for now.

"Yeah, I hope so."

We finish our meal and the bottle of wine, and by the time we stand to leave, I feel a slight buzz. "I have to get back to the library to finish some work, but I'd love to do this again. Maybe I'll come visit you at Colton's sometime," Flora suggests as we prepare to part ways.

"That would be great. Come anytime. We'd love to have you," I respond warmly, appreciating her company today.

Flora gives Chepi and me one more hug before disappearing in a cloud of red mist as she channels away. I decide to take a leisurely walk with Chepi through the village, enjoying the simple pleasure of being among people and feeling somewhat normal. As we stroll, I soak in the sights, allowing the vibrant life of the village to wash over me.

CHAPTER 14

NYX

I FIND solace only in drowning myself in work, letting the steady flow of whiskey numb the sharper edges of my thoughts. Ripping open another piece of mail, the complaints pile up—attacks across the kingdom have surged, relentless and chaotic. Despite Lyra's efforts in channeling her magic into the heart of Eguina, the demonic presence persists, unyielding. Soren mentioned the demons didn't emerge from the bridge during their last onslaught and had been already lurking within Eguina. How many more hide in the shadows?

As I down another shot, Bim's updates clutter my desk. He's been deploying troops across Nighthold, bracing for the storm to come.

The door opens, and without looking I know it's Colton—the familiar stench is unmistakable. "What are you doing here?" I ask, my voice flat, not bothering to hide my annoyance as he strides into my office with Twig. "I see you had the decency to knock and be escorted like a civilized person this time."

I finally look up as Twig closes the door, leaving us alone.

"We need to talk, brother," Colton says, his tone dripping with disdain. His use of "brother" grates on me, and I'm not in the mood for his games.

I lean back in my chair, feigning indifference as I swirl the whiskey in my glass. "Oh, we have nothing to talk about... Unless you're here to give back my mate."

Colton's jaw tightens. "We need to talk about the attacks, Nyx. This isn't about Lyra or our personal issues. It's about Nighthold's safety."

I smirk, setting my glass down with a deliberate thud. "Suddenly concerned about Nighthold? What changed, brother? Or is it that now you have something to lose, you're taking it seriously?"

His eyes narrow, and I know I've hit a nerve. "This is about protecting our people, Nyx. It's bigger than our quarrels."

Leaning forward, I rest my elbows on my desk, meeting his gaze with a cool challenge. "Is it? Or are you here because you're afraid I might actually find a way to prove I'm the one she should be with?"

His response is curt, a growl almost. "Lyra made her choice, Nyx."

I chuckle, "A choice made without all the facts is a guess, Colton. But go on, keep pretending it's all settled. We both know the truth isn't that simple. If I were you, I'd go enjoy the time with Lyra while you have it."

"What the fuck is that supposed to mean? You realize she chose me and is completing the bonding ceremony with me," he says, drawing the words out slowly. I clench my glass but try to keep my cool, not wanting him to see the effect he has on me. The thought of them together churns my stomach.

"Lyra doesn't know what she wants, but I plan on finding proof that I am the one she is fated to be with. Proof that will rid you from our lives once and for all. So run along now. We have nothing more to discuss," I wave him off, but he doesn't move, instead taking a step closer to my desk.

"She's not going to replace Zaelinn. You do realize that, right?" he says, and I get to my feet, fury threatening to boil over.

"I'm not trying to replace Z. Now get the fuck out of my office before I make you." I feel my magic pulsing, but instead of giving into his taunt, I let my lips quirk up on one side instead.

Colton retreats into himself. "I knew this would be a waste of time," he mutters, raking his fingers through his hair with a look of resignation.

"Indeed," I retort, reclining in my chair. I fully expect him to storm out or channel away in a huff, but instead he leans forward, placing his hands firmly on my desk, narrowing the distance between us.

His voice lowers, edged with a cold firmness. "I only came because she asked me to. I knew you were a lost cause, but after everything she still believes there's something decent in you. Consider this the only warning you'll get, Nyx," he says, his eyes igniting with a threatening glow as his magic simmers. "If you do anything to ruin our wedding, if you cause her any more pain, I'll fucking end you."

In a whirl of smoke, he's gone before I can utter another word.

The room falls silent, but I can't help the laugh that escapes me. The seriousness of his threat, the intensity in his eyes—I hadn't expected him to unravel so completely. He's truly ensnared by her, more than I thought. And he thinks his little display of bravado might actually intimidate me? Pathetic.

He's wrong on so many levels, especially about her being his mate. The prophecy, the one my father uttered so long ago, doesn't speak of Colton. It speaks of me. I'm the one destined to save Lyra, to be her true light. Now, I need to prove it. And when I do, this farce of a romance with Colton will crumble, and she'll see where her fate truly lies. With me.

I take one more long draw from my whiskey before setting the glass down with a decisive clink. It's time to check on my plans, the ones that not even Colton suspects. With a thought, I channel myself to the remote coast of Vision Valley. In the dimming light, the relentless waves crash against the jagged cliffs, a natural defense for the maneuvers I've been orchestrating.

While Colton has been preoccupied, reveling in his newfound happiness with Lyra, I've been making moves that will secure our futures. Drew, always a valuable ally despite her cryptic ways, has agreed to my request to keep ships anchored discreetly past the Center Isles. I've calculated the distances meticulously, from Vision Valley to these ships and then straight to the Sorcerer Realm, a strategic path designed for rapid movement of forces if needed. Channeling straight from Nighthold to Cloudrum has always been too far a distance.

Bim has been busy too, arranging army encampments atop these cliffs. Vision Valley is desolate, far from prying eyes, an ideal staging ground for what may come. I've sensed the darkness swelling across the lands, felt the increasing frequency of attacks—each a forewarning of the storm brewing within and beyond our realms.

And then there's the matter of Kaine's insidious flyers stirring unrest in Cloudrum, timed disgustingly close to Lyra's upcoming birthday. She could claim her right to rule as queen on that day, a move that would undoubtedly spark conflict given the current tensions.

As I stand here, overlooking the preparations, I'm more convinced than ever that we're edging toward a war that has been simmering beneath the surface for too long. And with the rumors of Samael's return—rumors that chill even the salted air around me—I know that my unresolved past with him must finally find resolution. Samael and I have a score to settle, and when we next meet, only one of us will walk away from that encounter.

"King Onyx, how may I assist you today?" Poe greets me immediately upon my arrival. Despite his youth, Poe is a soldier of notable promise, particularly skilled in elemental magic. I once witnessed him transmute rain into acid, albeit briefly—a potent ability indeed.

"Yes, Poe, could you direct me to Commander Bim?" I inquire.

Poe strokes his clean-shaven jaw thoughtfully before nodding and guiding me toward the heart of the camp. As we walk, I note the expansions and improvements. Bim has clearly been industrious, the camp bustling with activity and preparation.

We arrive at a larger tent at the camp's core, and Poe pauses at the entrance, giving the tent flap a respectful tap before announcing, "Commander Bim, King Onyx wishes to speak with you."

A moment later, Bim appears at the entrance, his face lined with the marks of sleepless nights but his eyes sharp and assessing. "Nyx," he greets with a nod, stepping aside to let me enter. The interior of the tent is a strategic war room. Maps and scrolls litter every surface, and the air is thick with the scent of ink and wax.

"Poe, that will be all. Thank you," I dismiss the young soldier with a nod, and he retreats, leaving me with Bim.

I approach the nearest table, which has a copy of Kaine's flyer on it, one Drew gave me. Kaine knows better than to spread such nonsense in Nighthold. I scan the text on the flyer once more.

"Protect our realms from the dark enchantress, Lyra Lewis. Do not be deceived by her guise of nobility. Underneath lies a heart governed by dark magic that seeks to dominate and destroy. She has already unleashed her terrifying power upon the Luminary Council, proving her willingness to slaughter those who stand in her way. We must act now to preserve our heritage and safeguard our future. Stand united against the tyranny of dark magic. Reject Lyra Lewis as queen. Protect our realm. Protect our traditions!"

As I trace my fingers over the detailed sketch of Lyra's face under the writing, the likeness is uncanny—her features are hauntingly similar to Z's. I shake the thought away. Soon enough, Lyra will reign as the queen of all Eguina, if I have any say in it. Men like Kaine and Samael are trying to turn her own people against her. I can only imagine how Lyra must feel about this...if she's even aware. We never had the chance to discuss her actions that day in the bunker, and now I'm not sure I can face her yet.

"The camps really have come a long way," Bim remarks, drawing me out of my reverie. I tear my gaze from the flyer, acknowledging his efforts.

"You've outdone yourself. Are the men growing restless?" I inquire, scanning the map of Eguina spread across the table.

"Nah, are you kidding? They're relishing the prospect of a fight. Most of them have been alternating between responding to attacks in Nighthold and honing their battle magic here, away from civilian eyes," Bim reassures me, and I nod in approval. The map is dotted with colored X's, each marking incidents that have occurred. We even have spies in Cloudrum, though mostly in the Sorcerer and Lycan Realms—Drew would have our heads if we dared infiltrate the Lamia Realm with spies. She's too sharp for that.

"Have any of the recent attacks in Nighthold been hordes?" I ask, knowing Bim keeps meticulous records while I'm away.

"No, it's been relatively quiet on that front. We've dealt with a couple of Sarrols stirring trouble on a farm, but that's about it. Otherwise, it's been isolated incidents. A Sarrol here and there, a few Monstrauths, and then there are those attacks by creatures no one can even identify," Bim explains, stroking his neatly trimmed beard thoughtfully. "When witnesses describe these creatures, it's like nothing I've ever heard of before."

I don't like the sound of that at all. Unidentified creatures could mean new threats or, worse, evolving ones.

"What did they look like? Can you give me a detailed description?" I prompt Bim, eager for information. He moves to a cluttered desk, thumbing through stacks of parchments with determination to provide a precise account.

"Here's what we have from the eyewitnesses. The entity appeared humanoid but with unsettling differences—its skin was a pallid gray, almost moist to the eye. It had a gaunt build, with a starkly pronounced ribcage and sharply defined muscles." He pauses, finding another relevant note. "Most disturbingly, these creatures are devoid of normal human features: no hair, no ears, no nose, and no eyes—only a gaping mouth. That's what really unnerved the witnesses, oh, and they move on all fours like an animal," he explains, disturbed.

Reflecting on my extensive knowledge and the myriad oddities I've encountered over the years, nothing quite matches this description. "I'm not sure what we're dealing with, but we should bring Flora into this discussion tonight. She's been deep in research at the elders' library and perhaps has stumbled upon something related to these creatures," I suggest, hoping for a breakthrough. Bim nods, his expression mirroring the weight of our growing concerns.

"You still want me to keep Colton out of the loop on all this?" Bim asks, raising an eyebrow.

I scoff. "That bastard stormed into my office asking about these attacks." Frustration seeps into my voice as I rub my temples.

"I still can't believe you two are half-brothers—all this time. It explains so much," Bim muses, looking genuinely surprised.

"What's that supposed to mean?" I snap, fixing him with a sharp gaze.

"Uh, it makes sense now. Both of you share that intense vibe, not to mention the unique wing structure. And let's not forget, both of you are stubborn as hell," he chuckles, and I can't help but shake my head at the comparison.

"Keep him out of it. This doesn't concern him, and I don't want Lyra to stress either. Let them live in their blissful igno-rance for now," I decide, realizing it's more for her sake than his. I know Lyra would be furious if she knew I was with-holding information, but she's not naive and must sense the unrest in the realms.

"Alright, if you say so. Are we still on for tonight at your place? Flora joining us?" he confirms.

"Yes, I need to do a few more things, then I'll head over," I respond, mentally preparing for the evening's discussions. With a nod from Bim, I channel away to pay Dorian a visit. We need to talk about our arsenal.

CHAPTER 15

LYRA

THE LAST FEW weeks have flown by in a blur, the days and nights melding together. Time really does pass quickly when you're enjoying life.

Since Rix and Rune have been away visiting family, Hollie has made it a regular occurrence to hang out with me while Colton's away during the day. He's often tied up with what he calls boring business matters, trying to mend peace with his mother, so I've steered clear of pressing him for details, opting to wait until he's ready to share on his own.

The tension with his family is rough, but he assures me that everything will settle down in due time. His parents have even invited us to their palace for an engagement party, and although I'm still uncertain about how I feel, we've agreed to attend.

"What are you thinking about over there?" Hollie asks from atop Chepi's back. It amazes me how he lets her ride on his back like that, but she is incredibly small.

"Oh, the party Elspeth and Granger are throwing for us and who might be there," I respond as we walk along a path by the creek. We've been exploring new trails every day, and the more I discover of the Dream Forest, the more I fall in love with its enchanting inhabitants and scenery.

"Like King Onyx?" she giggles, and I scold her.

"I doubt he'll be there. Celebrating my relationship with Colton is probably the last thing on his list. I'm nervous about how everyone will react," I admit.

Hollie stretches out on Chepi, soaking up the sun. "Who cares about their reactions? If anyone gives you trouble, unleash your shadows on them," she quips with a mischievous grin. I can't help but laugh. Hollie has been watching me practice my dark magic, and thankfully it hasn't scared her off.

"Did you hear that?" I whisper, crouching lower to peer through the dense foliage. This part of the Dream Forest feels more remote than anywhere we've ventured before, and a prickle of unease settles over me. Beside me, Chepi and Hollie hover close, their tiny forms tense with alertness.

"What are they doing?" Hollie's voice is barely audible as she squints at the group of five Fae men dressed in tan combat gear by the riverbank ahead. "Could there have been another attack nearby?" I murmur, more to myself than to them.

"I've never seen them in uniforms like that. It's usually Colton or his friends who patrol here, not King Onyx's soldiers," Hollie observes.

They seem to be merely stopping for water, filling their canteens before preparing to move on. "I'm going to follow them. You two should head back," I say, turning to them with a firm look.

Hollie plants her hands on her hips, defiance written all over her small face. "We're coming with you," she insists firmly.

Reluctantly, I nod. "Fine, Chepi can make you invisible if we run into trouble, as long as you are holding onto him," I concede, watching her relax slightly.

"I know he's a Glyphie, but he's the first Glyphie I've met with such cute little horns," she comments, reaching out to gently touch Chepi's head.

"He shares my dark magic too," I explain as the soldiers begin discussing channeling back to their camp.

"Camp? That means they might have a setup here in the forest. That's highly unusual," Hollie notes, her eyes narrowing with curiosity.

"Fuck, if they channel, I think I can track their magic, but only if we use the same spot immediately after they leave. Be ready to run," I instruct, my voice low and urgent as we inch closer, still concealed by the underbrush.

As the last man vanishes, the air still hums with residual magic, laced with an earthy, woodsy scent. We dash to the spot where he stood, and I focus on the lingering traces of his magic, my heart racing with adrenaline. With a deep breath, I channel us through.

We land softly on sandy terrain, surrounded by sprawling tents. Quickly, we duck behind the nearest one to avoid detection. "I've never done that before—tracked someone through channeling. That was incredible," I whisper, unable to hide my thrill.

"It looks like you've brought us to Vision Valley, the desert lands," Hollie observes, her voice low. She curls her lip as she lets a handful of sand trickle through her fingers, clearly unimpressed with the arid environment.

"Let's find out what they're doing here. Chepi can keep us invisible for quite a while now, thanks to his enhanced magic. Make sure you don't let go of him. Remember, they can still hear us, so we need to keep quiet," I instruct her, taking Chepi into my arms. Hollie clings to his fur at his neck and carefully settles down.

Once we are shielded from sight, I edge around the tent

and begin to tiptoe through the camp. It's bustling, filled with hundreds of soldiers milling about, their voices a constant buzz in the air. A distant roar and chanting draw my attention, and I follow the sounds, creeping closer until we come upon a large crowd. They're gathered around a makeshift arena where two men spar, their magic sparking and clashing as they fight.

"What are they doing?" Hollie whispers.

"I think they're training," I murmur in response, my eyes never leaving the action below.

"But why here? And why so many?" Hollie's questions are valid. The size and scale of this operation aren't ordinary.

"Preparing for war," I conclude softly, the realization settling heavily in my chest.

We watch intently as the two men in the pit, both shirtless and slick with sweat, circle each other. Each wields a sword in one hand while their other hand is hurling magic with calculated precision. The sun catches on the outstretched wings of one fighter, sending dazzling reflections our way. Their swords meet with a clang that echoes around the arena, sparks flying with each strike.

Suddenly, one of the Fae males gestures elaborately with his free hand, manipulating the sand beneath his opponent. The grains whirl and shift, rapidly forming a pit that begins to swallow the winged fighter, drawing him down until only his head remains above the surface. The victor bows to the applause of the onlookers before aiding his opponent out of the sandy trap. As they exit, two more warriors take their place, ready to spar.

The spectacle is mesmerizing, but it also presents an opportunity. With the crowd's attention focused on the new fighters, now might be the perfect time to explore the camp and uncover what's really happening here.

I tighten my grip on Chepi as we move stealthily through

the war camp, guided by the pressing urgency to uncover the camp's secrets before we're discovered. Each row of tents blends into the next, but it's the central, grandiose tent that catches my attention. It stands out with its imposing size and finer make.

Slipping inside, the lavish spread of furs across the floor and a makeshift bedroom in one corner suggest it's a command tent. The rest of the space is dominated by military logistics: maps, communications equipment, and piles of documents all over.

I approach the central table, its surface a detailed expanse of Eguina's map. Hollie, still perched securely on Chepi, whispers, "They must be tracking more than just Sarrol attacks."

Nodding, I release her and Chepi, taking a moment to ensure we're alone. My focus narrows on the Sorcerer Realm section of the map. The handwritten notes and markers scattered across it are a clear indication of active surveillance—not on random beast attacks but on something much more orchestrated.

Squinting to decipher the tiny script, the reality hits me hard. They're charting Samael's movements and the burgeoning insurrection he and Kaine are fostering—directly aimed against me.

"Lyra, look, it's a drawing of you!" Hollie exclaims from across the room, and I immediately know they must have one of Kaine's flyers. I join her and inspect the board in front of us, plastered with parchments. In a handful of weeks, more flyers have been distributed. Samael has been found, and he has retaken the throne, regaining quite a following, it seems. He was so weakened the last time I saw him, so how did he regain his strength and power so quickly? The people know he was a terrible leader. Do they truly believe I will be worse?

"Why are they so afraid of your dark magic?" Hollie asks, glancing over one of the flyers about me.

"Dark magic hasn't been around in a very long time. They fear what they don't understand, believing the stories they're told," I explain. The Sorcerers recognize Samael as a dark leader, aware that he practiced dark spells, but he never truly possessed dark magic.

They must think I will be like him, only worse. I can't entirely blame them. To my people, I am a mystery, and with Kaine pushing his narrative, their fears are only amplified.

I turn to see more papers on the table detailing troop movements and alliances with various minor lords in the Sorcerer Realm. It's clear that Kaine has been weaving a complex web, building up military and political support for Samael's return. I can't help but feel a pang of betrayal. These are my people, and yet they rally behind a known tyrant because of fear stoked by lies about my magic. I don't want to blame them, but the feeling of betrayal starts to fester in my chest.

"This is worse than I thought," I murmur, scanning the documents for any mention of plans directly targeting me or Colton.

Hollie hovers close, her tiny form barely casting a shadow over the parchments. "We need to tell Colton about this. He should know."

"No, not yet," I decide abruptly. "I need to understand the full extent of their plans. We can't alarm him without knowing our next move. Plus, he's dealing with his family."

Another alarming thought crosses my mind. What if Colton already knows about all of this and has been keeping it from me? We agreed—no more lies, no more secrets. If he knew and didn't tell me... I shake my head, not wanting to entertain the thought. There's no way he would keep this from me. Nyx might, given our strained relations, but Colton...

"Come on. I've seen enough of this place for now. Let's go back home," I tell Chepi and Hollie, and they fly over to me immediately. As I prepare to channel us back, a nagging thought lingers. Weapons are everywhere, and Dorian, Nyx's main weapons supplier, is also Colton's best friend—a man he meets with often. It's hard to believe Dorian would keep such secrets from Colton. How could Colton not know? The doubt seeds deeper as we vanish from the camp.

"Something's here!" I shout, grasping for Nyx's hand, but it's slipping away. The stage beneath us fractures, splintering wood and crumbling plaster plummeting into the abyss as unfamiliar shadows coil around my limbs, dragging me backward. The crowd blurs into chaos. Only Nyx's haunting white eyes pierce the darkness as I'm swallowed whole.

A chilling screech echoes, like a gate flung wide. Yet when I spin around, it's not the gates I face but an ancient throne room steeped in the weight of centuries. Each cautious step I take ignites the torches along the walls, their flames casting elongated, twisting shadows that murmur in an almost recognizable tongue.

At the room's heart lies a throne of black obsidian, ensnared by twisted branches that mirror those at the gates, surrounded by a moat of molten silver shimmering under a moonlike glow. It beckons, and as my hand reaches out, drawn to the intricate tangle of branches, my gaze spots a crown aloft in the shadows above. Crafted from the same dark tendrils and studded with shifting gemstones, it morphs under my stare, a living part of the darkness.

As my fingers stretch, yearning to touch the ethereal crown, a cold claw clasps my chest from behind. The grip is iron-tight, anchoring me in place as a raspy, malicious whisper grazes my ear, "Embrace your destiny, for you are the bridge between worlds." The words scratch through the air, sending shivers down my spine.

Gasping, I bolt upright in bed, my hand instinctively clutching my ear where the phantom breath still seems to linger.

As I search the room for Colton, I realize he isn't here. I must have drifted to sleep while waiting for him after my unsettling visit to the camps. Chepi, lying at my feet, seems at ease despite my turmoil. I scoop him up, cuddling him close, and his immediate soft snoring against my chest helps to anchor my frayed nerves.

My heart still races as I try to wrap my head around the vision that disturbed my sleep. Was it a glimpse from my midnight mind, reaching beyond the gates into unknown realms or simply my own fears weaving into my subconscious as my wedding day and future reign as queen draw near? The vision of a dark throne suited for my shadowed magic makes me wonder if it reflects how my people perceive me—or perhaps it's a deeper, more ominous prophecy about my destiny.

The thought of returning to Zomea, to confront those gates again, looms over me, but there are immediate challenges to face. My bonding ceremony is fast approaching, and I must step into my role to safeguard my realm, especially now with the uncertainty under Samael's reign. The weight of these realities presses down, mixing with the whispers of my dream, reminding me of the critical path ahead.

Only the gods know what truly awaits, and I must be ready for anything.

CHAPTER 16

LYRA

It's been a few days since my last dream, and the nightmare still haunts me. I can't stop thinking about the visions I'm having, which are oddly similar to what the Echosphere showed me. Tonight is our engagement party at Colton's parents' palace—the Elders' Palace—and I'm somewhat nervous, considering the last time I saw them was when I was in Drew's throne room.

Colton comes up behind me while I'm getting ready in front of the mirror and wraps an arm around my waist, bending to kiss the top of my head. "You've had so many late nights recently. I feel like we've hardly had a chance to talk," I say, looking at him in the mirror.

"I'm sorry. Tonight, after the party, I'll take you somewhere special," he replies, giving me a cheeky grin and winking in the mirror.

"I like the sound of that." I turn to face him. He's dressed nicely, beige pants with an off-white shirt, a black vest, and a black jacket adorned with fancy buttons. I reach up, putting my hands on his arms and savoring the feel of him as he leans down to kiss me. It's a quick kiss, and then he moves away to let me finish getting ready, but a part of me wishes he would take me back to bed.

"So what have you been up to these late nights? Sorting things out with your parents?" I inquire, applying a swipe of red lipstick. I've given him space, waiting patiently for him to share on his own terms, but my curiosity has been piqued—especially after witnessing the military camps with Hollie.

"No, not exactly. I've actually been spending these past nights assisting Dorian," he reveals.

"Oh?" I turn to face him.

"But let's not talk about that right now," he says, a smile emerging. "It's almost time to go, and I know you're already anxious enough as it is."

"I'm not that anxious, but I want to know," I insist.

He simply kisses the top of my head again. "Come down-stairs when you're ready," he replies, leaving the room.

I pout at my reflection in the mirror. He must know some-thing about the camps and all the other developments—I can't imagine Dorian would keep such things from him. And if Dorian is still supplying the military with weapons, Colton has to be aware that something significant is underway. What are you hiding, Nyx?

Shaking off my suspicions for the moment, I slip into an almost sheer pale-blue dress with delicate straps. It clings to my form down to the floor, elegant yet comfortable. I study myself in the mirror, pinning my hair back on one side while letting the rest cascade in waves down the other. Deciding that the red lipstick is too bold for my outfit, I switch to a soft pink shade instead. With a final glance, I slip into some strappy heels and head downstairs.

Colton's eyes start to glow as he watches me descend the staircase, and his gaze intensifies, warming me to the core. "I am the luckiest man in all the realms," he murmurs, and I can't help but smile as I wrap my arms around his neck, tilting my head to meet his lips.

"I can't wait to take this off you after the party," he whispers, his voice a low rumble. He pauses, his breath hot against my neck as he plants a trail of light kisses up to my ear. "Although, I have to admit, the dress doesn't leave much to the imagination. I'm not sure I want everyone else seeing you in this tonight. Are you trying to make me jealous?"

His tone is teasing, but there's a hint of real concern there too, making my heart flutter with a mix of delight and a touch of guilt.

"Maybe a little. I thought it might keep your attention on me all night," I tease, feeling his arms tighten around my waist, his fingers tracing circles on my lower back. "My attention would be on you all night even if you wore a flour sack," he murmurs against my ear, making me giggle. He gives me one more kiss, then asks, "Are you ready for this?"

I nod, resting my head against his chest, savoring our last moment alone before the whirlwind of the party. "Ready as I'll ever be," I whisper back, and he channels us.

THE ELDERS' Palace is nothing short of breathtaking tonight, transformed into a place of opulence and enchantment befitting a celebration of Fae royalty. As Colton channels us directly into the festivities, we step into a part of the palace I've never explored before—a grand ballroom that dazzles the senses.

The vast space is bathed in gold and ivory, with enormous vaulted ceilings from which delicate crystal chandeliers hang, casting a cascade of sparkling light across the polished marble floor. The air is filled with music and chatter as guests dance and mingle.

The room teems with at least one hundred Fae, each wearing their finest attire—gowns shimmering with gemstones and suits tailored in silks, at least half the crowd displaying their wings in a riot of bright colors. Servants glide through the crowd like wraiths, offering silver trays laden with exotic cocktails and canapés that seem almost too delicate to eat, crafted to delight both the eye and the palate.

"Let's greet my parents first," Colton suggests, guiding me through the throng. His presence commands respectful nods and hushed whispers, though many give us space, perhaps wary of me... Gods, I hope not.

The ballroom extends into a spectacular open terrace, transformed into a luxurious outdoor lounge with a bar set against the backdrop of the night sky. The air out here is cooler, scented with the heady fragrance of night-blooming flowers.

Descending the terrace steps, we pass a large pool area, where the water glimmers with blues and greens under the moonlight. Steam rises gently from the heated waters. Some guests mingle in and around the pool, their laughter echoing with the splash of water.

Beyond the pool, the palace gardens unfold—a beautiful maze beneath the stars. Lantern-lit paths wind through meticulously tended flowerbeds and over ornate bridges spanning small, gurgling streams. Each turn reveals hidden nooks with benches perfect for discreet conversations or a stolen kiss. I wonder how many women Colton has whisked away out here during his years of living with his parents. He squeezes my hand gently, as if somehow reading my thoughts, and pauses to give me a quick kiss.

"Lyra, Colton!" a voice calls out, and I turn to see his mother, Elspeth, approaching. Her chestnut-brown curls bounce lightly, and her unique golden eyes sparkle in the soft lantern light. She's accompanied by a few other people, including Colton's stepfather, Granger.

"Ladies, you all know Colton, of course," Elspeth says, smiling at us and introducing him to her friends. I notice she hesitates before mentioning me.

Colton, sensing the pause, wraps his arm around my lower back and says, "And this is my fiancée, Lyra." He turns to me. "Lyra, meet my mother's oldest friends—Rosalie and Odetta."

"Pleasure," Odetta responds, her tone carrying an edge. "Colton, you must remember my daughter Crimson. Do say hello to her tonight. It's been too long."

"It's lovely to meet you, Lyra. You look beautiful. The rumors don't do you justice," Rosalie adds, her smile warm and genuine.

"Thank you," I reply, appreciating Rosalie's kindness but internally questioning what rumors she's referring to.

"Colton, Lyra," Granger interjects with a deep, authoritative voice. He gives us a brief nod before excusing himself to join a group of men nearby, each holding a drink and engaged in conversation.

"Well, ladies, I'll let you get back to your gossip. The party is beautiful, Mother," Colton says, and I breathe a silent sigh of relief that our interaction is brief.

"Thank you, son. And, Lyra dear, we'll chat later. There are a few things we should discuss," Elspeth adds, her tone light but carrying a weight that settles uneasily in my stomach.

What could she possibly want to discuss that couldn't be said now? I manage a polite nod and a smile, masking my growing apprehension.

"Let's grab a drink," Colton says, guiding me away through the gardens. The farther we move from his parents, the better I feel—until he pulls me behind a sprawling moonflower bush into a secluded nook shrouded by blossoms.

The moment his lips find mine, the world falls away. His kiss is deep, insistent, and his hands roam over my body with a hunger that makes my knees weak.

"Colton," I whisper when we break for air, my voice thick with desire.

"Do you want to skip out? Forget the party and make love under the stars?" he murmurs, his breath hot against my ear.

Tempting as it is, I know leaving now would only strain things further with his family. "Shouldn't you introduce me to your friends first?" I tease, nibbling on his earlobe even as his hand slides up my dress, his fingers daring in their exploration.

"Only so they know you're mine," he growls, his finger slipping inside me, pressing into my heat. His touch sends a shiver through me, and I almost relent, almost say yes to leaving the party behind.

"Let's give it a bit longer," I manage to say, even as he drives another finger inside, sending waves of pleasure coursing through me.

"Your body seems to disagree, my shadow," he teases, finding my clit with his thumb.

The thrill of potentially being discovered adds an edge to his touch that's impossible to resist. "I love how you clench around my fingers. Later, I want to feel you tighten around my cock," he whispers, driving me closer to the edge.

I nod and begin to rock my hips against his fingers. His breath is hot against my ear as he murmurs, "Good girl. Fuck my fingers," he says, encouraging me deeper into the throes of my arousal.

I reach down, groping for his hardness through his pants. The contact stirs him further, and when I cry out, his mouth covers mine, swallowing my moans as I shudder and find my climax.

He eases his fingers out, allowing my dress to fall back into place. "I love you," I exhale, leaning into his embrace, feeling the unresolved tension in his body.

"I love you more—my queen, my mate, my everything," he responds, his voice rough with need.

I kneel down, unfastening his pants until his impressive length springs free. He's magnificent, and I can't help but wonder how I became so lucky. "I like when you look at me like that," he teases. Realizing I've been caught staring, my cheeks warm. With a playful smile, I extend my hand, running it along his length a few times, reveling in the feel of him. Then, locking eyes with him to see his reaction, I take him into my mouth, eager to taste him.

He grips my hair gently at the back of my head, urging me deeper, and I oblige. Swirling my tongue around the tip and then sinking down, drawing him in as deeply as I can manage. I'm relatively inexperienced, but the sounds he makes—a low, appreciative moan—encourage me to continue.

With each motion, I push my limits, drawing him in until he brushes against the back of my throat, and I gag slightly, but it only spurs me on. "Fuck," he breathes out, and I quicken my pace, using both my hand and mouth, keeping my eyes locked on his. His expression is one of sheer bliss, and it thrills me to know I'm the cause.

He reaches his climax, and I swallow, savoring the warmth then lick him clean. He pulls me to my feet, kissing me deeply, his taste mingling with mine. "Are you sure you don't want to leave?" he murmurs against my lips, his hand caressing my cheek tenderly.

I hesitate, torn by desire. "I do...but we should stay a bit longer," I admit, pressing my lips together. "Let's rejoin the others before I change my mind."

He laughs softly, "Alright, let's grab a drink then." I quickly adjust my hair and smooth out my dress, ensuring I look as composed as when we arrived. Slipping his arm around my waist, Colton leads me back through the gardens to the bustling terrace bar.

"Can I get you a Stardust?" Colton asks when we reach the bar. I let out a laugh, louder than I intended, drawing a few glances from nearby partygoers. I quickly cover my mouth, trying to contain my amusement, but the name Stardust brings back a flood of memories—it's the arousal drink I had at my first party here, the very night I met Colton, though I was with Nyx at the time. So much has changed since then.

"Maybe later." I wink, and he chuckles, picking up two amber glasses garnished with cherry and orange.

"Try this. It's alcoholic but nothing...altering," he assures me. I take a sip. It's like whiskey but sweeter with a pleasant hint of citrus.

"It's perfect," I tell him, finishing the drink quickly. I have a feeling it'll make the night more bearable.

He laughs softly, handing me another drink, and we start navigating the ballroom. He introduces me to a slew of people, but by my third drink, my head is spinning—not from the alcohol but from the sheer number of people he knows. I can't remember a single name after the first dozen.

"Lyra, darling," a familiar voice calls out, and I turn to see Flora approaching. Relief washes over me. She pulls me into a hug then looks at Colton. "We need to catch up. We'll find you later," she tells him. He nods, kisses my cheek, and lets me go.

Flora leads me back to the terrace and hands me a light-pink drink topped with smoky bubbles. She's in a tight, sparkly red dress that matches her hair and wings almost perfectly.

"So how are you holding up?" she asks, eyeing me closely. "You look amazing, by the way."

"So do you," I reply. "I'm doing okay, all things considered. I can't shake the feeling that Colton's parents really don't like me, and I've noticed a lot of odd looks."

"Looks?" Flora echoes.

"Yeah, or an energy I feel. I don't know. People are talking about me, and not in a good way," I explain.

"Of course they're talking about you. You're beautiful, engaged to an elder's son, and you're the dark sorceress, the shadowmancer of our time. They have too much to speculate about. Not to mention you also use to date the Fae king," she states matter-of-factly, making it sound like no big deal.

"When you put it like that, it makes me feel a whole lot better," I say dryly, finishing my drink.

"Sorry. Don't worry about it though. Most are curious or jealous. Powerful, attractive, and taking one of the most eligible Fae males off the market," she adds.

"Okay, point made," I say, raising my hands in mock surrender, and she giggles.

"I visited Seraphina earlier today. She wouldn't show me your dress, but she said it's nearly complete," Flora tells me, taking a sip of her drink.

"I can't wait to see it," I respond, excitement bubbling within me.

"Have you two settled on a date yet? Or a location? When I saw Elspeth the other day at the library, I suggested you should have the ceremony at that coastal property in Onyxland I told you about. She seemed keen on the idea," Flora says, her smile bright.

I return her smile, but a twinge of anxiety lingers within me. I really need to mend things with Elspeth and Granger, especially Elspeth. Perhaps tonight, if she seeks me out for that talk she mentioned, I'll have my chance.

"Hey, can I ask you something?" I venture, taking a few steps toward the edge of the terrace, away from the bustling crowd. Flora follows, placing her drink on the railing.

"Of course, what's on your mind?" she responds.

I hesitate, unsure if it's wise to bring this up, but trusting Flora feels right. She works closely with Nyx after all. "Do you know anything about the military camp set up in Vision Valley?" I ask cautiously.

Flora's eyes widen slightly. "How do you know about that?" she inquires, her surprise evident.

"It's a long story, but I've seen it firsthand," I admit, watching her closely for her reaction.

Flora takes a deep sip of her drink, seemingly weighing her words. "You should really speak to Nyx about that. I know things aren't great between you two, but he'd likely explain if you approached him directly," she suggests, sounding serious.

I nod, already dreading the thought of Colton's reaction to such a meeting. Perhaps it's better to wait until after I've spoken with him tonight to learn what he's been up to with Dorian. We all need to be aligned, especially now, and it feels like we're anything but.

Changing the subject to lighten the mood, I ask, "Is Bim here tonight?" I've always sensed a unique chemistry between him and Flora.

She brightens immediately. "He mentioned he might come, but I haven't spotted him yet."

A voice calls down from the balcony above us. "Flora, is that you?" a woman shouts.

Flora looks over, and her eyes widen. "Molly!" she exclaims. She turns to me with a quick smile.

"I'll catch up with you later. Go ahead and mingle," I encourage her, giving her a reassuring nod.

She gives me a hug and kiss on the cheek before dashing off to greet her friend.

I often feel awkward at events like this, likely a product of my sheltered upbringing. Being the subject of rumors and gossip certainly doesn't help. "Enjoying yourself?" a man's voice interrupts my thoughts, and I turn to see a Fae clad in all white. He's quite handsome, with short dirty-blond hair and hazel eyes.

"Sure," I respond, offering a half-smile.

"I hate parties like this," he confesses. "I never enjoy exchanging boring pleasantries with people I barely know. The only good things are the drinks and the food." His candidness makes me laugh, and I step closer to the bar to grab another of the premade drinks lined up.

"So are you friends with Colton?" I inquire, taking a sip of my drink.

"I don't really know him or the woman he's engaged to. My mother is friends with Elspeth, so I end up attending a lot of these parties. I'm Alaric," he introduces himself, extending a hand. "I don't think I've seen you before."

"I don't get out much," I admit, shaking his hand but withholding my name. It's refreshing to converse with someone who doesn't know who I am. "Nice to meet you, Alaric."

"Have you seen the couple we're here to celebrate yet?" Alaric asks, taking a sip of his drink and stepping closer. "I hear the woman is mad. Her name is Laura or something like that. My mother says she's using dark magic to trick Colton into bonding with her. Apparently, she's here because her own people can't stand her back in Cloudrum. There's even a price on her head," he whispers, cautious not to be overheard.

"Lyra. Her name is Lyra. And I've heard she's sweet and

misunderstood, and that Colton is madly in love with her, no magic involved," I reply, struggling to mask my annoyance.

"Interesting. I wonder if the wedding will really happen. If it does, maybe we could go together. I assume Elspeth will invite everyone she knows, like tonight," he muses, and I inwardly cringe, ready to end this conversation.

Elspeth's voice startles me from behind. "Lyra, there you are! We have so much to discuss," she says, catching me off guard.

I avoid making eye contact with Alaric as Elspeth hooks her arm through mine. "Let's find somewhere quieter to talk," she suggests, leading me away.

While led away, I glance back at Alaric and mouth, "I'm sorry." He looks slightly bewildered and embarrassed himself, his cheeks now flushed a bright pink.

CHAPTER 17
LYRA

"THANK you for hosting this lovely party for us. It's truly beautiful," I say, settling across from Elspeth on a settee that faces a large stone fireplace painted with intricate gold designs. She had guided us away from the festivities to a quaint sitting room.

"I didn't throw it for you," she replies crisply, and I jerk my head up, our eyes locking in a moment of tension. "I threw it because I love my son. But let's make this easier and forego the pleasantries. Can we speak frankly?"

I appreciate the directness.

"Yes, I prefer honesty," I respond, relieved to drop the facade.

She nods once then stands to prepare drinks at a cart in the corner of the room. Returning with two glasses filled with ice and a clear liquid, she hands one to me. I place mine on the table, undecided about drinking it.

"Let's clarify something. I don't like you, and I do not support your bonding ceremony with my son," she states flatly, delivering the words like a blow.

"Why do you dislike me? What have I done?" I scoff. "I'm sorry for how things went at the Luminary Council meeting, but I was under attack and coming to terms with my new powers. I couldn't control it then, but I can now." At least I can most of the time.

"It's not about the council meeting. I'm glad those who died are gone. My dislike isn't about that day. I've been in your head, Lyra. I know your heart," she declares, reminding me of her ability to mind walk—an ability she had used on me before to release my Fae magic after Euric buried it when I was a child.

Confusion clouds my thoughts. "When Nyx brought me to you, you were kind and helpful. I thought..."

"You thought wrong. I tolerated you when you were with Nyx. But then you shifted your affections to my son. I know what you're destined for..." She takes a long drink from her glass.

"What am I destined for? Is this about Callum's prophecy?" I ask, hoping to grasp the root of her disdain.

Elspeth sets her glass down with a clink, her gaze piercing. "You're destined for a path that doesn't suit what I want for Colton. You bring too much uncertainty, too much danger. And it's not about you—it's about the balance of power. You might think you control your dark magic, but it will influence more than your life."

The room feels colder as she speaks, her words hanging heavy between us. I grip my untouched drink for something to hold onto, feeling the weight of her judgment and the enormity of the forces aligning against my future happiness.

"Are you planning to interfere with the ceremony?" I ask, needing to understand her intentions clearly. Elspeth's lips press into a thin line, betraying her contemplation of the question. "I love your son. I would give my life for him," I insist, my voice steady despite the turmoil inside. "All I want is for him to be happy."

"Then let him go," she counters coldly. "Marry King Onyx instead. Colton will grieve, but he'll recover. He'll move on."

Her words sting like a physical slap, the suggestion that I abandon Colton to soothe her fears seems cruel and impossible. I feel something stir within me, my dark magic reacting to the emotional onslaught, my shadows yearning to protect me. I take a deep breath, striving to maintain control.

"You really think I should break his heart?" I ask, needing her to hear the absurdity in her proposal.

"I would do anything to protect him from you," Elspeth states bluntly. "It's not your magic that concerns me—it's you. Your very essence is tainted. You will bring nothing but death and destruction to Nighthold and beyond. The prophecy speaks of darkness and devastation, and you, Lyra, are its herald."

I impulsively squeeze my glass, downing the contents to quell the rising anger and hurt. The alcohol burns my throat, but it's a minor relief against the harsh judgment from the woman whose approval I once hoped to earn.

"And if I refuse to leave him?" I challenge, my voice steady, unwilling to show any weakness.

Elspeth's expression hardens, her resolve apparent. "Then I'll ensure you meet your end before the havoc you're destined to wreak even begins." Her smile turns sinister as she continues, "There's already a price on your head in Cloudrum, isn't there? And your charming step-brother Samael is quite eager to see you again...touch you again."

Disgust courses through me, my skin crawling with both revulsion and the creeping tendrils of dark magic seeking release. I rise, stepping closer to her, till we're nearly nose to nose. The shadows around my hands begin to coil with eager anticipation.

"You think you know me," I sneer, "but you have no idea. I have dealt with far more dangerous beings than a power-hungry elder. If you do anything to interfere with this wedding, to drive a wedge between Colton and me..." I lean in, my eyes locked on hers, my shadows slowly moving up her body. "I won't kill you because Colton loves you, and I won't hurt him through you. But believe me, Elspeth, I will make sure you regret it. I can make your life a living nightmare without ever touching you."

My shadows reach her throat and wrap around it, tightening ever so slightly. She holds my gaze, her fear momentarily visible despite her bravado.

"You've been inside my mind and must know what I'm capable of," I continue. "If I were you, I'd be very careful about how I sleep from now on. Darkness has a way of creeping in when least expected." My voice is a soft threat, a promise of retribution as I retract the shadows and step back, leaving the room with my head held high before she has a chance to respond.

I DISCOVER a secluded balcony at the edge of the ballroom, positioned high enough to provide a panoramic view of the entire celebration below—from the bustling ballroom to the vibrant pool area. It's half indoors and half outdoors, which offers a much-needed breath of cool air to soothe my frayed nerves. The space is thankfully deserted, affording me a moment of peace. It's also shrouded in shadow, allowing me to settle onto a couch against the back wall, hidden from the view of the partygoers below.

I had harbored a faint hope that my relationship with Colton's mother might improve, that she might come to accept me as her daughter-in-law. But tonight's events have dashed those hopes completely. The thought of disclosing this to Colton isn't an option. I can't bear the thought of breaking his heart. For now, I resolve to keep this burden to myself, hoping she won't follow through on her threats—but prepared to defend myself if necessary.

As I draw a deep, steadying breath, the sliding doors creak open, and a figure approaches the balcony ledge, peering down at the crowd. "Nyx?" My voice is barely a whisper, and he turns, his expression one of surprise.

"Lyra," he responds, his tone soft as he joins me on the couch.

"Isn't this supposed to be your celebration? Why are you lurking up here in the dark alone?" he asks, and I think I hear a hint of concern in his voice.

I manage a strained chuckle. "Let's say the evening is unfolding exactly as I feared," I confess, and his brow creases with worry.

"Do you want to talk about it?" Nyx inquires, sensing my distress.

I shake my head, barely managing to mutter, "No."

"Maybe this will help," he suggests, snapping his fingers. Instantly, two small glasses of whiskey materialize. I grasp one and take a hesitant sip, feeling the warmth spread through me. The liquor, I realize, is the only thing keeping my roiling shadows at bay tonight. I guess it's a good thing the Fae all like to drink a lot.

"What brought you here tonight?" I ask him, trying to sound casual. Nyx drains his glass, hesitating before he answers. "I felt a need to see you," he admits, his voice laden with an emotion he doesn't display. My heart aches slightly for the pain I've caused him. I catch his gaze, but he quickly looks away.

"There's something I need to talk to you about," I say.

He doesn't look at me, but his interest piques. "Oh? What's that?"

"I'm aware of the camps, Nyx—the ones in Vision Valley," I state, carefully observing his reaction. His eyes meet mine, flashing a mix of surprise and wariness.

"You've been there?" His voice is hushed.

"Yes, I've seen them firsthand," I admit firmly, holding his gaze.

"Why haven't you mentioned this earlier?" he probes, his eyes searching mine for an answer.

"What, because we were on speaking terms?" I retort with a hint of sarcasm. "What's the purpose of all this? Why the massive military buildup? Are you preparing for war with Cloudrum, with Samael?"

Nyx sets his glass down, his demeanor shifting as he considers how much to reveal. "It's complicated, Lyra," he begins with a mix of frustration and resignation. "Yes, there are preparations in place. We have to be ready for anything. Samael's return has destabilized the balance, and with Kaine rallying support against you, things are more precarious than ever."

He pauses, his eyes intense. "I didn't tell you because...I didn't want to drag you further into this mess. You've already been through so much because of your powers and the prophecy. Yes, it's about preparing for what might come, but it's also about protecting you. Whether you believe me or not."

"Protect me? By keeping secrets?" I challenge, unable to keep the hurt from my voice. "Or protect me as in...you still care?"

Nyx looks away briefly before meeting my eyes again.

"Both," he admits quietly. "I can't stop caring about you, Lyra, no matter how much I try. But understand, everything I do is to ensure your safety and the realms' stability."

"Does Colton know about the camps, about what you're planning?" I ask.

Nyx shakes his head, his expression hardening. "He doesn't need to know. The less I deal with him, the better," he replies coldly.

I reach out tentatively, the urge to mend the rift between us pressing on me. "We should be united in this, the three of us. Together, we make a strong team," I suggest gently.

He stands abruptly, brushing my hand away. "As long as you're with him, there's no us," he snaps with bitterness.

I close my eyes, exhaling slowly. "Nyx, please. If we face what's coming together—"

"No, Lyra. I really am sorry. I don't want to hurt you, but I can't stand by and watch, let alone work with him, not while you're together... I can't bear it," he chokes out, pain evident in his strained voice.

I rise, feeling his anguish echo within me. "Nyx, I'm sorry," I whisper, though I know it's of little to comfort him.

"I'm not giving up on us, on what could be our future. I'm close to proving why we belong together," he asserts, stepping closer. His hand cups my cheek, a tender gesture that feels like a goodbye.

"Nyx, stop. I've made my choice. I love him," I state firmly.

His expression darkens. "We'll see how far your love carries you when reality strikes," he retorts, dropping his hand.

"What's that supposed to mean?" I ask, my frustration mounting as I lean against the railing, looking down at the party below.

"You'll see soon enough," he says cryptically, a shadow of a smile flickering across his face. "Looks like your beloved is quite entertained with someone else."

Before I can respond, he gives a sardonic smile and vanishes, leaving me in a cloud of darkness, and the faint scent of him lingers in the air.

I gaze into the crowd, my eyes quickly finding Colton. He's surrounded by a group, but one woman in particular catches my attention—a young woman with straight brown hair, clad in a daringly revealing white dress, laughing and frequently touching his arm.

A surge of jealousy tightens my chest, an unfamiliar and unwelcome sensation that urges me to stride over there and claim what's mine. But I refuse to let Elspeth or Nyx spoil my evening. Instead, I'm going to join the fun.

I teleport myself directly in front of a server carrying a tray of the all-too-familiar Stardust drinks, grab two, and down them swiftly. If the night is going to spiral, I might as well steer it myself.

With newfound resolve, I weave through the crowd to Colton's side, sensing his immediate recognition. He turns, his eyes sweeping over me with palpable desire, then pulls me close, his arm securely around my shoulder. "This is my gorgeous fiancé, Lyra," he introduces me proudly, his hand slipping lower on my back to caress the bare skin there. "This is Lucrezia, Cyril, and Crimson," he continues.

Cyril, the smirk lingering on his lips, lets his gaze drift lower than appropriate. "My face is up here," I snap more sharply than intended. His eyes flick back to mine, chastened like a child caught misbehaving. Beside me, Colton stifles a chuckle, and Lucrezia, perhaps embarrassed, pulls Cyril away.

That leaves Crimson—the overly friendly woman and daughter of Elspeth's friend. Our eyes meet, and I steel myself, ready to handle whatever the night throws my way.

I can't believe that's even a name—it's a shade of red. "I think it's best I get a drink. You two enjoy your evening," she says, ducking away. She might be smarter than I initially thought, wise enough to leave and stop touching what's mine.

I turn to face Colton, his hands pulling me close. "You're scary when you want to be," he says, laughing.

"I guess you're not the only possessive one in this relationship," I tell him, and he laughs even harder.

I press my body against his, and an embarrassing moan escapes my lips due to the closeness. My breasts feel heavy, and I long for his touch. "I think we've shown our faces here long enough, don't you?" he suggests, and I nod, getting on my tiptoes to whisper in his ear.

"I may have had one or two Stardust drinks too," I confess, nibbling on his earlobe. His grip around my waist tightens.

"In that case," he replies, waving his hand as his own Stardust drink appears. He downs it quickly, and then his sweet citrus scent envelops us, accompanied by a swirl of wind as we channel away.

CHAPTER 18

LYRA

"WHAT IS THIS PLACE?" I ask in a whisper as I slowly turn, taking in my surroundings.

Colton flashes me one of his heart-stopping smirks. "Oh, my shadow, I could bring you to a new romantic location within the Dream Forest every night for a year, and we still wouldn't see all of its beauty," he declares, and gods, I believe him.

This secluded part of the forest forms a natural enclave, crafted by the dense canopy of towering trees and cascading wisteria vines. The ancient, majestic trees with their thick, gnarled trunks and broad branches intertwine, forming a vaulting ceiling far above. From this verdant arch, long clusters of wisteria blooms hang like curtains of rich violet, transforming the space into a cave-like sanctuary.

I walk along the small river's edge, looking up. The canopy is so lush that it nearly obscures the sky, allowing only speckled beams of moonlight to filter through. These beams illuminate the mist rising off the river, adding to the spectacular ambiance.

"It's so beautiful—this may be my favorite place yet," I tell him.

He tugs on my hand, drawing my attention back to him. His touch sends shivers up my skin, and a deep yearning starts to form in my core. The cool air, fragrant with the scent of fresh blooms and wet earth, heightens the sense of entering a hidden grotto. The tranquility is further enhanced by the soft murmurs of a modest waterfall behind Colton.

I glance past him to see its waters cascading into the calm river below, and the idea of getting into the water is suddenly very tempting.

He sheds his jacket and shirt, tossing them aside along with his boots, as if he's tuned into my unspoken desires. I slip off my shoes and start to tug at one of my dress straps, but Colton catches my hand, clicking his tongue in gentle admonishment. My brow furrows in confusion, but before I can protest, he lifts me effortlessly and carries me toward the water.

"Don't spoil all my fun. I want to undress you...slowly," he murmurs, his voice a warm caress as we wade into the shallow waters near the waterfall.

The water is pleasantly warm. The mist from the waterfall feels good as it splashes off the rocks and rains down on us. "I might actually make you work for it. You still have some explaining to do," I retort playfully, echoing him from earlier.

He responds by tightening his grip on my ass, pressing me closer to him in a way that nearly draws a moan from deep within me. The effects of the Stardust drink are intensifying, and my desire for him grows with each passing second.

"Is that so? Well, ask away, Princess," he challenges, his lips trailing a path of kisses up my damp neck.

"What have you been doing with Dorian? Do you know about the military camps Nyx has set up in Vision Valley? Is Dorian supplying them with weaponry?" I fire off my questions, each one punctuated by his kisses slowing as he processes them.

He pulls back to look at me, dipping us further into the water until it reaches his waist. "What exactly have you been up to yourself? Seems you've been quite busy lately too," he teases, desire still alight in his eyes despite the shift toward more serious conversation.

"I may have gone hiking with Hollie, and we stumbled across some Fae soldiers, so we followed them," I admit, noting his sudden concern.

"What were you two doing hiking so far from the villa? You must have been quite distant to run into soldiers," he says.

I pull back slightly, his tone igniting a flicker of defiance within me. "I didn't realize you intended to keep me locked up in the villa while you're away," I snap back more sharply than I intended.

"Lyra, that's not what I mean. You know you can do whatever you want. But I worry about you," he says quickly, trying to soften his previous implication. "I didn't know you and Hollie were hanging out so much or venturing that far. The Dream Forest can be dangerous."

"You don't think I can take care of myself? You don't think I can protect us if something were to happen? I think I've more than proven I'm capable," I retort, my voice firm. "Plus, I've been practicing my dark magic even more lately. Hollie and I venture far from the villa, away from prying eyes. The last thing I need is for more rumors to spread."

Then his words stun me momentarily, his admission an echo in the cool night air. "Gods, I want to fuck you so bad right now," he breathes out, his eyes locked on mine, blazing with a fiery intensity. He's trying to dodge this conversation.

"What did you say?" I laugh, surprised by his bluntness yet finding myself drawn deeper into his gaze.

"Oh, I think you heard me loud and clear, Princess. But I'll say it again because I think you enjoy it," he continues, each word deliberate, punctuating the air between us. "I want to fuck you so bad right now."

My cheeks burn with a flush of heat, my body responding despite the serious undertone of our conversation. "Don't think for a second you're going to distract me away from this conversation," I manage to say, though my voice comes out breathier than intended, betraying my own desires.

He doesn't miss a beat, addressing my earlier questions as he pulls me closer. "Yes, I know about the camps. Yes, Dorian is supplying them, and I've been helping him, working with Bim a bit too. Bim doesn't like lying to Nyx about my involvement, but he knows he's irrational when it comes to you," he confesses, his words mingling with the misty air around us.

"It seems both of you make irrational decisions when it comes to me. Why did you keep this from me, especially after we agreed no more secrets?" I ask, the effects of the drink muddling my frustration.

"I wasn't hiding it, honestly. We've both been so busy, and I only found out about it recently myself. They were reluctant to tell me because they didn't want to provoke Nyx," Colton explains, his voice earnest. "Things are getting serious in Cloudrum, Lyra. We're all going to have to make tough decisions soon, especially you. I wish I could keep you hidden away here forever. If you asked, I might even try to find a way to make that happen."

"All the more reason to cherish nights like tonight. Who knows how many we have left?" I say, gazing up at the slices of moonlight filtering through the canopy.

"Have you really been practicing your dark magic more? Why wouldn't you ask for my help?" he suddenly asks, shifting the conversation.

"I didn't want to unsettle you," I whisper, avoiding his gaze.

He gently cups my cheek, compelling me to look at him.

"Hey, I've told you before—nothing about you could ever unsettle me."

I look down, uncertain if I believe him. I'm not sure why I'm letting Nyx get to me, especially right now. Colton moves his hand to my chin, coaxing me to meet his gaze, and I finally do.

"I'll prove it to you right now." He pauses, and a wicked smirk starts to spread across his face. "Let your dark magic out right now. Let your dark side fuck me, and I'll show you exactly how little it unsettles me," he says, and I feel my shadows stir under my skin at the invitation.

His suggestion sends a thrill through me, a mix of fear and excitement. He watches me, his eyes intense, filled with an earnest hunger that leaves little room for doubt.

"Are you sure?" My voice is barely a whisper, the weight of my power pressing against the confines I've imposed on it.

"Absolutely, my shadow," he breathes, his expression unwavering. "I want all of you, Lyra. Every shadow, every sliver of darkness. Show me."

Emboldened by his acceptance, I let the darkness seep through the surface, my shadows spilling out of me and curling around us both like a tangible embrace. The air around us thickens, the atmosphere charged with the raw essence of my magic.

I let my shadows tighten around us, pressing our bodies closer together, and his smile widens.

"See?" he says, his voice rough. "Nothing about you could ever push me away. Let go—I've got you, always. Show me all of you."

I'm wary, but his encouragement is all I need. I release my hold further, allowing the dark magic to intertwine with my desires. My need for him becomes frantic as I press my lips to his and drink from him as if I am dying of thirst. I clasp his arms, and the feel of his muscles beneath my hands sets me off.

He pulls my straps down, freeing my breasts and taking them into his hands, massaging me before breaking our kiss and teasing my nipples with his lips and teeth. I let my head fall back, the tension in my body building for him.

I don't know if it's the Stardust drinks, my dark magic, or perhaps a potent mix of both, but I'm consumed with a fervent hunger for him. I thread my fingers through his hair, gripping tightly at the back of his head, pulling until his head tips back. This allows me the perfect angle to kiss him fiercely.

I bite down on his bottom lip hard enough to draw blood, eliciting a deep growl from his throat. His response is instant. His hand finds my neck, pulling me into a harder, more desperate kiss, the taste of blood only spurring him on. As the intensity escalates, I close my eyes and channel us to the river's edge, where his back hits the soft grass.

My shadows react, tearing my dress into shreds while Colton, with a wave of his hand, makes his pants disappear before I can rip them myself. I pout briefly at his quick action, but my frustration is fleeting—I need him too much, and I can feel my power stirring within, still holding back, not yet ready to surrender completely to its dark embrace.

There's no time for foreplay. My body craves more of him, a desperate need to cling to what I have, to be closer to my mate. I can tell I'm ready, and without hesitation he steadies my hips as I lower myself onto him. The sensation of him filling me satisfies my deepest need. I brace my hands on his chest, beginning to ride him in a tantalizingly slow rhythm.

He reaches up to grab my hips again, but I weave my shadows around his wrists, pinning them above his head. A soft chuckle escapes him, and I meet his gaze with a look that says I'm in control now, a notion he seems to relish. I increase my pace, lifting off him then sinking back down, each movement more intense than the last.

I glance down and notice the tips of my hair darkening to black. *Don't lose control,* I remind myself, but it's challenging. He feels too good, and my grasp on restraint is slipping away rapidly.

Colton flips me onto my back. I don't know how he broke free, but in a blink he's on top of me, his fingers tracing my face and around my eyes as he examines me. I catch sight of my own reflection in his eyes—my pupils swirling black—and he must be feeling the inky veins that have started to spread across my face.

"Now, it's my turn to show you that no matter how dark and powerful you think you are, I can always take control, because you're mine," he declares, thrusting into me. The force takes my breath away, each movement more dominating than the last.

My body craves his possessiveness, and the darkness within me purrs in pleasure as he asserts himself. Colton takes control in the most intoxicating way.

He grips my thighs tight, holding my legs apart, pushing and pulling my body with his, as if seeking to bury himself even deeper inside me. I cry out, throwing my hands up, desperately searching for something to ground myself. I latch onto his biceps, holding on for dear life as he drives me into oblivion.

I climax twice before he finally slows his pace. This is not making love; this is Colton claiming what belongs to him—and I fucking love it.

He releases my legs, and they fall to the grass, limp as overcooked noodles. He leans over me, his face inches from mine, his expression intense, his emerald eyes fiercely glowing in the moonlit night. "I love you, Lyra, all of you, no matter how dark.

You're mine," he declares, sending my heart into a joyful flutter.

"I love you, Colton, and you're mine," I respond, reaching up to caress his face. He kisses me tenderly for the first time tonight, his tongue slowly exploring my mouth as if memorizing every contour.

His arousal remains firm inside me, and he resumes moving, slowly this time. I revel in the sensation of him withdrawing and then pressing back in deeply.

"Come inside me. I want to feel you," I urge him, pulling away from his kiss. I've already climaxed twice and feel a twinge of selfishness. Looking down between us, I watch us merge into one. His hand travels from my breast down to my center, where he begins to circle my clit. I bite down on my lip, my hands digging into the grass.

Colton tugs gently at my lip with his teeth and kisses me again, his movements drawing moans and cries from me until I climax once more, quivering beneath him.

"Good girl," he murmurs, tasting myself on his finger. His stare locks onto mine, not kissing me, watching as he reaches his own climax. I hold his piercing gaze, letting it delve into my soul as he releases inside me, leaving us both panting in the aftermath.

I never want to leave this position, but after a few moments he gently pulls out and settles beside me, tugging me to rest on his chest. "Colton," I whisper, my voice nearly drowned out by the chorus of frogs echoing through the night.

"Yes, my shadow," he replies. I throw an arm over him and hook one leg around him, yearning for the closeness we shared moments ago. He wraps his arm around me tightly, holding me as if he too can't bear the distance.

"My dress is shredded to ribbons, and I'm too exhausted to move," I confess, and he chuckles softly. I swat at his chest, but it's a feeble gesture. I'm spent after the day's events, the night's passions, and the surge of magic. My body cries out for rest.

"I've got you," he murmurs, the last thing I hear before his essence envelops us. Suddenly, we're in his bed, his body wrapped around mine, cradling me in his embrace—safe.

CHAPTER 19
COLTON

"How long has she been out there?" I ask Rix and Rune as they prepare dinner in the kitchen. I can see Lyra through the window, seated on the grass, her feet dipped in the water, gazing into the distance. Chepi, as usual, is snoozing beside her.

"She's been out there for a couple of hours," Rune comments without looking up from chopping vegetables.

"Hasn't really moved much either," Rix adds from the pantry.

It's been nearly a week since the party at my parents' estate, and Lyra hasn't been herself. She seems distant, lost in thought, and it's been weighing on me. With all the time I've spent managing the fallout from Nyx's schemes, maybe it's time to try talking to him again, to mend things so we can discuss the looming battle openly.

I've been trying to keep Lyra out of the darkest parts of this. I know she doesn't want any more secrets between us, and I'm not hiding anything, just shielding her from the stress of what's coming. I want her to be happy, lost in plans for our wedding, not burdened by the imminent threat of war.

Yet she will be queen of Cloudrum someday, and perhaps it's unfair to keep her from the realities of her kingdom. I wanted her to enjoy the Dream Forest, to have some peace before the storm. And every time Samael's name comes up, I see how it affects her. That bastard is living on borrowed time, and I intend to end his reign myself—for good this time.

"Are you in trouble?" Rix teases, emerging from the pantry with a bag of flour in hand.

"Guess I'd better find out," I respond, receiving a scolding look from him. I kick off my boots and head out the back door.

Lyra doesn't turn as I approach, but I know she senses my presence. Sitting next to her, I dip my feet into the water beside hers. "What's wrong, Princess? You've got Rix and Rune back there thinking I'm in some kind of peril," I chuckle, noticing the corner of her lips twitch upward, though she still doesn't face me.

"I like keeping you on your toes," she teases, her foot playfully brushing against mine under the water.

"And what are you doing out here all by yourself?" I probe further.

"Thinking about life...and our future," she replies.

"A future with lots of sex, I hope?" I jest, earning a light giggle from her. "Seriously, what's on your mind?"

"I'm figuring out what I need to do," she says, and I wrap an arm around her shoulder.

"What we need to do, you mean. We're a team, remember?" I squeeze her a little tighter. Her recent melancholy weighs on me. I wish I could break through her defenses, understand her thoughts and feelings every second of the day—especially now. "Let me in."

"I think we should meet with Nyx and have a serious talk, all three of us," she suggests, and I close my eyes, dreading the thought. Nyx is insufferably stubborn and righteous, but for Lyra, I'd walk through fire.

"How about I invite him to join us for dinner tonight?" I propose instead.

"Here?" she turns to me quickly, a flicker of a smile crossing her face that unexpectedly stirs a hint of jealousy within me.

"Yeah, Rix and Rune are cooking enough to feed a small army, so why not tackle this tonight? It might ease your mind," I say, noting the slight furrow of her brows.

"But how will we get him to come here?" she asks, her concern palpable.

"Leave that to me. Why don't you go freshen up for dinner and let Rix or Rune know that Nyx will be joining us?" I suggest. She nods, leans in to kiss my cheek, then hurries inside. Chepi, stretching leisurely as I give him a couple of pats, glances at me before bounding after her.

"WELL, isn't this like old times?" I chuckle as I materialize in Nyx's study, skipping the pleasantries—I know he adores it when I channel directly into his sanctum But he's currently preoccupied. A blonde woman is bent over his desk, and Nyx is rather...engaged with her. She looks up at me and smiles. Her face seems familiar, but her name escapes me.

Nyx hastily adjusts his pants, and I can't help but stroll leisurely toward his fireplace, taking in the room. "Don't stop on my account. I can wait... I'm sure it won't take you long."

Nyx's tone is sharp as he dismisses the woman. "Leave us," he commands. She quickly pulls her dress back on and vanishes, and by the time my gaze shifts back to his desk, she's gone.

"What the fuck are you doing here, Colton?" Nyx snaps,

clearly irritated. I revel a bit in catching him like this. Lyra's always worried he's sulking over her, yet here he is, clearly not suffering too much.

"I came to invite you to dinner," I say, my smile smug and wide.

"Well, you've wasted a trip. I have no desire to dine with you," Nyx states flatly, settling into his chair and pouring himself a glass of whiskey.

"That's a shame. I'd hate for you to have dismissed...whatever her name was...for nothing." I take a seat across from his desk, near the fireplace, making myself comfortable.

"She can easily be summoned again," he retorts, downing his glass with an air of defiance.

"Naturally. Well, Lyra sent me in hopes you would attend dinner with us, but you're preoccupied," I say, pressing my hands against the chair arms, poised to stand.

"What did she say?" he asks, a trace of eagerness betraying his usual reserve.

"She wants to talk to you. Not sure why though. Maybe she'll worry less about your poor broken heart when I tell her how I found you," I chuckle, enjoying the rise I'm getting out of him. He slams his fist down on the table, ruffled.

"Give me a moment to change, and I'll come with you," he concedes, snapping his fingers and instantly appearing in a clean black tunic and pants.

I roll my eyes. "Who are you trying to fill the void for this time, Nyx? Still Lyra, or are you ready to admit you miss—"

"Don't speak her name," he cuts me off sharply. "Let's go."

We both materialize outside the back door simultaneously. Striding into the dining room, I find Rix and Rune absent, though the table is laden with food. Lyra is seated at the head of the table. Her smile blossoms as she sees me, and she rises to greet me. I walk over, leaning in for a kiss that I deliberately prolong, pressing against her a bit longer than necessary—a small jab at Nyx, who I'm aware is behind me.

Lyra allows this moment, but as I finally pull back and move to take my seat, she catches sight of Nyx. Her eyes widen slightly, her cheeks tinting a brighter shade of pink. If only she knew what he was just up to...

"Nyx, you came," she remarks, stepping toward him then halting as if unsure of how to proceed. He nods stiffly and takes the seat opposite me, Lyra settling between us at the head of the table.

Preferring to let Lyra lead the conversation, since she's the one eager to speak with him, I start piling my plate with food, hoping the others will follow suit to cut through the tension. The spread includes fish garnished with fresh lemon, pasta, and a vegetable casserole—looks like Rix and Rune went all out.

Thankfully, someone had the foresight to place a decanter of whiskey at the end of the table. Nyx seizes it, quickly filling his glass, then courteously offers it to Lyra. She accepts with a smile, her glass brimming under his attentive pour. The bastard doesn't bother to offer any to me, simply setting the decanter back on the table.

I clear my throat conspicuously as I grab it and pour myself a generous amount. "So, my shadow, what would you like to talk about?" I ask, the affection in my nickname for her hanging in the air.

Nyx scowls at the term. He's always despised the pet names I have for her; they rile him up so easily. Lyra takes a sip from her glass then shifts her focus to Nyx.

"I really want us all to get along and work together," she starts, her voice threading through the silence. "Nyx, I know I've hurt you, and I know you two have your differences... your history...but you are brothers. Please," she pleads, her voice punctuated by several long pauses, her nervousness evident.

Nyx looks down at his plate, as if weighing his words carefully. Before he can respond, I quickly interject, not wanting him to say anything that might hurt Lyra. "Nyx was in the midst of some important work when I found him this evening. Perhaps now isn't the best time for this discussion. He seems eager to return to it," I say, giving him no room to maneuver.

He shoots me a sharp look, his gray eyes flickering with a light that suggests his irritation at my insinuation. Knowing that I can now hold this over him brings a twisted sort of satisfaction —after all, Lyra chose me, and yet he clings to a desperate hope of swaying her.

"Maybe we should talk without him," Nyx suggests directly to Lyra, ignoring my commentary. "You could come back with me for a nightcap."

I can't help but laugh at his audacity, which earns me a sharp look from Lyra. I close my mouth, offering her an apologetic glance.

"There's something I need to do, and this would all be much simpler if we could rely on each other. We don't have to enjoy each other's company, but can we at least be civil and discuss the future of Eguina? We all have crucial roles to play," she insists, her tone firm yet imploring.

My interest is piqued. What does she need to do? What is she up to?

"Lyra, you can always count on me, no matter where we stand. What is it?" Nyx says, his voice smooth, always ready to play the devoted ally.

"You both are well aware of the military camps being established in Vision Valley. Colton has been collaborating with Bim and Dorian, and it seems everyone has been tiptoeing around the two of you, so let's lay it all out now," she states, rising to her feet with a resolve that marks her readiness to dive deep into the discussion.

"I know you both try to shield me from the realities of my situation, but I do not need it. I do not want it, so stop," she declares, pausing dramatically to let her words sink in before she begins to pace the room. Nyx's eyes follow her every move, and I can't stand the way he watches her, knowing his history with her.

"I'm fully aware that Kaine is fostering animosity among my people. I know Samael has reclaimed the throne, and I understand that violent attacks are escalating across the realms for reasons yet to be discerned. I am not oblivious to any of this, despite your incessant efforts to shield me from my own life," she continues, her voice climbing with each revelation.

Her frustration is palpable, and I remain silent, giving her the space to express all that's been weighing on her.

"My nineteenth birthday is quickly approaching, and I know I need to be ready to fight for my throne. I need to ensure we are aligned, that I can count on both of you when the time comes," Lyra declares, her gaze shifting rapidly between me and Nyx. Her eyes linger on mine a moment longer. She knows she has my allegiance.

"Lyra, a major reason I am even assembling my army is that we've been teetering on the brink of war for far too long. You can trust that, no matter what, I am on your side, and my forces will fight for you," Nyx says.

"Thank you." She nods at him and resumes pacing. "I need to return to Cloudrum, to see my people and assess how dire the situation is in the Sorcerer Realm. Not only that, but I will also be returning to Zomea for a short time," she adds.

"What?" Nyx and I interrupt in unison, our voices sharp with concern.

She pauses, her eyes scanning our faces. "I've been plagued

by distressing dreams, visions that come to me in the night. My midnight mind is... Understand this is something I need to do, and I will be doing it alone," she explains.

I immediately want to protest but decide it's better to discuss this privately after Nyx leaves, so I bite back my words.

Nyx looks from her to me, incredulous. "You're going to let her go back to Cloudrum, knowing the hatred brewing there for her? And back to Zomea, where only the gods know what dangers await, alone?"

Lyra is beside him in an instant. "Don't look at him. He doesn't control me. I am my own person, and it's high time you both stop treating me like I'm fragile. I will not break," she asserts fiercely, her stance resolute.

Her declaration reminds me of a time when she was much more vulnerable, at least internally. She has grown significantly since then, though I know deep wounds still linger under her resilient exterior.

"Colton will accompany me to Cloudrum, but I must go alone to Zomea. I can't explain now. Trust that it's something I need to do by myself, and I'll be alright," she says.

To my surprise, Nyx nods, accepting her decision without further argument.

"I look forward to seeing you when you return. Until then, my people will continue to monitor the situation with Samael, as well as the increasing Sarrol attacks in Nighthold and across all the realms," Nyx says amicably.

"Have the attacks been mostly Sarrols?" Lyra inquires.

"Mostly, yes. There have been Monstrauths and other creatures involved, but the Sarrols seem to have the most numbers for now," he replies.

Lyra tucks her hair behind her ear then lets her hand glide down her neck—a clear sign of her concern. Catching Nyx's expression, which holds a different kind of intensity, I decide it's time for him to direct that gaze elsewhere.

"Great, so we can do this again soon. I look forward to it," I interject with a hint of sarcasm, drawing a slight smile from Lyra.

Nyx rises, and rather than channeling directly out of the dining room, he opts to walk to the back door—a show of decorum, as always. I roll my eyes subtly, which Lyra catches with a quick.

She calls out to him, "I'll walk you out."

I nod, taking another sip from my glass before gathering our plates and heading to the kitchen, which has a window that offers a clear view into the backyard, and wouldn't you know, it's open—allowing their voices to drift in.

"Thank you for coming tonight," Lyra says as he turns to face her.

"I'll always be here for you, even when it's hard to bear," he replies, taking a step closer. She holds her ground, not stepping back as he raises his hand to touch her cheek. Watching from the kitchen, I clench my jaw, barely restraining myself from storming out there to break his damned hand.

"I know, and I appreciate it. Take care of yourself," she responds, her voice steady.

Oh, if only she knew just how well he'd be taking care of himself—with a queue of women, no doubt, eager to assist him. He looks up then, his eyes finding mine. There's a taunting glint in them as he leans down and kisses her on the top of her head. My teeth grind, and he winks at me, a smug gesture, before disappearing in a cloud of night.

Lyra turns and spots me in the kitchen, immediately coming back inside to wrap her arms around my waist and press her face into my chest. I hold her close, my hand gently stroking her hair. "That went better than I thought it would," she murmurs, looking up at me with a hint of relief in her eyes.

I bend down to kiss her softly. "Come, let's go to bed, and you can tell me all about this solo trip to Zomea," I suggest, feeling the weight of the night start to lift.

She laughs, a light, melodious sound that fills the room. "I might need you to remind me you're mine while you're at it," I tease, enjoying the playful spark in her eyes.

"Feeling a little jealous tonight?" she asks, rising on her tiptoes to kiss me again, her lips teasing mine.

"Maybe a little," I admit, though the lingering image of him touching her stirs a deeper unease within me.

"Then come to bed and show me who I belong to," she whispers, her teeth gently tugging at my bottom lip.

CHAPTER 20

NYX

I FIND myself wandering the dimly lit corridors of the Elders' Palace library. It's late, and perhaps I should have stayed home, entertained by Tansy's company, or had Twig concoct a potion to ease me into sleep. Yet here I am, compelled by an urgent need to uncover answers about Lyra.

I suspect Elspeth and Granger are asleep, if they're even at home. Relief washes over me as I enter the vast library and find it deserted. I'm not in the mood to encounter anyone tonight, especially since this place stirs memories of Colton, which I'd rather avoid.

Flora's searches have turned up nothing useful regarding Lyra's future, and I refuse to believe my father's prophecies were mere inventions. They originated from somewhere, and I'm convinced there must be additional writings about the dark Sorcerers or the prophecy concerning Lyra specifically. I am determined to unearth them, even if it means dismantling every library piece by piece.

With the recent revelations of Elspeth's infidelity, it wouldn't surprise me if she's kept more of my father's journals hidden here. Colton managed to procure one of Callum's journals, and if there were more, he likely would have handed them over to Lyra by now...unless he's concealing something himself. Or perhaps the journals cast him in an unfavorable light.

Dinner tonight was excruciating. Watching them together is unbearable. I know I should want Lyra to be happy, but I can't—not when she's with him. Perhaps that reveals a flaw in my character, but I yearn for her happiness to be intertwined with mine. Colton simply doesn't deserve her, and I'm fucking tired of him constantly mentioning Z, as if my feelings for Lyra are not real, merely an attempt to fill the void left by her.

I don't want to dwell on Zaelinn. She's gone, and pondering what might have been is futile. She's not coming back. Overwhelmed by frustration, I kick over a stack of books and let out a huff of anger. Perhaps I should head to the training ring at the army camps—unleash some of this pent-up rage on soldiers who could really benefit from the practice.

"Don't stop on my account. Please knock down the whole library if you think it will help," she says from behind me.

I roll my eyes before turning to face her, not in the mood for whatever games Elspeth wants to play tonight. Normally, she's timid and level-headed, but ever since her secret was revealed, I can barely stand to look at her. This woman, who pretended to be my mother's friend, was having an affair with my father. Really, this mess is all her fault.

Granger has been a wreck. Since the council meeting, I haven't been able to discuss any political strategy with him. He's taking this all very hard. I'm surprised they are even still together. For all I know, they might not be—it could all just be for social appearances.

I used to look up to Elspeth after my mother passed, sought her advice and help, even once when Lyra needed her Fae magic awakened. But now I don't know how to feel about her.

"It won't help," I drawl, running a hand through my hair in an attempt to ease the tension building inside me.

"What is it that brought you here tonight? Don't think I haven't noticed how often Flora has been visiting too. What are you hoping to find?" she asks. I really don't feel like having this conversation with her. I look down, grappling with how to respond, when she presses on. "You're searching for a way to get her back, aren't you?" she probes, catching me off guard.

My eyes snap to hers—what does she know about it? "What if I am?" I reply, striving to keep my voice nonchalant.

"Then I'd say maybe I want to help you," she offers, taking me even more by surprise.

"Why would you want to help me get Lyra back when she's engaged to your son?" I ask cautiously. Elspeth is a scheming woman, but her love for Colton is undeniable.

"You don't need to worry about why. Do you want my help or not?" she says, making me feel like this could be a setup. I glance around the library, extending my essence to confirm we are truly alone.

"I need to know what's in it for you," I tell her, not trusting Elspeth to offer help without having her own agenda.

I'm not sure if I care what her agenda is if she truly has something that could help me win Lyra back, but I'm curious if she'll reveal her motives.

"I don't want that girl bonding with my son. I don't want him anywhere near her or her dark magic. Colton can do far better, and I will do whatever it takes to ensure that. But Colton can never know I helped you," she confides.

I mull this over. Colton can do far better? I suppress a laugh. Clearly, Elspeth's love for her son is blinding her, maybe driving her a bit mad given all the recent events. Regardless, her reasons are her own—I don't care as long as I get what I want from the deal.

"Fine. I won't reveal your involvement to Colton. Now, what do you have that can help me?" I ask, hoping it might be exactly what I suspect.

"Follow me," she instructs, leading me to the bottom floor of the library. It's always colder here, and the smell of old books is pungent. She navigates to the back of the room and turns down one of the aisles. At the end, she tugs on two books simultaneously, and magically a door appears in the aisle itself, hidden until now.

Of course. No wonder Flora isn't finding what I'm looking for—this cunning woman is hiding everything right under our noses. I keep my mouth shut, half-expecting her to tell me to wait here, but instead she allows me to push through the door behind her.

The door opens into a hidden vault, not merely filled with books but shelves packed with jewels and artifacts. I wonder if Granger is aware of this concealed chamber beneath the library.

"What is all of this? Why hide it?" I ask, frustrated that she thinks she can conceal books in my kingdom because she's an elder. Deciding this isn't the moment to escalate tensions, I keep my tone controlled, casually masking my irritation.

"Some texts are not meant for public eyes. Some histories are better left buried. As for the other items," she says, her voice as cool and composed as ever, "I've simply collected my fair share of trinkets over the years. Nothing special."

I suppress the urge to roll my eyes. I don't believe for a second that everything in this room is merely trinkets.

"Listen, I know what I'm about to show you may upset you, but I want you to understand that I loved your father. However, I also love my husband and my son. I kept these things hidden to protect the ones I love," she says, confirming my suspicions that she might have one of my father's journals hidden here.

"I understand that love can drive us to do crazy things," I tell her, meaning every word. She smirks at me, perhaps understanding my feelings more than I realize. She walks over to a large cabinet, pulls open one side, and retrieves a stack of books —a stack of journals. It's unbelievable how many there are.

"After your parents passed, I hid away every journal of Callum's that I could find. I feared they might reveal our relationship or Colton's lineage. I'm sorry for keeping a piece of your father from you all these years." She hands me the stack, and I glance down, counting roughly sixteen journals.

"Perhaps in death, he will help you get what you truly desire," she says. Eager to leave, knowing I have many sleepless nights ahead to go through these, I watch as she returns to the cabinet for more. Could there really be more?

"These are letters he wrote. I haven't read them all myself. His mind was fragile at the end. Take them if you wish," she continues, handing me a small stack of old envelopes, some wax seals still intact.

I nod and leave without another word. I can't bring myself to thank her—I'm too furious she hid this from me for so long, my father's possessions, rightfully mine. Yet I know maintaining her as an ally might be beneficial, so I restrain my anger for now.

I channel back to my bedroom, not wanting to leave these items scattered around my study, especially since Colton has been appearing there lately. My bedroom is safer. I start to set the journals and letters out across my bed, doing a quick inventory of everything.

I wonder how much of this might be the ramblings of a man troubled by delusions. Perhaps my father wasn't as deranged in his final days as everyone believed. Maybe there was a kernel of truth in his madness, his struggles exacerbated by our disbelief in his predictions and the many prophecies he knew. With these thoughts swirling in my mind, I kick off my boots and grab the first journal from the pile. Settling back against my pillows, I open it to the first page, eager to uncover whether wisdom or madness lies within its worn pages.

This prophecy, these scribblings—they will call it the delusion of a disturbed mind. Let them. For in the truth of these words lies the salvation of those who dare to heed them. Beware, for the night grows darker, and its terrors do not sleep...

CHAPTER 21

LYRA

"Have you thought about when you want to have the wedding yet? You need to set a date," Flora says from her padded chair in the backyard.

"She can take all the time she needs. Don't rush her," Colton chimes in from behind me, shooting Flora a pointed look. I lean back against him, stretching my legs out in the sun. We had planned to leave for the Lamia Realm this morning, but Flora's unexpected visit prompted us to enjoy the day outside and leave tonight instead.

"It's okay. I don't need more time. I honestly don't know when to have it," I tell her, and Colton wraps an arm around me, idly tracing circles on my stomach.

"Well, have you thought about anything specific you want for the ceremony? Have you made any decisions at all since I last saw you? It's a good thing I took you dress shopping when I did, or you would probably have worn something out of your closet," Flora teases, and I laugh at her dramatic tone.

"You went dress shopping?" Colton asks. We've both been so busy lately that I forgot to tell him.

"Yes, Seraphina is designing a dress for me. I picked out some fabric and let her take my measurements. I haven't seen the dress yet though," I explain. Colton hums in response, and I place my hand over his, giving it a gentle squeeze, hoping he understands that my lack of involvement in the planning doesn't mean I'm not excited.

"And I have decided a few things about the ceremony," I add to Flora, who props herself up on her elbows, eager for me to continue. "I want the ceremony to be small, and I think having it on the coast at Colton's family home you told me about would be perfect."

I pause, and when neither of them protests, I continue, "I know your mom wants to invite all her friends and make it a big event, but I want the ceremony to be inti- mate, close friends and family. If Elspeth wants, she can throw a reception afterward and invite whoever she wants."

"It's our day, not my mother's. You can do whatever you want, and I will tell her to stay out of it completely if that makes you happy," Colton says, his voice firm. His support brings a smile to my lips.

"Well, it's settled then. Elspeth can throw an after-party, and I get to plan the ceremony for you," Flora squeals with excitement.

"That would be amazing. Are you sure you have the time?" I ask, surprised yet relieved that she wants to take on the planning.

"Are you kidding? I love planning parties. I'm going to make it the most beautiful intimate ceremony ever," she assures me, and I trust her completely.

I lean my head back to look up at Colton. "Are you okay with this?" I ask.

"I'm okay with anything as long as I have you," he replies,

leaning down to kiss me. I melt into him, feeling completely content.

Flora clears her throat, and I break away from our kiss, giggling. "Now, about the date," she prompts.

"What do you guys think?" I ask, unsure of how long these things take or what's a good date to get married.

"How about we do it on your birthday, October 19th? It will be extra special, and that still gives me enough time to get everything in order," Flora suggests.

I mull the idea over. My birthday—I've never really done anything special for it, no big celebrations or anything. I've always looked forward to my nineteenth birthday, anticipating it as the day my sorcerer powers would awaken. Now, with all my powers already active, I like the idea of looking forward to it for a different reason. It could be the day I complete the bonding ceremony with the man I love. My wedding day.

"I love the idea. Yes, let's have the ceremony on October 19th," I say. Flora emits an excited squeal that makes both Colton and me laugh.

BEING BACK in the Lamia hive, I already miss the sunshine. I'm glad Flora visited today. We spent a few precious hours hanging out and talking about wedding plans instead of the usual topics like impending wars, attacks, and prophecies that have been plaguing my mind these days.

"Now that we're here, are you going to tell me what plans you have?" Colton asks, standing by the closet unpacking our small bag of belongings.

"I don't have a plan, exactly. I want to have a look around the Sorcerer Realm in disguise," I reply.

"Disguise?" He turns to me, a smile spreading across his face.

"Well, yeah. With those flyers out, it feels like everyone is looking for me, and the gods know what else has transpired since we left Cloudrum. I can't go out there looking like this," I say, making exaggerated motions over my body. Colton chuckles while tossing a cloak at me from the closet.

"This should be more than sufficient," he says, and I tie my hair back for extra precaution. Slipping on the black cloak, I pull the hood up to cover most of my hair. "Let's leave Chepi here. He's tired," I suggest, watching Chepi burrow into the covers on the bed, making a cozy nook for himself.

"As you wish," Colton replies, stepping close to me. Instead of a cloak, he opts for a black jacket. He places his hands on my hips and looks down at me with a hunger that prompts me to chew my lip anxiously.

"Let's go. The sooner we leave, the sooner we can get back," I say, pressing my hand against his chest and channeling us to outside Alchem Hollow, the village I'm most familiar with now in the Sorcerer Realm.

The village is bustling as usual, with the sound of frogs croaking from the nearby creek and children playing in the distance. Dusk settles over us, and the colorful lanterns strung overhead begin to glow softly against the evening sky. I inhale deeply, savoring the warm air mixed with the scents of fresh water, burning fires, and herbs.

"You always smile when you come here. You say this place isn't your home, but look at you—so fucking beautiful and happy the moment our feet touch the ground," Colton observes, his voice warm.

"I'm not smiling because this feels like home," I tell him, my smile growing even brighter. "I'm smiling because I love the crisp scent of the fire and the softness of the summer breeze. The sound of the frogs mingling with the laughter of children— it feels joyful, like what home should feel like."

Without warning, he kisses me, backing me up until I'm pressed against the side of one of the shops. His hands roam beneath my large cloak, seeking me out. When he finds my waist, he tugs my top up enough to caress my skin, and I revel in how we can never keep our hands off each other. I wrap my arms around his neck and stand on my tiptoes, yearning to be closer to him. We lose ourselves in the kiss, and I absolutely love it.

As I'm ready to suggest we head back to our room and explore the village tomorrow, my breath catches. Colton feels my body stiffen and breaks the kiss to search my face.

I can't quite explain it, but I sense something evil, a presence that is not of this world pressing down on my chest. The sudden silence when the playful laughter of children and the croaking of frogs once filled the air confirms my fears.

I don't need to voice any of this to Colton, who sees the alarm in my face and feels it in his own keen awareness.

"Fuck," he can barely mutter before he whirls around to fend off a creature that lunges at us from the shadows. He presses me back against the building, shielding me with his body as if I were made of glass instead of the formidable dark sorceress that I am. I try to peer around him, desperate to see if it's another Sarrol attack, but he keeps me fully blocked from the action.

Colton's movements are a blur, his arms swinging with trained precision as he confronts the dark silhouette darting toward us. When did he pack a dagger? I hadn't noticed until now. Frustrated by his attempts to shield me, I push against his hold, desperate to see and understand what we're up against.

"Sarrol? Tell me what it is!" I demand, my voice low but firm.

"It's not a Sarrol," he shouts back, his voice strained over the clash of his movements against the creature's advances. His eyes flick back to mine, wide with alarm. "I have no idea what this thing is!"

As he swings again, I slip under his arm as the creature lunges. Its form becomes clearer in the dim lantern light, and what I see horrifies me. It's not a Sarrol or a Monstrauth; it's something else entirely, something that might once have been human. Its skin is a wet and pale gray, stretched tight over its emaciated frame with no distinct features until you reach its head. Gods, its head—it has no eyes, no nose, only a giant mouth full of razor-sharp teeth and a black pointed tongue.

The creature hisses, its enormous mouth snapping at Colton's arm. He reacts quickly, plunging his dagger into its chest. Inky black blood seeps out, pooling on the ground. I swallow hard, staring down at the creature.

"What the fuck?" I murmur under my breath, a sentiment echoed by Colton as he stands beside me.

A pit of worry starts to fester in my chest as I slowly turn toward where the children had been playing on the edge of the forest. Silence descends, punctuated only by the heavy beat of my heart thudding in my ears. My breathing stops as I spot two small bodies on the ground in the distance. Without looking at Colton, I channel instantly to their side, and the moment my knees hit the ground, I have to clamp a hand over my mouth to stifle the scream rising in my throat.

How did this happen? These kids were only playing mere feet from the back of one of the shops—a place that should have been safe.

I start to shake my head, tears welling in my eyes, as the

gravity of the scene overwhelms me. Then Colton's hand is on my back, as he kneels next to me.

"Why?" I manage to whisper, my voice breaking.

He curses softly under his breath.

"I never even heard them scream," he says, and he's right—one minute I heard their laughter in the distance, and the next only silence. What was that thing, and how did it strike so swiftly and undetected?

"Neither did I," I reply

A man's voice, panicked and urgent, calls out from behind us, "What happened?" He races toward the children, dropping to the ground and frantically shaking one of them, screaming his name in a desperate bid to wake him. My heart shatters at the sight.

A crowd begins to gather around us, and I step back as another couple collapses near the other child's lifeless body. Colton places his arm on the small of my back and leans in close. "Maybe we should go," he whispers, but it's too late. In the commotion, my hood has slipped off, and whispers are already swirling through the crowd.

"What have you done?" a woman on the ground exclaims, pointing directly at me. Oh gods.

I freeze, shaking my head frantically. "This wasn't us. This was..." I glance toward where the creature was moments ago, only to find it gone.

"It's the dark sorceress," another voice shouts, and panic begins to set in.

"It's the dark princess, the one with shadows," someone else adds, and Colton's grip tightens around me.

I sense Colton's essence gathering, ready to channel us away, but I push away from him before he can act. "I didn't do this. I would never hurt a child," I plead, my voice rising over the murmurs of the crowd. "You have nothing to fear from me.

I'm on your side. This was a monster." I'm desperately trying to convince my people that I am not the enemy that Samael and Kaine have painted me to be.

"You're the only monster here!" a man in the crowd yells back, his voice filled with conviction and anger.

"The king put a price on her head. Capture her!" another man shouts, and panic surges through the crowd like a wave.

Before I can attempt to calm the situation or defend myself further, the crowd surges forward. The air is thick with fear and accusation, and in moments they are upon us.

"Don't harm anyone!" I yell to Colton over the roar of the crowd, but he's nowhere in sight. I'm encircled, the air crackling with charged magic. "Please, listen to me!"

That's when the first strike hits me—a bolt of magic slams into my back. I hunch over, absorbing the blow, striving to maintain composure. Spells are hurled at me from multiple directions, and a woman swings a branch at my head. I dodge the branch, but another spell strikes me. Panic rises. I should channel out, but I can't spot Colton, and I'm surprised by how quickly the situation has spiraled out of control.

Suddenly, someone yanks my hair from behind, jerking my head back painfully. I cry out as the dark magic I've been holding back unleashes itself.

In an instant, darkness explodes from me, not seeping out slowly but bursting forth violently. My shadows swallow the entire crowd. Everyone freezes. I straighten up, and as the darkness recedes, I see my shadowy tendrils have shot out into dozens of branches, sealing every mouth except Colton's, who I hear chuckling somewhere in the distance.

I clear my throat and stand a bit taller, my voice firm and resolute.

"People of Cloudrum, look at me and see your future queen, not as a figure of dark tales, but as one of your own. Yes,

I possess powers that many fear—powers that could, if I wished, bring devastation upon those who stand against me. But look around you—none are harmed because I choose peace over violence, healing over hurt.

"I could unleash destruction, yet here I stand, imploring you to see the truth. I am not your enemy. The very magic that courses through me, the shadows that respond to my call, are the same forces I harness to protect, not to persecute. Samael has painted me as a monster, a creature to be feared and hunted. Ask yourselves why."

I gradually draw my shadows back into myself. The crowd remains silent, attentively following each word. It seems I have captured their attention. Now I need to earn their respect.

But as I begin to sense a shift, I'm abruptly interrupted by a man in the crowd who yells, "You are a monster!"

A woman shouts, "We know what courses through your blood." Chaos erupts anew, the brief silence shattered by screams and accusations.

Before I can react and lose control of my temper, Colton is by my side. This time, when he wraps an arm around me, I don't protest. I let him channel us back to the safety of the hive. Even after we arrive in our bedroom, the harsh voices continue to echo in my mind, the faces twisted in hate and fear haunting me...and the lifeless bodies of those two children, their laughter a ghostly memory in the chilling silence.

"Lyra, you can't let them get to you—" Colton begins, but I cut him off before he can continue, the urgency in my voice cutting through the air.

"No, you don't understand. They are getting to me. All of this—everything—is getting to me." I feel my eyes well with tears, but I swallow hard, reining in my emotions.

"Come here." He reaches for me, and every fiber of my

being yearns to go to him, to let him hold me and reassure me that everything will be okay. But I can't.

"Colton, you can't save me from this. You can't protect me from everything. I need to figure things out for myself. I'm going back to Zomea, and I'm going back now." I throw my cloak on the bed and grab a sweater from the closet, pulling it over my head.

"It's late. Come to bed, and we can talk about this in the morning. Don't act rashly while emotions are heightened," he tries to soothe me, but he doesn't understand.

"I'm not acting rashly. I need to do this. I always planned on going to Zomea alone. I know what I need to do, and I'm going to be alright," I say firmly. He takes a step closer, his eyes pleading, ready to follow me, but I shake my head. "Please, don't follow me. I'll be back as soon as I can."

"How long are you planning on staying there?" he asks, sounding worried for the first time.

"As long as it takes to find the answers I need," I respond, picking up a sleeping Chepi and cradling him in my arms. "Stay here or go back to Nighthold. I'll find you when I return."

"I thought you wanted to talk to Drew first," he reminds me. True, I had intended to, but after what happened, I feel like I'm running out of time. I need answers before things escalate further.

"I'll talk to her when I return."

I stand up on my tiptoes and kiss him, and as he wraps his arms around me, pulling me in for a deeper kiss, I surrender to the moment. I let myself savor the taste of him, lingering in the embrace. When he finally releases me, I see the acceptance in his eyes—he's letting me go.

"I love you," I say, meeting his gaze.

"I love you too. Hurry home to me so I can marry you," he

responds, effortlessly drawing a smile from me. He always knows just what to say.

With one last glance, I channel to the bridge, departing without another word. His smile and the sweet taste of our last kiss linger with me as I make my way to Zomea.

CHAPTER 22

LYRA

I HAVE BEEN SEARCHING Zomea for days, perhaps even weeks now. It's easy to lose track of time in this forgotten place.

My father's old palace stands deserted. If it weren't for Chepi's constant companionship, I might have succumbed to the solitude, driven mad by the echoing emptiness.

I'm beginning to doubt everything. Are Gholioths even real? The legends of Moirati—the supposed oldest Gholioth to inhabit Zomea—do they hold any truth, or are these creatures mere myths? I came here seeking answers, hoping to find Moirati or another Gholioth who could enlighten me, but so far my search has yielded nothing.

Despite the desolation of this palace, I've discovered that Zomea is not entirely abandoned. I've encountered many Lycans and a few Sorcerers during my wanderings. However, none have been particularly helpful. It seems most who dwell here are like me, souls adrift, searching for answers, longing for something more.

My father had a purpose here and lived in Zomea as he would have in Eguina. But the others I've met are aimless, their lives an endless quest for meaning in the shadows of forgotten magic.

I can hardly believe this place is really the afterlife. What happens to those who don't make it here? Or those who arrive and then perish—where do they go next? If Zomea was truly the afterlife, surely it would be teeming with souls. Yet it feels deserted. I haven't even run into Athalda. I wonder what corner of the world she's causing trouble in now.

Covering the entirety of Zomea seems an impossible task. This place is larger than Eguina, and I am but one person, yet I had hoped to uncover some sign by now. I can't return to Eguina without understanding my purpose. Deep in my bones, I feel drawn to this place, as if an inexplicable force has been pulling me here for weeks.

I cannot marry Colton or plan to ascend as queen of Cloudrum until I find the answers I seek.

I kick off my shoes and climb into bed next to Chepi, who has already drifted off to sleep. For the first time, perhaps ever, I find myself praying. I pray to Ryella—the Goddess of Darkness and Shadows. I plead with her to send me a sign, anything to guide me, as I'm running out of ideas. My prayers linger in the quiet of the night until at last sleep finds me.

SOMETHING'S HERE! I feel it as a prickle up the back of my neck. I'm standing on a terrace, the sound of waves crashing in the distance. Colton is only a few feet away, his gaze fixed on me, an expectant air about him.

I start walking down what seems like an aisle, but then a voice, delicate yet resonant, whispers in my ear, "I would have helped you long ago. All you had to do was ask."

I turn to see Ryella, the Goddess of Darkness and Shadows.

Contrary to her title, her strawberry hair cascades in vibrant waves around her freckled face, radiant and paradoxically bright. She extends her hand invitingly. As our fingers touch, the terrace warps, dissolving into a dark forest where we stand isolated in an eerie silence.

I release her hand, spinning to face her with a torrent of questions on my lips, but my voice fails me. She places a finger to her lips, silencing the unspoken words. "You know where to find the answers you seek," she intones mysteriously. "Fear has kept you from the path you must walk. Don't be afraid, Lyra."

I shake my head, confusion and denial mingling within. I have no idea what place she speaks of, where the answers lie waiting. As my uncertainty mounts, the forest begins to transform. It's not merely changing; it's melting away. The trees contort, the landscape shifts transporting us, and my mind struggles to grasp the surreal vision.

Once the world settles, Ryella smiles and points behind me. I turn slowly, and there they stand—the gates. Drawn by an inexplicable force, I approach them, each step resonant with foreboding. When I'm close enough, I extend a trembling hand and let my fingers caress the cold bars of the gates.

As soon as my fingers brush the cold iron, a force from within awakens, resonating deep in my core. My hand clasps around the bar uncontrollably, gripping it as if magnetized by some ancient, unseen power. The pressure intensifies until suddenly it ebbs away, leaving a tingling echo in my palm. With an eerie creak that pierces the heavy silence of the forest, the gate slowly begins to swing open.

I bolt upright in bed, my sudden movement startling both Chepi and myself. A sheen of sweat covers my skin, and I glance down at my hand, which still feels icy from the touch of the iron bars. Midnight mind visions aren't supposed to occur in Zomea, unless they're meant to lead you further—beyond the gates my father once said. And Ryella, she was there in my vision, responding to my call.

"Come here, boy. It's okay. Go back to sleep," I whisper, pulling Chepi to my chest as I settle back into the bed. His warm presence is comforting against the chill that lingers. "Tomorrow, I think we finally have to visit the one place I've been avoiding." Chepi licks my cheek and nestles into my neck with his wet nose.

AFTER A RESTLESS NIGHT haunted by visions, I stand before the ancient gates, Chepi by my side. "Well, boy, are you ready for this?" I murmur, his eager yip grounding me slightly. These gates—towering structures, entwined with gnarled roots and decaying branches that seem to pulse with a life of their own, dripping a dark viscous substance—loom before us.

I had thought to avoid this place forever, to bury its memory deep within the recesses of my mind. But it seems the fates have other designs. The gates have infiltrated not only my waking thoughts but also my deepest, darkest dreams.

Now, as I confront them once again, a surprising calm settles over me. There's an inexplicable rightness in standing here, as if these ominous barriers were meant for me all along.

Upon closer inspection, the gates are a marvel of foreboding artistry. The dark iron from which they are crafted is not merely shaped but seems to be alive with a haunting animation. The bars themselves are twisted and contorted, their surface wrought into intricate, swirling patterns that resemble the agonized movements of souls ensnared in perpetual torment...it's slightly horrifying to gaze upon.

Each swirl and twist of the metal tells a silent tale of despair, the patterns flowing into each other like a river of lost spirits. The designs are unsettlingly organic, as if the iron itself had once been living entities now transformed and bound into this eternal, metallic form. Shadows seem to flicker and move within the crevices of the designs, as though the souls themselves are still writhing under the gaze of any onlooker.

If this is truly where the gods live like Euric believed, then perhaps these gates stand as a grim testament to the ultimate price of ambition—the tortured souls of those who dared to ascend to divine heights, now forever bound in this iron tapestry of agony. Among these writhing figures, could my father's soul be entwined?

I step closer, driven by a force I can't quite understand but cannot resist. This time, as my fingers trace the cold, foreboding metal, there's no fear, no hesitation.

The gates creak sinisterly, the sound echoing like the world cracking open, as they swing open slowly, inviting—or perhaps daring—me to step beyond.

With a deep breath, I lift Chepi into my arms, and we cross the threshold.

CHAPTER 23

NYX

I MUST HAVE READ through my father's journals and all the letters several times now, each reading filled with a vain hope that the words might somehow change. I shudder to think about the revelations they contained—the secrets kept from me and the grim path of my future. Everything has fallen apart, and now I see only one way forward. I resolve not to speak of the journals until I can discuss everything with Lyra. She must know what I've discovered, but with her still in Zomea, I'm compelled to take action.

I find myself knocking at Colton's back door, because unlike him I maintain a semblance of courtesy—even in urgency. My patience wears thin as he fails to answer after the initial knocks, prompting me to bang harder on the door. I know he's here, likely brooding in Lyra's absence—he's the fool who let her venture back to that cursed place alone. Had she been with me, I would never have allowed her to return to Zomea without company.

"Not used to anyone knocking on your door the proper

way, are you?" I remark as he finally pulls the door open, his expression amused.

"No, I had a feeling it was you," he replies, and I chuckle.

I follow him into the living room, and when he doesn't inquire about the reason for my visit, I make my way to sit in front of the fireplace. "Are you going to offer me a drink?" I demand, a reminder of my rank—after all, I am his king.

"Get one yourself. I'm not in the mood, Nikki. So why don't you tell me why you're here," Colton retorts, his tone dismissive.

I rise, pouring myself a glass of whiskey from the drink cart. The alcohol, I decide, will be necessary to swallow my pride. After taking a long sip, I set my glass on the mantle, my gaze fixating on the flickering flames as I contemplate my next words. Perhaps I should handle this without him.

"What is it, Nyx? If you're here to ask about Lyra, I haven't heard anything," he interjects, now reclined on the couch, his casual posture underlining his lack of concern for the gravity of my visit.

"I may not have started this war, but I fully intend to finish it. Tonight, we begin our plan of attack. I'm not waiting any longer for Samael to make his move. I am taking the men to battle," I declare, pacing in front of the fire, feeling the energy for the impending battle building inside me.

"War hasn't started. What are you thinking?" Colton rises to his feet, his confusion apparent.

I shake my head at his naiveté. "The first attack may not have taken place yet, but make no mistake—war has been brewing for far too long. Don't pretend you don't know. Don't tell me you can't feel it," I insist, locking eyes with him, seeing the recognition of the truth in his gaze.

"I thought you didn't want to discuss any of this with me.

You cut me out when I tried to help," he counters, his voice tinged with a mix of resentment and challenge.

He's not wrong. He is one of the best fighters we have, and though I may not want to admit it, I need him on my side. "Things are different now. Lyra would want us to work together, so I'm willing to make an exception," I say, opting for pragmatism over pride.

He scoffs, skepticism written all over his face. "You want to wage a war against her realm while she's in fucking Zomea," he accuses.

"That's exactly what I want to do. Don't you see? We need to act first, strike while Samael is not expecting it. And if we manage to get through this before Lyra returns to Eguina, all the better. She will be out of harm's way the entire time," I explain, laying out my plan clearly.

I watch as realization dawns on his face, knowing he understands the strategic advantage. I also know how deeply he cares for Lyra, how her safety gnaws at him. He will do whatever it takes to keep her safe. If we can keep her out of this war altogether, it's a win-win for both of us.

"You know she's going to be furious with both of us when she gets back and realizes we did this without her," he says, and I shake my head.

"Yeah, well, at least she'll be pleased we're working together. That's what she's been asking for," I tell him, finishing the last of my drink.

"She'll be happy about that, sure, but she'll be pissed she missed out on all the action." He summons a pack and slings it over his shoulder. "Let's go," he says with a resolve as if he had been ready for this moment all along.

"Alright then." I shrug and channel us both to the Vision Valley army camps.

I stride toward the large tent at the center of camp, the one Bim has been using as his command post. Colton walks beside me, his steps betraying a familiarity with this place. The thought irks me. He thinks he's being discreet, but I'm aware of everything that transpires in my kingdom and choose my battles wisely. If Bim and Dorian saw fit to keep him informed, I was prepared to overlook it, knowing I'd call upon his aid in battle regardless.

As we enter the tent, Bim and Drew are huddled around a large table, poring over a map of Eguina that's spread wide with marked positions and notes.

"Fancy seeing you here," Colton quips with a wink at Drew as he takes a seat next to her. His ability to charm everyone he meets grates on me—most find his sarcasm endearing; I find it merely irritating.

"Have you heard from Dorian? What's the status with the Lycans?" I ask, settling into a chair beside Bim at the head of the table.

"I sent two men to fetch Rhett for this meeting. They should be arriving any minute with him. As for Dorian, he's around, last I saw him instructing some of the men outside on how to wield the new weapons he designed," Bim reports.

I nod, then Colton starts to speak, "Lyra met with Rhett, and she hinted that things didn't go smoothly."

"It doesn't matter," I state firmly, catching Colton's eye. "We need to understand where the Lycans stand, and I'm prepared for either scenario."

Colton presses his lips together and mutters something to Drew under his breath. I decide to let it slide. Now is not the time for petty squabbles; it's time to lead and strategize for victory—to put an end to Samael once and for all.

"Looks like they've retrieved the wolf. I can smell him without even seeing him," Dorian comments as he ducks into the tent, settling into the seat at the far end of the table opposite Colton.

"You can wait right inside there," one of our men outside says, unaware that we're all assembled and waiting. Rhett walks in next, and I remember him clearly from when he assisted Lyra and me on our journey to Aidan's. He still has the same tall frame, dark hair, and blue Lycan eyes, but now there's a weariness about him, a certain aged look that seems out of place. It hasn't been nearly long enough for such a change. Perhaps it's stress.

"King Nyx," he greets with a nod.

I wave, indicating for him to take the seat at the head of the table opposite me, flanked by Dorian and Colton. Following him closely is another Lycan, a younger one whose expression is both angry and hardened. He says nothing as he boldly takes the seat next to me, between Dorian and myself.

With no seats left at the table and every key player now present, I take a deep breath.

"Thank you, everyone, for coming. As you all know, we have teetered on the brink of war for far too long. Under Samael's reign, Cloudrum has suffered—his leadership marked by dark spells and deranged ideals has left our lands and people in despair. Now that he has returned to power, it is imperative that we stop him once and for all.

"The darkness that Samael spreads has seeped into every corner of Cloudrum and now threatens even Nighthold. The entire realm of Eguina bears the scars of his relentless assaults. We cannot afford to remain on the defensive, reacting to his every move. It is time for us to take decisive action, to restore our lands to their rightful, thriving state and purge the corruption that seeks to dominate us.

"I will not stand by while Samael or Kaine attempt to dictate the fate of Cloudrum. That is why today, I am calling for unity and action. I need your unwavering support, your keen strategic insights, and the might of your armies. Together, we can end this turmoil and reclaim the peace that has been so cruelly stolen from us.

"Let's show Samael that his reign of terror is over. Together, let us unite our realms once again and fight side by side, not just to restore Eguina, but to ensure a future where such darkness can never take hold again."

I clear my throat and lean back, my eyes sweeping across the faces before me, ready to gauge who will speak first, preparing to address any concerns or rally further support.

"You speak of darkness and dark spells as if eliminating Samael will rid Eguina of it, but am I incorrect in saying the last time I saw you, you were quite entangled with Lyra—the so-called queen of darkness herself, according to Kaine?" Rhett challenges, and I swallow hard to maintain my composure, silently hoping Colton doesn't act rashly against the provocateur beside him.

"You are correct that when we last met, I was in a relationship with Lyra. We remain friends and allies to this day," I respond calmly, meeting his skeptical gaze. "That gives me all the more reason to assure you that her dark magic is grossly misunderstood, and the rumors being spread about her in Cloudrum are nothing but lies."

He remains unswayed, but frankly I don't care. We don't need him or his packs to win this war. My invitation was merely to gauge where his allegiances lie.

"If I may," Drew begins, her gaze shifting from me to Rhett as she commands the room's attention, "I have spent considerable time with Lyra recently, and she has always spoken of you in the highest regard, Rhett. She valued you as a friend and was overjoyed when she learned you had become the leader of the packs. I believe her exact words were, 'Finally, someone with a good heart is leading the Lycans.'"

She pauses, allowing her words to sink in. For the first time since his arrival, I notice a flicker of softness in Rhett's stern features.

"After what she endured in the Lycan realm, after how Aidan abused her and the ceremony your people witnessed without intervening, I'd imagine if Lyra truly were the evil, dark enchantress you seem so ready to believe she is, she would have incinerated your entire realm by now," Drew continues, her tone sharpening. She flashes a wicked grin, her fangs visible as the candlelight gleams off her pristine canines. "Frankly, I know I would have."

"Are you going to let her talk about our packs like this? This woman," the young Lycan next to me howls.

I haven't bothered to learn his name yet, but his rash outburst only makes me smirk.

"I suggest you watch your tone when speaking about a lady, or you might not make it back to your packs," Colton says, his amusement mirroring mine.

"I'm not afraid of you. You Fae think you're so tough," the young man retorts.

I stifle a chuckle, reaching for a glass of water to mask it.

"Oh, it's not me you should be afraid of," Colton laughs, glancing at Drew, whose red eyes now glow ominously in the dim light, though her expression remains impassive.

"Ryder, enough," Rhett says, and I struggle even more to contain my amusement. Rhett and Ryder, these young boys really are in over their heads.

"Quite enough, I think," I interject, setting my glass down and sitting up straighter. "You may believe whatever you like. I need to know if you will fight with us or not. If you prefer to stay out of this, I can have my men escort you back to the Lycan Realm now, and no harm will come to you. It's your choice."

My gaze remains fixed on Rhett as he deliberates for a few moments before responding. "As I told Lyra before, I do not wish to be her enemy, but that doesn't make me her ally either. The Lycans wish to remain out of this war. Enough death and destruction have come to our packs in trying to protect the realms from the evil creatures once confined to the Shifting Forest."

He rises, Ryder quickly following. "No longer will my people die protecting Sorcerers, Lamia, or Fae alike. It's time we look out for ourselves. May Bellor be with you in the coming days," he says, surprising me by invoking the god of war. The Lycans are so often fixated on the moon's powers. I hadn't realized they held such reverence for the other gods.

I nod once to Rhett as Bim walks him out and speaks to the men outside, the ones who will channel them back home. When Bim returns and sits next to me, I let out a sigh.

"Well, fuck," Bim mutters.

I look around at those who remain—Bim, Colton, Drew, Dorian, and myself will be the ones planning and delegating for the rest of this meeting.

"We didn't need them. It's better this way. The Lycans are unpredictable anyway," I remark, scanning the table.

"Do you think they will choose to fight for Samael?" Dorian asks.

"Not if they know what's good for them," Colton replies sharply.

"No offense, King Onyx, but I believe it would be unwise for us to enter this battle assuming victory is guaranteed," Drew begins, her voice steady and earnest. "While it's crucial for us to maintain a positive outlook, there's a fine line between confidence and overconfidence, which could lead us to underesti-mate our enemy."

She isn't wrong. With the forces I've gathered, it seems inconceivable that the Sorcerers could defeat us, especially if Samael hasn't fully regained his strength. However, her caution resonates with a part of me that knows the unpredictability of war.

"Samael will be defeated. I plan to kill him with my own hands for what he's done to my mate," Colton declares from beside her, his use of the word "mate" making me inwardly cringe.

"Let's stay focused," Bim says, smoothing over the growing tension. "I'll begin by outlining what we know about his where-abouts and the current positioning of his army, based on the latest intelligence our scouts have provided."

Bim leans in, his eyes scanning the map spread out on the table before us. "Samael has been keeping all of his troops close to home. It seems he's more concerned with protecting himself than his people," he states with a hint of disdain.

Colton, standing beside him, mutters under his breath, "No surprise there."

Bim points to a location on the map, marked with a circle and pin. "He has established two military encampments within Tempest Moon. The first is situated here, outside the castle's boundary." His finger lingers on the spot before sliding across the map to another marked location. "The second is further out, positioned right on the border between the Sorcerer and Lycan Realms, near the river."

I turn to Drew, hoping for any insight she might provide on Samael's condition. "Drew, do you have any updates on Samael's state? Has he regained all of his strength since he emerged from hiding? What about Citlali—have you heard from your daughter?"

Drew's expression tightens slightly, a shadow of discomfort passing over her. "I haven't spoken to her, but it's safe to assume Samael is back to full strength. It's been long enough for him to heal." She pauses, her voice lowering. "Unfortunately, my daughter has persuaded some of her old friends to join her cause."

The room falls silent for a moment, all eyes on Drew. She straightens her shoulders in her chair, and Colton sits back down next to her, a resolute look crossing her face. "Don't worry. The Lamia will fight alongside you. I will personally join you with my best warriors. However, a couple dozen of my own have joined Citlali, and I anticipate they will fight for Samael."

A couple of dozen might not seem like a significant number, but having witnessed the ferocity of Drew and other Lamia in recent battles against the Sarrol attacks, their prowess is undeniable. The Lamia are vicious fighters. Their loyalty to their own could shift the balance of power if we are not careful.

"The weaponry I have supplied will not disappoint, even against the Lamia," Dorian declares, his gaze shifting from Drew to me with a confident glint. "I've committed my entire stockpile of magic-infused blades to our cause—swords, throwing knives, daggers, you name it. Not to mention, I've designed and forged a selection of exceptionally powerful swords for your elite fighters."

I nod, well aware of Dorian's reputation for having the best armory in all of Eguina. "I also have something special set aside for each of us," he adds, a secretive smile playing on his lips.

"So along with physical weapons for close combat, we all have our Fae magic, of course. Were you able to acquire all the bows and arrows you mentioned before?" Colton asks, looking toward Dorian with an expectant raise of his eyebrows.

"Of course, I got everything I wanted and then some," Dorian confirms with a nod.

"The men are ready, we are fully stocked, and everyone is in a good headspace. Honestly, this is the best time for us to act. Samael won't be expecting it. We've given him no reason to suspect we would go on the offensive."

Bim concurs with a firm nod, his expression resolute.

"We attack tonight," I declare.

AFTER SEVERAL MORE HOURS OF intense deliberation, we finalize our course of action. We decide to launch a three-pronged attack: one group will target each of the military camps in Tempest Moon, and a third will strike directly at the castle itself.

Colton will harness our father's magic, leveraging his unique ability to create multiple illusions of himself. This will allow us to position a Colton in each group, ensuring seamless communication across the battlefield. The real Colton will be able to see and speak through his illusions, coordinating our movements and strategies in real time.

We will all channel to the Lamia Realm together, where Drew will then distribute her fighters among our three groups. Each group will be accompanied by Fae who will channel the Lamias to their respective locations.

Channeling is one of our greatest assets in this war, though it comes with limitations—the Fae cannot channel to locations they have never visited, necessitating a strategic approach to deployment. We must coordinate meticulously, moving in waves to ensure every fighter is properly positioned.

I will take command of the first group, with Bim and Dorian leading the second, and Colton alongside Drew heading the third. Our plan is to initiate the attack just after midnight. If all proceeds as intended, we anticipate declaring victory by mid-morning.

"It's all decided then," I declare with finality. "Bim, notify the men to prepare for battle. Dorian, ensure all ranking officers are briefed on the plan. I've already informed Flora of my intentions, and she's coordinating with Twig to hold things down until we return. I've kept this from the elders and everyone else. The element of surprise is crucial."

I stride over to the shelf, grabbing the decanter and pouring each of us a glass. As I distribute them, the weight of the coming battle settles over us. I raise my glass.

"To Eguina and to restoring the balance," I proclaim, the irony of what I've learned about Lyra from my father's journals momentarily surfacing in my mind.

"To killing that bastard Samael," Colton adds.

"To all my life's work finally paying off in the face of battle," Dorian chimes in, his anticipation palpable.

"To peace," Bim interjects, lifting his glass higher.

All eyes then turn to Drew, the last to speak. She smiles—a rare expression that lightens the tense atmosphere. "To none of you fools getting yourselves killed," she says wryly.

We all down our glasses in unison, the sharp clink of glass echoing our resolve. Without another word, we split to don our armor and gather our weapons, ready to converge outside the tent in thirty minutes, united for the impending assault.

CHAPTER 24

COLTON

CLAD in my cuirass and armed with my favorite weapons, I feel a surge of eagerness rather than the usual pre-battle anxiety. We've divided into our three groups in the Lamia Realm. Drew and I lead about a hundred fighters, including roughly twenty Lamia besides Drew.

Although I often train with Lyra, it feels unusual to head into battle with so many women. Nighthold's armies rarely include Fae women, despite having many powerful female Fae. Tonight, only six are in my group.

Utilizing my magic, I cast two identical illusions of myself, sending them to join the other groups. With that task off my mind, I focus solely on the team I'm leading. We are tasked with assaulting the camp furthest from the castle. Nyx, naturally, has chosen the castle for his own team. While we target the camp near the Lycan Realm, I can still tap into what's happening at the other locations, and I'm ready to channel directly to Samael if needed.

Clearing my throat, I address my fellow fighters. "Tonight, we battle Sorcerers, and it's crucial to remember the stark differences between their magic and ours. Sorcerers cannot cast through mere gestures or sheer force of will like we can. They rely heavily on spells that require more time to cast, giving us a tactical advantage.

"We attack under the cover of nightfall because powerful Sorcerer spells necessitate whispered incantations, often causing their lips to glow. If you see anything glowing tonight, move quickly out of the way and prepare to defend yourself." I see a collection of affirming nods.

"When we land outside the camp, we'll split into smaller squads to encircle it before methodically advancing toward the center. Eliminate anyone you encounter," I instruct, scanning the faces of my team for understanding.

I glance over at Drew to see if she has anything to add. With a quick wink, she signals her approval.

Turning back to the group, I announce, "We channel on my mark."

Drew and I are the first to arrive, pausing in the cover of the tree line as the rest of our group assembles behind us. It's shortly after midnight, and a warm summer breeze whispers through the trees, carrying the fresh scent of pine. I breathe it in, savoring the sweet aroma, fully aware it will soon be over-powered by the acrid stench of death and destruction.

The enemy camp lies ahead, shrouded in a deceptive calm. A small handful of guards are gathered around a fire, their laughter and the soft shuffle of cards punctuating the quiet night. Unbeknownst to them, their tranquil evening is about to be engulfed in flames—quite literally.

With a subtle gesture, I signal my group to fan out and encircle the camp. The disciplined silence of my team is palpable as they stealthily position themselves, knowing not to engage until they receive my command. I take a moment to anchor myself in the stillness, listening to the distant murmur of the river and the crackle of the fire.

Then, with everyone in place and the camp unsuspectingly secured within our grasp, I open my eyes and give the signal.

Silence reigns as I step forward, the shadows of the trees cloaking my movements. I draw two throwing knives from my belt, my fingers brushing against the cold metal imbued with ancient Fae magic. I spot the first two guards, their backs turned, oblivious to the impending doom. In one fluid motion, I hurl the knives, watching them spin through the air and embed themselves between the eyes of each guard.

Before their bodies hit the ground, I flick my wrist, igniting the knives. Flames burst forth, enveloping the guards in a fiery shroud that stifles any sound they might have made—a gurgled moan of blood-flecked breath extinguished in an instant.

The initial shock of our assault allows each member of my team to dispatch at least one enemy silently. However, the stillness of the night is abruptly shattered as an alarm pierces the air—a spell cast by a Sorcerer sentinel. In response, the camp transforms before our eyes.

Tents that appeared mundane seconds ago ripple and shimmer, revealing hidden enchantments that harden their fabric to the strength of steel. The ground beneath our feet begins to tremble as earthen walls erupt around the perimeter, attempting to enclose us within a makeshift fortress. Sorcerers emerge from their shelters, hands aglow with the buildup of potent spells, their lips moving in silent incantations.

From my peripheral vision, I see Brady—one of the men I trained with many years ago—channeling his own formidable magic, his hands weaving through the air as he summons vines that burst from the ground. They snake around the emerging barriers, tearing through the spell-forged earth with supernatural force.

The air crackles with magical energy, a tangible tension that feeds the chaos. I dive into the melee, my own Fae magic pulsating through my veins. With another wave of my hand, I conjure a gust of wind that snuffs out nearby torches, plunging sections of the camp into darkness. This elemental manipulation gives us the cover we need to advance.

"Push forward!" I shout to my fighters through the cacophony. I leap over a fallen log, landing amidst a trio of Sorcerers. My sword—bathed in a radiant, ethereal light—slices through the air, meeting the magical shields they conjure with sparks and the shriek of stressed energy.

Fuck me, the new sword Dorian forged for me is proving its worth, melding seamlessly with my magic, almost anticipating my movements. In the midst of the fray, I kick out at an approaching attacker to gain some space, and then with a swift arc of my blade, I slice cleanly across his neck. He clutches at the gaping wound, but it's too late. He crumples silently to the ground.

As I whirl to face his comrades, I see the other two Sorcerers already casting. Before I can interrupt, one of them blows through his cupped hands, unleashing a dark swarm of shadow moths that surge toward me. My vision blurs as the swarm envelops my head, their tiny bodies biting into my flesh. This isn't a normal Sorcerer spell—manifesting creatures in such a tangible form requires a dark spell, revealing that Samael's twisted practices are spreading.

With urgency, I reinforce the shield around my connection to Lyra, ensuring our mission remains hidden. With a furious wave of my hand, I incinerate the swarm assaulting me. Moments later, as one of the men hurls a bolt of magic aimed straight for my chest, I dodge to the left. In the same fluid motion, I call upon the roots below. They burst from the ground, wrapping tightly around the men's legs and anchoring them in place.

Seizing the moment, I strike—my sword cuts through them with lethal precision. As their bodies hit the ground, I pause, using this brief respite to connect with my illusions and check on the progress of the other two groups.

The feedback from the illusions is clear: the battle rages fiercely on all fronts, but our strategy holds. With renewed determination, I ready myself for the next wave of combatants, my sword thirsty for the justice we've come here to deliver.

Some of these Sorcerers might be innocent, mere pawns blindly following their leader, but I'm acutely aware that many, especially those loyal to Samael, have committed atrocities against the creatures and women of Cloudrum. The thought alone sends my blood boiling, fueling a raging tempest within me as I navigate the battlefield.

I round the next tent, my senses sharp, searching for a rightful target for my pent-up fury.

The clash of weapons fills the forest, and the air hangs heavy with the mingled scents of magic and metal. Although we're outnumbered two to one, our superior strength keeps me from worrying. Scanning the area for Drew, I note she's moved to the far end of the camp when the chaos started. I push aside my concern for her. She is far more experienced and formidable than most.

Suddenly, a man emerges from behind the tent, now rein-forced with steel, and lunges at me with a dagger. I dodge effortlessly, and as he starts whispering a spell, I quickly punch him in the face, interrupting his incantation. With a snap of my fingers, I summon the river's water. It gushes forth, engulfing him, and he begins to drown under my magical command.

It's far too easy to use my elemental magic when this close to the waters edge.

I halt, alerted by a growing whooshing noise. The man, choking and gasping, begins to laugh—a deranged, unsettling cackle. His laughter unnerves me, but it's the sound that truly alarms me. I look up as the moonlight dims, clouded by hundreds of arrows arcing overhead.

Without hesitation, I conjure a protective shield above me and drop low.

"Take cover!" I yell, urging those nearby to shield themselves as the sky darkens further with the descending volley of arrows.

The arrows make contact, and to my shock, my shield is penetrated instantly. I brace for the pain, but instead of piercing my skin, the arrows combust into a cloud of golden mist. Holding my breath, I anticipate some kind of poison, but as the mist subsides, I see no immediate effects. The man in front of me, previously choking on water, is now laughing, unaffected by the river I had summoned.

Frustrated, I try to call upon the river again, but nothing happens. Desperate, I look down and envision roots breaking free to entangle him—still nothing. I attempt to check in with the other two groups, closing my eyes and seeking that familiar connection, but find only silence. It hits me like a wave—the Sorcerers have found a way to nullify our magic. It seems impossible, yet here I am, stripped of my abilities, isolated from my illusions and cut off from the others.

In a swift motion driven by urgency, I reach out and snap the man's neck, silencing his laughter instantly. The camp falls eerily silent, the shock of our sudden powerlessness hanging heavy. How long will this last? I wonder if the Sorcerers are also affected. If so, hand-to-hand combat will still favor us due to our training. But if this spell selectively targets Fae magic, they might have tipped the scales in their favor—a devastating blow none of us anticipated, especially not in the heat of battle.

I immediately unsheathe my sword and start pushing my way through the camp. Instead of working toward the center as planned, I pivot, searching for Drew. I dispatch several Sorcerers before they even register my presence, leaving a trail of bodies in my wake.

Suddenly, a bolt of pure, hot power slams into my right shoulder from behind. I whirl around to face my attacker—a Sorceress with long black hair draped in a purple cloak. Her lips move silently, and beneath her hood, a subtle glow emanates from her mouth, confirming my fears about the magic.

Seeking cover, I duck behind a nearby tree. It's clear now that their magic is still functional. I attempt to summon my own powers once again, but nothing stirs within me. Resigned, I realize I'll have to handle this the old-fashioned way. My shoulder burns painfully, a stark reminder that without my magic, I lack any advanced healing abilities.

Gritting my teeth, I prepare for her next spell. As I peek around the tree, she hurls another fireball. I dodge in time, and before she can begin another incantation, I'm upon her.

Our swords clash, sparking in the dim light. Her agility surprises me. She is far more acrobatic than anyone I've faced, leaping and flipping over my blade with a speed I hadn't anticipated. This Sorceress is clearly more skilled than the men I've taken down before.

She lunges at me with her sword and a dagger in her other hand. I duck and roll to evade her attack, and when I turn back, Drew is there. The sight never fails to startle me—Drew's jaw extends unnaturally as she bites into the Sorceress's neck, spewing blood in a gruesome display. The Sorceress collapses, and Drew turns to me, her eyes glowing fiercely red, her face smeared with blood.

"Did the arrows take out your magic?" she asks, wiping her mouth.

I nod, still reeling from the shock. "Did they affect you?" I inquire, knowing that while Lamias don't possess magic like the Fae, they have other supernatural abilities.

"No, they only seem to affect Fae. It can't last for long. No one has that kind of power," she responds confidently.

"How many casualties have we suffered?" Although I haven't witnessed any of our side fall, Drew might have seen more from her vantage point.

She frowns slightly. "Can't say for sure, but I know we lost some when the arrows hit."

The sudden stillness of the battlefield sends a chill down my spine. I can feel the magic pulsing around us. We exchange a glance, a mutual understanding flashing between us, and instinctively start scanning our surroundings, ready for whatever spell is coming next.

A dense fog begins to seep from the ground, enveloping us in a thick, white shroud that obscures everything beyond a few feet. The mist grows, swallowing the sounds of battle and isolating us in a ghostly silence.

"As soon as I get my magic back, I'm going to check on the other groups. Stay with our people," I tell her, though the fog has thickened to the point where I can no longer see her face.

"As you wish," her voice floats back, barely audible over the whoosh of wind that follows as she moves swiftly to rejoin our fighters.

Howls pierce the dense fog, their eerie cries slicing through the spell-enshrouded battlefield. The realization hits me—if the Lycans are joining the fight, they've been compelled to pick a side. I battle past a few more Sorcerers, tension coiling tighter within me. Suddenly, a large gray wolf darts past, and I hesitate, unsure whether to strike or stand down.

A low growl resonates behind me, and I spin around to face a giant black wolf. Lyra has often spoken of Rhett's imposing wolf form, and there's no mistaking this beast for any other.

"I thought the Lycans were staying out of this battle," I challenge, eyeing him warily.

Instead of responding, he bows his head slightly—an almost respectful gesture—before lunging not at me but at a Sorcerer poised to strike me from behind. The wolf's massive form barrels into the Sorcerer, thwarting the attack meant for me. In that moment, the allegiance of the Lycans becomes clear, and I mentally note to thank Rhett next time our paths cross.

With the Lycans in wolf form and the Lamias unaffected by the spell, I realize I can't remain here any longer. My group seems to be handling themselves well, but I have no such assurances about the others. Bereft of my magic to conceal them, my wings are on full display, and I decide it's time to use them.

I extend my wings to their full, impressive span and launch into the sky, rising high above the white blanket of fog below. Though the castle is an obvious destination, I first need to check on Bim and Dorian's camp within the boundaries of Tempest Moon.

I REACH THE SECOND CAMP, and from my vantage point above, the battlefield is a sprawling canvas of chaos and ruin. Below, the land is torn asunder, a grim theater of war where clashing armies embody the fierce struggle for supremacy. Flames devour what once were proud structures, now reduced to smoldering ruins that cast a baleful glow over the scene.

The ground itself seems to bleed, muddied and gouged by the feet and fallen of countless warriors. This camp is far larger than the one we attacked, and I can only hope the fae magic wasn't affected here.

Scores of combatants, each a mere speck from my height, swarm over the field like ants in a disturbed nest. Steel glints under the somber sky as swords clash, spears thrust, and bodies fall. Small bursts of color speckle the ground as spells are executed. The clamor of metal, the cries of the wounded, and the shouts of command rise to form a din that reverberates through the air, a symphony of destruction.

Dark figures maneuver through the disarray, and as I scan the crowd from above, I believe I spot Dorian. Without hesitation, I dive lower, plunging into the heart of the fray to join him.

CHAPTER 25

NYX

THIS HAS STRETCHED FAR LONGER than I expected. The castle grounds are unrecognizable—Samael and Kaine have clearly not been idle. I had thought they'd be unprepared for our assault, but the extensive preparations suggest either paranoia or anticipation. Perhaps they fortified the place against Lyra's eventual return. The thought makes me laugh aloud. Lyra wouldn't be deterred by mere enchanted barriers and traps.

Frustration mounts as I realize our lines of communication are still down—Colton's illusion vanished not long after our arrival. Damn him, probably slacking off with his magic, or perhaps... No, I quickly dismiss the darker thought of his demise. Despite everything, he is my brother, and his death would crush Lyra. Yet life would be simpler without him.

As if summoned by my thoughts, his projected self materializes within our ranks, and I can't help but shake my head at the sight.

It's eerie, seeing him like this—so lifelike yet so detached, moving mechanically until he chooses to engage. The fighters beside me still seem unnerved by it. I've only grown accustomed to it because my father used the same ability often.

Colton hurries over, and I brace myself for whatever comes next.

"Nice of you to join us again," I remark as he approaches.

"I lost my magic. Were any of you affected?" His question catches me off guard.

"What? No," I reply, scanning our surroundings for any immediate threats and not seeing any. "How?"

"Arrows," he explains, "shortly after the battle began, hundreds of spelled arrows rained down on my group, turning into golden dust that nullified our magic. That's why my illusion disappeared. I regained my powers moments ago."

Fucking Samael. This reminds me of the time Lyra and I were captured and restrained with specially spelled metal bars and chains, crafted from a deal he struck, selling a piece of his soul to Euric for the power to strip my magic. Now, it seems he's found a way to harness that same spell for mass deployment, which does not bode well for us.

"Have you checked on the other team?" I ask, hoping they've fared better but preparing for the worst.

"Yes, I'm with—" Then his illusion vanishes again. Godsdamn it.

"Everyone, watch out for arrows. They can nullify Fae magic. Spread the word, and don't get hit by one, for fuck's sake," I shout to the men closest to me.

The castle looms on the hill in the distance, but Colton's warning forces us to proceed with even greater caution. "Fan out," I command, gesturing for the men to take different paths through the shadowed gardens.

It's deep into the night, and with only a sliver of moon overhead, visibility is minimal. I navigate a narrow footpath leading through a gazebo, pausing outside as a prickling sense of being watched crawls over me. Surveying the small grassy area before me, centered by a softly murmuring fountain, I try to calm my nerves—water's gentle sound being the only soothing element tonight.

With a surge of urgency, I dash across the open space, feeling dangerously exposed, and enter the rose gardens. These gardens are eerie, filled with angelic statues that add an unsettling touch to the landscape. Who thought this was a good design?

A sudden movement catches my eye—a childlike figure holding a bow and arrow seems to twitch. I blink, convincing myself it's a trick of the light or my strained nerves. But as I take another step, reality strikes hard and painfully: a stone arm swings out, striking me across the head. Holy fuck, it's not my imagination. The statues are spelled, animated now, descending on me.

I'm surrounded by a veritable army of these flying, child-like statues, all armed with bows. It feels like I've stumbled into a nightmare, one concocted by Samael in his most deranged moments.

I waste no time with these monstrosities and simply fix my gaze on two of them and obliterate them with a burst of my power. As another statue draws its bow, aiming a stony arrow at me, I take no chances. I swing my sword, cleanly decapitating the eerie little figure, then with a sweeping gesture of my arm, I reduce the remaining four to rubble.

Straightening up, a smug smile creeps across my face. The ease of it almost makes me laugh—it felt too simple, almost trivial. Stepping over the scattered remnants of my adversaries, I aim to continue down the path when suddenly, a rose bush lashes out, its thorns slicing through my tunic and cutting into my arm. After all the sophisticated traps I've navigated tonight, it's absurd that a fucking flower draws first blood.

The sound of ceramic reassembling begins quietly at first. Reluctantly, I turn, dreading what I know is happening. The shattered pieces on the ground are pulling themselves back together, reconstructing the angelic figures I'd destroyed. I catch what looks like a smirk on one statue's face, even though half of it is still missing, and that's enough for me. This is too damn creepy.

With a renewed sense of urgency, I dash through the rose garden, my arm outstretched, shattering every statue in my path—spelled or not, I'm not sticking around to find out. I can't shake the eerie feeling as I flee, the sound of reforming statues echoing faintly behind me in the dark, twisted garden.

"King Onyx, the men on the other side of the property have been attacked by guards—dozens of them," Poe gasps, crouching next to me, breathless from his dash. The young officer is reliable, and I can't help but feel protective of the kid.

"Better you stay with me then. We'll head through the gardens toward the back entrance. The team can handle the other side," I advise him firmly.

"Yes, sir," Poe replies as we navigate the dark, zigzagged path. I keep silent about the statues. No need to relive that horror or scare him unnecessarily.

"Stop," I whisper suddenly, extending my arm to pull Poe down behind some bushes. I've spotted movement on a distant balcony that I recognize as Lyra's parents' old chamber, likely now occupied by Samael, given its size and grandeur.

"What is it?" Poe whispers back.

I nod toward the balcony where I saw a light flicker. As if on cue, several lanterns blaze to life, illuminating the figures of Samael and several others. It's difficult to make out faces from this distance, but the presence of Kaine and his wife are discernible. No sign of Citlali or any other Lamias though. Samael, donning a large mask that obscures his face, steps forward confidently, his hands gripping the railing as he surveys his domain.

The urge to hurl a blade at his head surges within me, but I know better. Magical shields and protective spells are undoubtedly in place, and who the fuck knows why he's wearing a mask?

"Oh, King Onyx, I know you're out there somewhere," Samael calls out, his voice unnaturally high-pitched and grating, echoing across the courtyard to our hidden spot. "Do you have my little bird with you? Oh, I do hope she's with you. I've missed my pet," he croons maliciously.

I clench my jaw so tightly I fear it might crack, repulsed by his possessive words about Lyra. Beside me, Poe's eyes widen in alarm. I shake my head slightly, signaling him to stay silent.

"Nothing to say? Not ready to beg for my forgiveness and bow to me? I imagine you'll be regretting that decision by sunrise, especially after what my men have told me about how your people are faring at my other camps." Samael's laugh rings out, a chilling echo mingling with the distant clash of battle.

I glance at Poe, ensuring his silence. Samael's penchant for deception and provocation is well known. I don't believe his claims that our other teams are struggling. Even if their magic has been temporarily nullified, my troops are far more adept at combat than the Sorcerers.

The lights abruptly extinguish, and all I hear is Samael's dismissive, "Suit yourself." Then the real onslaught begins. Guards pour from every corner of the castle into the courtyard, and I immediately grasp the unfolding scenario. I don't bother to shout a warning about taking cover. It would be futile.

Arrows rain down around us, and as Poe starts to panic, conjuring a shield, I shout over to him, "It's no use! The arrows themselves won't hurt you. It's the golden mist they release that takes away our powers temporarily. There's no avoiding it out in the open like this." The mist will penetrate our defenses, seeping into our very skin, even if we hold our breath.

The battle intensifies as we reach the hill's crest, the eerie golden mist swirling around us like a premonition of doom. It's a scene pulled straight from the darkest of fables, with shadows and fog dancing together under the moonlight, transforming the castle grounds into a living nightmare.

As I unsheathe my weapons, a sword in one hand and a dagger in the other—Dorian's magic ensuring it returns after each throw—I'm momentarily reassured by the familiar weight and the faint hum of magic still alive within them. Despite Samael's cursed arrows, our weapons remain potent, a small but crucial advantage.

With Poe close behind, we charge forward. Sorcerers, their robes billowing like dark specters, descend upon us. I waste no time. My strategy is simple—attack before they can utter a single incantation.

My sword slices through the air, finding its target with deadly precision. A head falls, the body collapsing into the mist, barely making a sound over the clash of battle. Without missing a beat, I hurl my dagger at another Sorcerer. It strikes true, embedding deep into his throat. As I spin to face my next opponent, the dagger flies back to my hand, slick with blood.

The mist thickens, a desperate attempt by the Sorcerers to diminish our onslaught, but it does little to quell the ferocity of our advance. Each step I take is a calculated dance of death—parrying, thrusting, and moving with a grace born of countless battles and many years of training.

I glance back to ensure Poe is keeping up. His young face is set in a mask of concentration, his actions mirroring my own as he fends off attackers. Our rhythm is synchronized, a testament to the countless hours of training and battle we've shared.

Sorcerers fall one by one as I weave through the gardens up the hillside, the castle growing larger as we near it.

The ground beneath us cracks, a spiderweb of dark energy spreading with alarming speed. I brace myself, planting my feet firmly on the earth, ready for whatever Samael's twisted magic might conjure.

Without warning, the ground tilts, a sudden steep incline throwing many off balance. I watch as the levitating Sorcerers begin to chant in unison, their voices a haunting melody that chills the blood. Above us, the sky darkens further, clouds swirling into a vortex directly over the battlefield blocking out the moonlight.

"Samael's manipulating the terrain," I shout to my men, my voice barely carrying over the crescendo of rising winds and the Sorcerers' incantations. "Stay alert. Keep your footing!"

The Sorcerers, now mere silhouettes against the darkened sky, start to hurl bolts of energy toward us from their elevated positions. Each bolt hits the ground with the force of a meteor, sending shockwaves through the already unstable ground.

I dodge a bolt, feeling the heat singe the air where it passes. The rumble beneath us grows more violent, and I realize Samael's attacks are an appetizer—something's coming.

"Poe, stay close!" I yell, not taking my eyes off the floating adversaries. We need to disrupt their concentration, break their formation. I hurl my enchanted dagger toward the nearest Sorcerer. It strikes true, and for a moment his chanting falters— but the dagger returns to my hand, and his levitation resumes as if nothing had happened.

The ground shifts again, more violently this time, and a new crack opens up, spewing a foul, sulfurous gas. I cough, the acrid air burning my lungs, and glance around, realizing that Samael's spell is more than an attack; it's a trap meant to disorient and weaken.

"We need to move!" I command, slicing through another bolt of energy with my sword. "Head for higher ground away from the cracks!"

As we maneuver, the realization hits me—we're up against the very landscape we stand on, twisted by Samael's dark spells. How has he gotten this powerful?

"Brace yourselves!" I shout to my comrades, barely getting the words out as the ground beneath us seals shut. Suddenly, a torrential rush of water cascades down the hillside like an avalanche, striking with the force of a boulder. I grab onto a nearby tree, anchoring myself as the deluge hits, threatening to sweep me away. Glancing around, I see several of my men aren't as fortunate, carried off by the newly formed moat swirling violently around the castle's base.

Enough of this madness. As the water subsides, leaving a slick, muddy mess, I drop from my makeshift perch into the mire. My boots sink into the mud with a sickening squelch, each step a struggle against the thick sludge. But Samael's magic has to have limits. He can't sustain this level of power indefinitely.

The Sorcerers, visibly fatigued and now grounded again, struggle to remain upright. "Attack now! Push forward. They're weakening!" I command, rallying my troops as we advance through the muck.

My blade meets the next opponent with a satisfying crunch. The Sorcerers' earlier poise has evaporated, their spells now desperate attempts to ward off our relentless assault.

We press on, and Poe and I finally clear the gardens, reaching the castle boundary. All entrances are heavily guarded, but they stand no chance against us. I swiftly take out the first two guards at the bottom of the stairs.

"Cover my back," I instruct Poe as I start my ascent. Three guards charge at me simultaneously. I kick one squarely in the chest, sending him tumbling down the stairs. His fall won't be fatal, but it buys me time.

The other two come at me, swords drawn. I fend off one with my dagger while stabbing the other in the chest with my sword, which gets stuck and fucking goes over the side of the stairs, still impaled in the guard. "Poe, my sword!" I grunt, pointing over the side with one arm while holding off the other guard with my dagger, not looking back but hoping Poe gets the message. If only my sword were imbued with magic to return to me as well.

"You're all going to die tonight. He can't be defeated," the guard I'm fighting says between gurgled breaths, blood spurting out of his mouth with his last words as I strike him in the collarbone, bone crunching as I retract my blade.

"Can't be defeated, my ass." I kick his body over the side and turn back as Poe runs up the first few steps, reaching out with my sword in his hand.

"I have it, King On—" His voice cuts off as a blade pierces through his chest from behind.

"No, Poe!" I scream, catching his collapsing body. The world narrows to the point of that blade as rage seethes within me.

Rolling Poe gently to the ground, I grab my sword and unleash hell on the man at the bottom of the stairs, who is laughing mockingly. I know he's dead after the first vicious swipe of my sword, but rage fuels me, driving my blade through him again and again until his laughter is choked out by his own blood.

Even after his body goes limp, I continue pounding his face with my fists until my knuckles are raw and bleeding, the pain a dull echo compared to the agony of losing Poe.

Breathing hard, I return to Poe, his body still warm. I kneel beside him, pressing my hand against his chest, futilely wishing for the magic that could save him. His eyes flutter open, a weak smile playing on his lips.

"Do you remember the first time we sparred off in the ring together?" I ask, my voice cracking as I clutch his hand, trying to distract him from the inevitable.

"I kicked your ass. You never saw my acid rain coming," he murmurs, his voice fading.

"I told everyone I let you win. Truth is, you really did kick my ass," I chuckle, gripping his hand tighter. His smile flickers with pride then dims as the light fades from his eyes, his chest falling still.

In that moment, something within me hardens—Samael will pay for this.

CHAPTER 26

COLTON

THE CAMP outside the castle's boundaries lies in ruins, a stark testament to the fierce battle that raged here. Everywhere I look, remnants of destruction meet my gaze: small fires flicker in the darkness, casting an eerie glow on the shattered landscape. The smell of death hangs heavily in the air, clinging to my senses as I tread through the debris. Each step is a grim reminder of the cost of this battle, of lives lost.

The war still rages on in the distance. Every so often, an echo of howls from the Lycans reaches my ears, and I find myself hoping for victory at the other camps. I trust Drew has everything under control. Bim and Dorian are nowhere to be seen. We'd all split up when the arrows hit and had to resort to physical combat.

Suddenly, I feel it—my magic returns, the remnants of the spell wearing off. Thank fuck. A few Sorcerers lie groaning on the ground in front of me. Without hesitation, I wave a hand, setting their bodies on fire.

Feeling satisfied that my people here will be triumphant, I channel to where I last saw Nyx through my projection before our magic was cut off. I wish I could channel directly into the castle itself. That would make this a lot easier.

The ground is sodden with water and decay. The once-beautiful gardens are now a flattened wasteland. Commotion echoes from within the castle. It must be nearing morning, and I find myself longing for this wretched night to end. Too many lives have been lost on both sides—a grim testament to the futility of this conflict. Shaking my head at the devastation, I channel to the outskirts of the castle.

Climbing a flight of stairs, I step over bodies strewn across the steps, making my way to one of the side entrances. Inside, the commotion continues from all directions, yet the halls are eerily deserted. I curse myself for not paying more attention to the castle's layout during my last visit with Lyra.

As I pass, the wall sconces flare to life, lighting my path. I check each room along the corridor. Most are empty, though a few host skirmishes—our forces holding the upper hand. I press on, determined to find Samael.

As I reach the other side of the castle, I pause, noticing a shift. The vibrant flooring is now dull, blanketed with dirt and rot as if abandoned for years. Trailing my gaze up the walls and down the hall, I see cracked sconces and roots piercing the stone—signs of decay mirroring the rot we found in Athalda's quarters at Euric's palace in Zomea. It's clear now that dark spells have been cast here, their corrupt essence seeping into the crevices, decaying the castle from within.

I press forward into this decrepit wing, the air thickening around me, filling with the stench of corruption. It's a tangible reminder of Samael's horrors—what creatures might have been harmed here, what souls tormented under his reign. My disgust mounts with each step, fueled by the high-pitched echo of his voice. It's a sound that grates, a reminder of why I'm here.

Tightening my grip on my weapon, I quicken my pace, driven by the urgency to end this for good.

The castle reeks, and I step over at least a dozen corpses as I rush down the hall toward Lyra's parents' old bedroom, where the voices seem to be coming from. Surprisingly, I encounter no living guards as I approach the door, which suggests they've already been dispatched—Nyx must have been here. Pausing outside, I listen for any signs of what lies ahead. Suddenly, a loud crash from within spurs me into action. I kick down the door and burst in, both blades ready.

Immediately, I'm confronted by two Sorcerers. I thrust my blade into the side of one's throat without hesitation. As I turn to face the other, he flings a handful of golden dust at me. Godsdamnit. I choke on the golden mist, feeling my magic drain away again.

"I'm getting real tired of this shit," I grumble, taking a moment to assess the room.

Nyx and Citlali are engaged in a deadly dance near the windows, while Samael sits nonchalantly at a table in the corner, a mask obscuring most of his face.

"He knows he can't stand a chance against us if we can use our magic," Nyx calls out, narrowly dodging Citlali as she lunges at him, her jaw agape.

Where are all his other men? How has no one else reached this far? They can't all be dead.

"Why do you look so confused, dear Colton? Surprised your men didn't fare as well as you thought they would against my forces?" Samael teases in his unnaturally high-pitched voice. The Sorcerer who threw the dust at me edges backward, and a smirk tugs at my lips—killing him will definitely be a highlight.

"I always knew you were the brawn of the operation, but it

seems Nyx snagged all the brains," he continues, his voice dripping with derision. I shrug off his barbs.

"Good thing killing you is a no-brainer." I step closer to the table, my gaze flicking between Samael and the clash between Nyx and Citlali. Part of me wants to see her fall by Nyx's hand, but we made a promise to Drew—I'll let her deal with her daughter.

I'm sure that's the only reason she still stands now. "Where are all your followers now, Samael? And what the hell is that on your face? I mean, it's a relief not having to see your usual scowl..." I watch as he bristles under his mask.

Nyx and I lock eyes for a split second, but his nod is all the confirmation I need. I lunge at the Sorcerer to my left, driving my blade through his armor and deep into his chest. He coughs up a torrent of blood as his body hits the ground.

Simultaneously, Nyx grabs Citlali, slamming her head against the wall with enough force to crack it. She slides to the ground, unconscious, leaving her for Drew to deal with later. I kick the fallen Sorcerer onto his back and yank my sword from his chest, wiping the blood on his garments. Samael laughs from where he sits, a cackle that makes my skin crawl, clearly thinking he's beyond our reach.

"Easy to laugh when you still have all your magic. Why don't you stand and fight us like a man?" I challenge him, stepping beside Nyx.

"Because he isn't a man. He's a sick freak, in love with his sister and abusing his power," Nyx adds with disgust.

Samael stands, clapping his hands mockingly. "I guess we all have something in common then, don't we?" he taunts.

I scoff, shaking my head. "More like sick infatuation, and last I checked, I wasn't in love with my sister. Hell, I don't even have a sister, and I could never be that sick."

Samael continues clapping, laughing maniacally, and Nyx

and I exchange a look that says it all—this guy has lost his fucking mind.

"Stop checking the door, my dear King Onyx. No one's coming for you. Did you really think I wouldn't cast spells to ensure we have some privacy?" Samael taunts, his gaze flickering between us.

"I don't need help to finish you," Nyx retorts, his temper flaring visibly.

"Enough chatter. Shall we?" I throw a wink at Samael, who mutters under his breath, his arms undergoing a grotesque transformation. Flesh and bone contort in a vile display as his limbs morph into blackened blades. Clearly, he's not planning to fight us without his magic. And I didn't think he could look more ghastly, but apparently I was wrong.

I glance at Nyx. We both know what we have to do next. We need to get that mask off him. It might be enhancing his powers. We start circling him slowly. It's two against one, but no one's playing fair in this fight.

We both charge simultaneously, and as my blade clashes with his, a jolt of electricity courses through the metal, shocking me so intensely that I'm hurled back into a bookcase. I clutch my chest as my heart skips a beat. Nyx fares no better, thrown across the room and tumbling over the bed.

Recovering quickly, I lunge again, managing to nick his thigh. His smug smile vanishes, replaced by a tight press of his lips as he charges toward me. His arms revert to hands, conjuring an orb of dark power that he hurls in my direction. I dive out of the way in time, the orb colliding with the wall and sending debris flying as it obliterates the adjacent bathing chamber.

"I hope you've got more of that gold dust because you won't be so tough once our magic returns," Nyx growls, charging Samael. He grabs him by the waist, tackling him to the ground.

Seizing the moment, I grip my sword and rush to join the fray. If Nyx can pin him down, I could end this—cut his throat. But Samael's not done yet. He casts another spell that blasts us backward, shattering the windows around us.

I wipe blood from my face, my jaw clenched, as we circle him again. Nyx and I alternate attacks, and I manage to drive my blade deep into Samael's calf. He staggers, yanking the sword free, and to my horror, the wound heals instantly.

"Do you see now? You cannot defeat me. Bend the knee, and perhaps I'll let you live," Samael taunts. "Maybe I'll even let you watch as I take my new bride to bed."

His words ignite a seething rage within me, a disgust for what he's threatened against Lyra. I lunge at him again, but Nyx, driven by his own fury, beats me to it. He screams, tackling Samael to the ground with such force that it seems to catch him off guard.

A flicker of motion in the corner of my eye pulls my attention to the balcony door, which stands eerily open—had it been that way before? My focus snaps back as I see Nyx grappling with Samael, his fingers clawing at the mask, desperate to rip it free.

Then I see Athalda. My vision blurs momentarily, and as she raises a magically sparking spear over Nyx's back, my body reacts before my mind can catch up, hurling myself over to shield him from the blow.

Nyx shoves me off, leaping to his feet, and as I stagger to my knees, the taste of blood in my mouth makes me cough. Nyx's gaze meets mine, wide with a fear I've never seen in him before. "What were you thinking?" he bellows, his eyes darting from my face to my chest.

I force myself to look down where searing pain radiates from my core. The tip of the spear protrudes from my armor, having pierced me from back to front. "I was thinking...I was saving your ass," I choke out as I spit blood onto the floor.

Samael's laughter fills the room, his claps sarcastic. I turn my head slowly to face my attacker, her marred face and dark, soulless eyes boring into me. "So we meet again, boy," Athalda says, her voice dripping with venom as she surveys the damage she's inflicted.

"You old fucking bitch," I spit out, blood pooling at my lips. "Lyra took pity on you, and this is how you repay her?" My voice is ragged, edged with betrayal and pain.

"This is precisely how I repay her, all I've ever wanted is for her to reach her true potential," Athalda cackles, a sound so vile I wince. "That girl was a fool to think banishing me was enough. Then you thought leaving a mortal boy guarding the bridge was a good idea."

Soren is usually tasked with guarding the bridge. Fuck, I hope he's okay. The cold metal of the spear shifts inside me as I attempt to breathe. "Maybe once you and King Onyx here are dead, she'll finally unleash her full potential," she muses with a twisted smirk.

I clench the spear with both hands, steeling myself to yank it out, but Nyx drops beside me, grabbing my wrist. "Don't," he hisses. "Without your magic to heal, pulling it out will make you bleed out in seconds." He's right, and as this sinks in, I realize how dire my situation is. Thoughts of Lyra flash through my mind—leaving her alone, not getting to say goodbye.

Samael's mocking voice cuts through. "Are you going to tell me where my little bird is now? Should we wait for her to arrive before we finish this?" His words ignite a fury in me, but it's Nyx who responds, voice thick with anger.

"Lyra's not here, she's not coming, and you're never going to touch her again." His glare shifts to Athalda, his expression one of betrayal and rage. "Why?" he chokes out, barely able to articulate his shock as he stares at her.

"Please, don't act like you haven't wanted to do it yourself. You should be thanking me for eliminating the competition, not questioning why," Athalda sneers, and I grit my teeth, feeling the life drain out of me, but I'm not ready to give up—not yet.

The world blurs around the edges, but I force myself to stand, each breath a battle against the spear impaling me. "If I'm going out, I'm not going alone," I growl through clenched teeth, seizing Athalda's throat before she can react.

Her smirk only ignites my rage further. I quickly scan the room for Samael, ensuring he isn't positioning to strike from behind, and catch sight of him cornering Nyx.

Turning back to Athalda, I see her face growing paler under my grip. Despite this, she reaches out, her bony fingers cruelly twisting the spear inside me. A searing pain shoots through my entire body. I stagger, nearly collapsing, the spear's metal grating agonizingly close to my heart.

In this moment of sheer agony, I lower my shields, searching for the tether that binds Lyra and me. Even diminished as I am, the connection pulses, a faint beacon between us. For a fleeting second, I'm surrounded by the essence of Lyra— the subtle sweetness of young roses and honeysuckle, so vivid that for a moment I forget the blood and the pain.

"You know, killing you is far easier than I thought it would be," Athalda taunts, her voice echoing as if from afar.

I shut her out, focusing solely on that ethereal link to Lyra, clinging to the sensation of her presence. But reality bends around me, walls seemingly warping, as if the castle itself is collapsing—or perhaps it's just my failing senses from the blood loss.

"It's working. Get ready," Athalda shouts over me. I lack

the strength to turn back to see Samael or Nyx, but they must be around behind me.

"Colton, no, keep your shields up!" Nyx yells urgently, but it's already too late.

I feel it—the rage, pure and unfiltered, radiating through me as if it were my own. It steals my breath away. The entire castle starts to vibrate, a hum of energy that raises the hairs on my neck. Deep down, I recognize this power—it's her, my shadow, my mate, and she is consumed with fury. As if summoned by my thoughts, the corner of the castle is ripped apart.

Rubble falls all around us as part of the roof is torn clean off, revealing the moon overhead. Athalda curses under her breath, and despite my wounds, a wave of satisfaction washes over me. I will live to see her end at the hands of my fierce mate.

Lyra lands on the balcony, her presence immediately sending Athalda crashing against the wall, held there by an unseen force. As Lyra approaches me, her movements are slow, deliberate. Her head tilts slightly, her eyes—now swirling pools of black shadow that vein out and stretch across her face and neck—scan over me intensely. Streaks of black bleed into her hair from the tips, tracing lines back toward her roots.

I struggle to rise, but my strength fails, and I remain kneeling. Lyra's expression softens, a rare vulnerability crossing her features despite the dark power radiating from her. She sinks to her knees in front of me and gently cups my face. Dark tears stream down her cheeks as she takes in my wounded state. I reach up to wipe them away, my thumbs brushing her skin.

"My shadow," I choke out, my voice rough. "I'm grateful...to see you, to touch you one last time." Each word is a battle as my lungs fill with blood.

She shakes her head, fiercely determined, standing swiftly.

"You're not dying," she asserts, her voice gaining an other-worldly resonance, the one she gets when her dark magic has completely taken hold of her.

"You'll be better off without him," Athalda hisses from her pinned position against the wall. Without breaking her fierce gaze from mine, Lyra's tendrils of shadow tighten around Athalda's neck, eliciting a guttural choke. "I'll deal with you in a moment," Lyra mutters, her voice cold as the shadows themselves. I want to turn to see what happened to Nyx and Samael, but I can't look away from her. She brushes her hands against her pants—those familiar black leather tights and bodice we used in our training sessions in Zomea. What has she been up to?

She kneels beside me once more, and suddenly Chepi is there, nuzzling against my cheek with a concerned whine. I'd pat him if I could, but my body is rapidly weakening, each breath more laborious than the last. If only I could summon my healing magic.

"Hold on," she commands me, her voice slicing through the haze of my pain. With a dramatic flourish, she thrusts her arm skyward, unleashing a maelstrom of darkness from her palm. It swirls around us, cocooning us in a globe of shadow more solid than stone.

Inside this dark sanctum, the chaos of the outside world is silenced, as if we're wrapped in the eye of a storm. The shadows churn violently around us, yet within this sphere, there's an eerie silence. All I can focus on is Lyra, her hair whipped up by an unseen wind, her eyes—dark pools of infinite depth—locked onto the spear in my chest.

Her lips move in a silent incantation, a whisper to the dark powers she commands so effortlessly. I feel a chill emanating from the core of my being, a creeping frost that spreads from the spear's entry point, seeping deep into my veins.

As the shadows tighten their grip around the spear, they begin to infiltrate the wound, intertwining with my very essence. Pain and cold intermingle, a paradoxical sensation that's both terrifying and mesmerizing. Lyra's shadows, alive with a dark energy, weave through my flesh, beginning a battle against the brink of death itself.

I've seen Lyra wield her shadows to heal herself, but never another. Doubt had me questioning whether it was even possible. Yet as her shadows twist beneath my skin, her dark magic begins stitching my flesh back together. I inhale sharp as the spear shatters under the force of her inky wisps, falling to the floor in shards.

I expect my next breath to be clear and strong, free from the pain of the weapon that once impaled me. But as I look up, I see Lyra's eyes widen in shock. I follow her gaze to her abdomen, where my blood has spattered across her. A wet, crackling cough escapes me as the last bit of life seems to drain away.

"It's okay," I manage, my voice barely a whisper as I collapse back onto the floor. The cold stone feels oddly comforting under me.

My body and mind succumb to an overwhelming tiredness, a pull toward sleep I can't resist. Lyra leans over me, her face etched with panic, her words lost to me. I reach up, my hand trembling, to touch her face—her beautiful face, the last thing I'll see, and I'm grateful for that.

"Find your light and live," I whisper with my last ounce of strength. Then, slowly, her face begins to blur and fade from my vision.

CHAPTER 27

LYRA

I CAN'T FEEL the tether! Colton's hand falls from my face as life drains from his features. He's so pale, and now I can't feel him, can't sense the tether connecting us. Panic threatens to seize me, my chest constricting so tightly it feels as though my heart is being ripped out.

Desperately, I press my hands to the wound on his chest, pleading for my power to surge into him, for my shadows to heal him. I grab his shoulders, shaking him violently, but he doesn't respond, and I'm starting to lose it. The safety net my magic has woven around us falters with my heightened emotions, and I let my shadows fall.

"Colton, wake up!" I scream through a sob.

"He's dead, girl, can't you see? Dark magic brings only death and destruction," Athalda taunts from behind me.

Tears blind me as I feel Nyx's hands, steadying me from behind, but I shove them away, desperate to escape the suffocating grip of sympathy. No, this can't be happening. The pain is a tidal wave, overwhelming, crushing every breath I attempt to take. I double over, the contents of my stomach spilling out in violent heaves, each one a brutal reminder of the life draining out of Colton. Nyx's touch lingers on my back, a futile attempt to comfort me.

I force myself upright, my legs trembling. The room spins chaotically—my shadows pin Athalda against the wall, her eyes wide with fear. In the corner, Samael watches, adorned with the cursed mask of my father, a relic from my past.

My gaze falls back to Colton—his once vibrant eyes now dull and lifeless, Chepi nestled against him, whining softly. A visceral scream tears from my throat, raw and shattering, as a surge of grief wracks my body. My heart doesn't just break; it detonates, scattering shards of pain through my very soul.

Hyperventilating, I clutch at the air, trying to grasp the remnants of my sanity. I can't endure this agony. With a desperate gasp, I surrender to the dark magic swirling within me, letting it encase my heart in ice. As the darkness consumes me, I bury my emotions so deep that nothing but a chilling calm remains.

When I reopen my eyes, they're empty of tears but full of lethal resolve. I'm no longer a heartbroken princess—I am the fury of the night, and I will devastate everything in my gods-damn path.

I tilt my head toward Samael, where Nyx stands, sword drawn. "Don't worry, dear brother, you'll get your turn," I murmur, my voice cold as I stride toward Athalda. Nyx remains silent, and I can almost feel Samael's jealousy, his awe at the darkness that bends to my will. I withdraw my shadows from Athalda's throat, allowing her to touch the ground once more.

"Still not strong enough to kill me," she rasps, laughing. "Oh, I know a place that's been waiting far too long for you."

I let a wicked smile spread across my face, and I think I see true fear in her features for the first time.

"You want death and destruction," I hiss through clenched teeth, unleashing a surge of my dark magic directly into her. Athalda's screams fill the room as her skin begins to bubble and sizzle, her flesh melting away in a grotesque spectacle.

"I trusted you! I showed you mercy, and you—you killed him!" I grab her by the throat, her skin sloughing off under my grasp, pooling at our feet. "You did this to me!"

My eyes, dark voids of writhing shadows, bore into hers as they dissolve beneath my gaze. As she withers before me, I thrust my hand into her chest, seizing her heart.

With a brutal tug, I rip it from her body. She collapses, a pitiful heap on the floor, and I crush her heart until it disintegrates into dust in my clenched fist. Then, with a whisper of dark power, I incinerate her remains, reveling in the rush of destruction. The shadows within me purr with satisfaction.

A choked sound from behind snaps my attention back. I turn slowly, my full wrath now directed at Samael.

"My pretty bird, how I've missed you," Samael coos in that sickeningly sweet voice of his. I shoot a glance at Nyx, wondering why he hasn't made a move yet. Catching my look, he lifts his hands in surrender. "I don't have my magic right now," he admits.

"Leave us," I command Nyx, and there's something in my tone, or perhaps the look in my eyes, that makes him comply without protest. He moves toward the door, and though I can sense he doesn't stray far, lingering by the threshold, it grants me the space I need.

"I can see now one of us may have underestimated the other," Samael comments, his voice sickeningly high-pitched but laced with a slight tremor of uncertainty. I merely tilt my head, eyeing him like the predator I am. The mask covers his entire face.

"Think of all we could accomplish together, my sweet.

Ruling with dark magic, all of Eguina could be ours," he proposes, sounding deranged.

I ready myself for the inevitable. Sure, I could turn him inside out where he stands, but where's the fun in that? I want to draw this out. With a casual flick of my hand, I send a surge of my power crashing into his chest. Had he not been braced against the wall, he would've stumbled.

Samael laughs, shaking his head as if in disbelief. He steps toward me, whispering an incantation and sending a shockwave that barrels into me. It throws me back, and the pain searing across my shoulder is almost a relief compared to the anguish gnawing at my heart. I crave more.

A smile curls my lips, unsettling him further. He retaliates, his power slamming me against the wall. My head thuds against the stone, and as I reach up to wipe away the trickle of blood from my nose, I laugh. Death, if it were possible, would be a sweet release right now.

"You're going to have to try harder than that," I giggle, mocking him. The challenge shatters his composure.

He charges, a scream tearing from his throat as he hurls another spell, the force crumbling the beam overhead. I casually disintegrate the falling debris with a mere glance, protecting myself effortlessly.

"Get them out of here," I command Nyx, trusting his compliance. I feel his gaze locked on me, unwavering. Samael doesn't obstruct him as he moves Colton and Chepi to safety.

Giving Samael a minor display of my power, I unleash my shadows, which playfully form a hand and slap him across the face—a mere tease of my capabilities. I withhold from seizing the mask, wanting him to keep his increased power, relishing the challenge it presents. It's the only thing allowing him to evoke any sensation from me.

With a furious roar, Samael charges, his hands casting

spells that shove me back before he can reach me, knocking me to the ground. In an instant, he's atop me, his hands clamping around my wrists, pinning me down.

"We belong together. When are you going to give in?" he hisses, leaning in so close I can feel his breath. Panic flares within me, but I react swiftly, tearing the mask from his face. He strikes, trying to retrieve it, but I simply laugh, crushing the mask into dust in my palm.

His scream of defeat is delicious to my ears. He strikes me again, desperation coloring his blows, but I only laugh harder. My power is too immense, my shadows healing me faster than he can inflict any real harm. His repeated hits become futile, his frustration boiling over into a frenzied yelling.

"Lyra, enough!" Nyx intervenes, his voice cutting through as he reenters the room.

"It's never going to be enough," I snarl, forcefully kicking Samael away and bracing for his inevitable counterattack. My desire for the darkness to envelop me, for my dark magic to take absolute control, wars against the acute pain of loss for Colton. My insides are a tumult of agony and rage that I barely contain. Suppressing the urge to collapse in tears, I release a piercing scream instead.

The chamber reacts violently. The roof tears off and the wall crumbles. I barely register Citlali's body tumbling with the debris—I hadn't even realized she was still there. Exhausted and overwhelmed, I tilt my head back, gazing at the moon as hundreds of Sarrols swarm overhead, descending upon the castle and the surrounding camps.

"Fuck," Nyx mutters beside me, his voice barely audible over the chaos.

Samael gasps, his eyes widening at the apocalyptic scene unfolding above us. I step toward him, the wind whipping fiercely around us, embodying the storm within me.

"Do you see it now? You can never defeat me," I proclaim, as powerful and relentless as the gale that surrounds us.

Samael's last desperate attempt to gain control unfolds chaotically. He screams, his feet stamping in a tantrum as he releases a horde of dark creatures. Black snakes and bats, formed from smoke, fill the room, but his spell backfires.

The creatures, recognizing the darkness within me, turn on him instead of attacking me. They swarm the room, bats diving into his body and disintegrating into clouds of smoke, snakes wrapping around his legs as he tries to shake them off in a fit of rage.

He slams his fists into the ground, and fire erupts, spreading flames across the floor and up the walls. I stand amidst the inferno, the heat searing but strangely welcome. Nyx's voice breaks through, though it's almost lost in the tumult.

"Lyra, it's not all lost," he says, though I can barely hear him over the cacophony. Suddenly, Nyx is before me, his hand on my chin, forcing me to look at him. "Come back to me. Come back for him. Let's end this together," he says, and I nod, our eyes locking with a shared resolve.

"This reminds me of old times, the three of us in here together," Samael croaks, a twisted smirk on his face. Both Nyx and I turn toward him, disgust mounting inside me.

Nyx unsheathes his sword with a swift, fluid motion, metal gleaming under the flickering light from the flames licking the walls around us. Samael follows suit, his blade drawn with a sinister hiss. They circle each other warily, eyes locked in a deadly duel of wills.

With a sudden lunge, Nyx strikes, his sword slicing through the air toward Samael. Their blades clash with a resounding clang, sparks flying as steel grates against steel. They move rhythmically, almost gracefully, each parry and thrust a duel of fates. Samael counters with a vicious swipe aimed at Nyx's head, but Nyx ducks under the blade, rolling to the side and coming up ready to strike.

The room echoes with the sound of their battle, each strike more desperate and forceful than the last. They are a whirlwind of motion, each fighter anticipating the other's moves.

It's time to end this, to cast all the pain he's inflicted into the annals of history, permanently. I summon an obsidian spear, its dark sheen glinting with lethal intent. Nyx steps aside, granting me a clear path. I lunge, the air whispering past the spearhead before it finds its mark.

Silence descends, the chaotic winds cease, and the flames waver as my weapon pierces Samael's chest. His eyes, dark pools of malice, lock onto mine. A twisted smile plays on his lips, even as the life fades from them. With a nod from me, Nyx acts—his blade arcs through the air, severing Samael's head with clinical precision. It lands with a thud at my feet.

I stoop to pick it up by the hair, examining the sneer frozen on his face. Nyx, his magic restored, nonchalantly kicks the body before launching a fireball straight at it. I toss the head into the flames, and together we watch as Samael's body disintegrates into ash, ensuring his reign of terror is extinguished once and for all.

CHAPTER 28

NYX

WITH THE FLAMES EXTINGUISHED, the war finally ends. I place my arm around Lyra's shoulders, and for a brief moment she leans into me before pulling away abruptly.

"Colton," she breathes out, her voice thick with emotion as she whirls around. I follow her into the small study across the hall. She falls to her knees beside Colton, and I have to steady myself against the doorframe, hardly believing my eyes.

He still lies on the floor in the center of the room, with Chepi nestled by his side, yipping at us and wagging his tail. I blink several times and take a step closer. Lyra's shadows—the darkness she poured into him when he was dying—still remain.

Small inky wisps swirl around him, stitching up the last outer layer of skin on his chest. His color is restored, and when she leans over and kisses him on the cheek, I see his chest visibly rise as he takes a breath. I've never seen anything like it. I saw him die. His heart stopped. I am certain of it, and yet her dark magic has brought him back.

She feels his chest rise in tandem with my observation and starts to cry again, kissing him frantically on the cheeks and forehead until his eyes flutter open and he steadies her with his hand. Reaching up to cup her face, they lock eyes while everything seems to pause, even time itself, and in this moment I truly grasp the depth of their love for one another.

It doesn't alter the fact that I need to have a serious discussion with Lyra about what I discovered in my father's journals, nor does it change that I cannot allow her to marry him. However, I can grant her this moment of joy amidst the pain. When he sits up and pulls her into his lap with a kiss, I step out of the study, leaving them to bask in their moment.

It's been a few weeks since the battle ended, and I think all of us are ready to leave—myself especially. Lyra and Colton have been staying with Lili while the castle's reconstruction is underway.

It seems most of the Sorcerers were not truly opposed to Lyra's leadership. It was all due to Samael's control over them with that artifact, the mask. Adira, Drew's right-hand, managed to take Citlali into custody and return her to the Lamia realm to face her own punishments.

Drew and Dorian killed Kaine and his wife but allowed the other higher council leaders to live once they swore allegiance to our side. Bim is going to stay here for a while to oversee things in the Sorcerer Realm until Lyra is ready to ascend as queen. Her birthday is fast approaching, and she will soon be of age to rule. I haven't had any time alone with her yet to talk, and there has been too much requiring my attention here, so I think I'll put it off for a bit longer.

"I think I have things under control here if you want to head back to Nighthold. Most of the men have already returned home, and there hasn't been a violent attack since that night," Bim says from where he sits at the conference table.

I lean against the window, looking out at the pine trees. "Yeah, I think I'll do that. You'll reach out if you need anything?" I ask, turning to look at him. He's sorting through paperwork, and I don't envy his job.

"Yeah, we'll see each other at the ceremony too. Unless you've changed your mind about attending," Bim says, and I pause, not wanting to divulge anything to him yet.

"Yeah, I'll see you," I say and channel down to the foyer.

I debate whether to say goodbye to Lyra and ask how long they plan to stay but decide it's better not to. I need time to gather my thoughts and see what's been happening in Nighthold while I've been away. After a brief stop at Drew's, I finally make it back home, only to face Flora's scrutiny when she storms into my office.

"What's going on, Nyx? I know that look, and I know you're planning something," she says from across my desk.

I run a hand through my hair, feeling the weight of exhaustion. "It's been a long few days, Flora. I've barely slept. Can this wait?" I ask, hoping for a reprieve.

She shakes her head, her arms crossed, her foot tapping in impatience. "No, it can't wait. I'm serious. If you're planning to crush that poor girl again..."

"I thought you were on my side," I counter defensively, but her expression softens slightly.

"I am on your side. But this isn't about sides. This is about letting Lyra be happy. She loves Colton and has made her choice. Don't ruin this for them," she advises, her eyes narrowing as she tries to convey the seriousness.

"I don't want to ruin anything. Why would you say that?" I respond, irritation creeping into my voice.

She sighs, uncrossing her arms. "Because it's important.

You may resent him, but your feelings shouldn't cost them their happiness. Remember, he is technically your older brother—you usurped not only his throne but also his first love, Z. Don't rob him of Lyra as well. You can despise him if you choose, but don't let your anger dismantle their lives."

That hits a nerve. I pour myself a glass of whiskey, the liquid's amber color doing little to calm me. "Don't talk about Z," I say sharply, pouring more whiskey than intended.

"You never want to face anything that's painful. Remember, I lost her too, Nyx. She was my best friend, and I loved her," Flora adds quietly.

I close my eyes, taking a deep breath, struggling to contain my frustration inside before I say something I might regret. I did love Z, but I prefer to keep that buried. There's no bringing her back, so dwelling on her feels pointless.

"I only want to do right by Lyra, I promise. And as much as you think I hate Colton, I don't. He saved my life, had my back, and I won't forget that," I say, which seems to appease her for the moment.

"Good, because I've been planning their ceremony and am taking Lyra to try on her dress soon. The last thing I want is to worry that you might ruin her day," she says.

I nod, pressing my lips into a thin line. I don't want to talk anymore and have a lot to think about. She sighs heavily then channels out of my study. Finally alone, I relish the peace and quiet, ready to strategize my next move.

Everything is aligning now. With Samael and Kaine gone, the Sorcerer Realm seems ready to welcome Lyra's leadership. I'm sure Drew will support it, though she's been quite reserved about her thoughts—at least with me. She and Colton always seem to share some inside joke, leaving me feeling out of the loop.

Nonetheless, I believe she respects Lyra and would support

her leading Cloudrum, even if Lyra weren't with Colton. The Lycans have been unpredictable, but hearing that Rhett ultimately joined our cause gives me hope that they won't oppose us.

I'm anxious about what Lyra discovered in Zomea and clueless about why she even went there. If she knew what I do, I imagine she'd have returned to me by now.

The situation with Colton is complicated. Despite everything Flora said, I don't hate him—hell, he was ready to die for me... He did die for me. I need to sort out my plans thoroughly. There's no scenario where everyone escapes this unscathed.

I must visit Elspeth soon, before she potentially sabotages my plans. I run a hand through my hair, considering the need to review the journals again. I have to be absolutely certain of my course before facing Lyra alone. If she rejects my plan, I might have to take drastic measures. Capture her, confine her—if it comes to that, how far am I prepared to go to save her? I'd raze the world for her.

Rising, I start pacing before the fireplace. I'll have Twig concoct something to help me sleep. Yes, I'll rest tonight and revisit everything with fresh eyes in the morning. I'm going to need to bring evidence with me when I confront Lyra.

CHAPTER 29
TWO MONTHS LATER
LYRA

I wake with a gasp, the sensation of hot breath on my ear startling me. Instinctively, my shadows surge outward faster than smoke, engulfing the room in darkness and pinning my intruder against the wall. My heart pounds as I blink rapidly, disoriented by the sudden awakening.

A low chuckle fills the room, and I jump out of bed, clasping my hand over my mouth as I reel my shadows back.

"Oh my gods, I..." I start, a nervous giggle escaping me.

"My dark enchantress indeed," Colton says, his face lit by a cheeky grin as the soft candlelight seeps back into the room. "Don't call your shadows back yet. I think they had the right idea, tying me up like that," he winks, and I close the distance between us with a few quick steps.

"What are you doing in here? I thought we agreed to sleep separately the night before the ceremony. You know Flora will have both our heads if she finds you here," I chide him irreverently. Flora's obsession with the wedding details has morphed her into a delightfully tyrannical figure, and I adore her all the more for it.

Falling asleep alone tonight, in a house unfamiliar to me, must be why my magic felt so on edge. Colton wraps his hand around my lower back, pulling me close. He cocks one knee slightly, and I seize the moment to straddle it, tilting my head to meet his gaze.

"I'm willing to take the risk of her wrath if you are," he challenges, his voice a low murmur. I reach up, threading my fingers through his hair, and pull him closer.

"How could I resist?" I tease, tracing his bottom lip with my tongue. He growls, a deep, primal sound, and his tongue meets mine with a fervor. As our kiss deepens, I begin to grind against his leg, the growing heat inside me igniting a fierce desire.

"It's our last night as two separate souls," I whisper, our lips barely parting as we move together, gravitating toward the bed.

"Darling, my soul has belonged to you from the moment our eyes first met," he responds with a depth of feeling that sends shivers down my spine.

I slip out of my chemise, letting it pool at my feet, and unleash tendrils of shadow to ensnare his waist, drawing him irresistibly close.

"Assuming command already, My Queen?" he teases, his voice a low murmur as he eases me back onto the bed, spreading my legs with a reverent touch. "Then permit me to worship at your altar, my dark enchantress." He sinks to his knees with the grace of a predator.

His lips trace a searing path up my thigh, igniting tiny fires of desire under my skin. When he reaches the apex of my thighs, I let my head fall back, lost in the sensation as he expertly circles my clit with his tongue then slides a finger inside me.

"Oh gods." A moan escapes me, hanging in the air.

"I think you mean, 'oh King,'" he teases, his voice low as he adds another finger, pushing me closer to the edge. "Not yet."

He clicks his tongue as he withdraws and rises, conjuring an illusion of himself. The second form of him binds my wrists, stretching me out beneath him, utterly exposed and deliciously vulnerable. The real Colton stands at the foot of the bed, a predator's smile playing on his lips. "You think you're the only one with tricks up your sleeve? You've got your shadows, and I've got...well, more of me." He smirks.

His illusion captures my lips in a demanding kiss, overwhelming my senses before granting me a moment to breathe. Colton discards his clothes with a snap, and his illusion mirrors him instantly. "I thought there were always three of you when you replicate," I tease, breathless under their intense gazes.

"Are two of me not enough?" he chuckles, climbing onto the bed to join his illusion. My heart races at the prospect of what's to come and sends a flush of heat across my skin. He laughs softly at my flustered state then captures my lips in a kiss that promises both passion and a profound connection, his green eyes alight with mischief and love.

The situation is wickedly delightful, and I remind myself they are both him. One man, doubled in form but singular in intent—double the hands, double the...pleasure. My face heats at the provocative thought, thankful for the room's dim lighting. But Colton, ever observant, catches the slight change in my expression.

"Imagining what it'd be like with both of us, aren't you?" he probes, his voice a delicious challenge. I bite my lip, overwhelmed by the surge of desire.

"Now, with you so beautifully restrained, where should I begin?" he muses, his lips finding my right breast. His duplicate does not relent, capturing my left breast with equal demand. They suck and tease, perfectly synchronized, drawing gasps and moans from me that I should be embarrassed about, but I feel too good to care right now.

The duplicate trails kisses up my neck, eliciting shivers that Colton watches with rapt attention, his eyes dark with desire. "I love how your body responds to me," he murmurs, as his illusion nips at my ear, sending sparks cascading down my back.

I feel his arousal pressing against my thigh, ramping up my own need for him. I shift invitingly, signaling my readiness. He meets my movement with a smirk, aligning himself at my entrance. The illusion captures my lips, his tongue diving deep as the real Colton enters me—slow at first, then with a growing urgency. He holds my wrists firmly above my head as I wriggle beneath him, each thrust pushing me to the brink of ecstasy. As I near climax, he pulls back, teasingly prolonging the moment and leaving me craving more.

The illusion releases my wrists and moves to stand beside us as the real Colton gently withdraws, only to guide me to the bed's edge. He lifts me effortlessly, my legs wrapping around his waist as he sinks into me once more, deeper this time. I moan into his kiss, his hands firm on my thighs, guiding the slow, intoxicating rhythm that builds toward a crescendo.

My fingers tangle in his hair, the intensity of our connection deepening with each thrust. "I want more," I gasp, pulling away from his lips. The illusionary Colton's hand glides up my back, fingers weaving into my hair to gently tilt my head back.

"Are you ready to take more of me inside you?" he whispers huskily, his breath warm against my neck. My response is a desperate whimper. I nod fervently, my body alight with anticipation.

The real Colton tightens his grip on the back of my neck, his touch both commanding and tender. "Look at me," he commands softly. "I want to see your eyes as I fill you." I lift my gaze to his, finding a storm of desire there, and he holds my eyes intently as he begins to move.

The illusion at my back embraces me tightly as he starts to

press into me from behind. I draw in a sharp breath, the sensation new and intense. I keep my eyes locked with Colton's as he fills me slowly, deeply. The initial pressure gives way to a pulsing pleasure that radiates through me.

They move in a careful rhythm, one advancing as the other retreats, creating a mix of sensations that leaves me breathless. With each coordinated movement, the space within me adjusts, accommodating the dual presence that both overwhelms and exhilarates.

Colton's gaze never wavers from mine, his eyes holding a mix of concern and intense passion. Each time he withdraws, the illusionary Colton fills the void, maintaining the exquisite pressure. The rhythm builds slowly, meticulously, until I find myself nodding slightly, a silent signal that I'm more than okay —I'm consumed by the pleasure of it all.

They accelerate, and I cling to Colton, my nails digging into his shoulders as waves of pleasure roll over me, culminating in a shuddering orgasm. After thoroughly fucking me senseless and driving me to orgasm multiple times, the illusion behind me vanishes.

Colton gently lowers me back onto the bed, maintaining our connection. His demeanor softens. His movements become tender as he cups my cheek, kissing me slowly, deeply, making love to me with a measured rhythm that once again escalates our pleasure until we both climax together.

Exhausted, he eases out of me and rolls onto his back, drawing me close so I'm sprawled across him, my body spent. His fingers tenderly stroke my hair and trace soothing patterns on my back.

In the quiet aftermath, he whispers declarations of his love and excitement for our future. His words, filled with emotion and promise, lull me into a peaceful sleep nestled against his heartbeat.

"ARE you ready for the most fabulous day of your life? Did you sleep well?" Hollie exclaims, perched on a pillow next to Chepi at the foot of my bed.

I twirl a strand of hair around my finger, staring at my reflection. "Actually, I had a nightmare and woke up at 3 a.m. Couldn't fall back asleep after that. I guess it's nerves, you know...but the good kind," I reply, examining the bags under my eyes that Flora will undoubtedly magic away with makeup later.

I don't bother mentioning the part about Colton giving me the best sex of my life before my midnight mind woke me with a nightmare. But he was gone when I woke at 3 a.m., having slipped back to his room to avoid a confrontation with Flora.

"It's natural to feel that way. I wonder how Colton slept last night. Or better yet, how King Onyx slept—gods, isn't he handsome? I hope he shows up today!" Hollie muses, drifting into a daydream about him.

"He mentioned he'd be here," I say, pausing as I frown at my reflection. "Well, he said he needed to talk to me before the ceremony, so I assume he'll stay. But I wouldn't hold it against him if he chose not to."

Hollie's face falls into a pout, sparking another round of laughter from me.

"If he stays, I'll make sure he sits next to you during the ceremony," I assure her, watching her cheeks bloom with excitement as she flutters over to land on my shoulder.

"I love you, you know that? Have I mentioned it lately?" she giggles, her voice bubbling with joy.

"You know, I haven't spoken to Nyx alone since that night —the night we defeated Samael. It feels like a lifetime has passed, and we've been worlds apart. I meant to talk to him before today, but time slipped away," I admit, a pang of guilt shadowing my expression.

"I'm sure he understands, Lyra. Don't beat yourself up. You're on the brink of a monumental change, stepping into power and mystery—he couldn't possibly grasp all that's weighing on you. And let's not forget, he's been wrapped up in his own kingly duties as well." she reassures me, fluttering back to Chepi to stroke his head. "I'm going to miss you two. The Dream Forest won't be the same without you."

A frown tugs at my lips. "I'll miss you too, Hollie. I'll visit when I can, though I'm not sure how my new responsibilities will shape my time. But one way or another, we'll see each other again. I promise," I say, sinking down onto the pillows beside them.

"Does it feel weird, staying here knowing Elspeth hates you?" Hollie asks as we lie back on the bed, gazing up at the elaborately painted ceiling. This coastal home, one of Colton's family's many properties, is beautiful. Flora chose it for the ceremony, and honestly I couldn't care less about the location as long as Colton and I are together.

"It feels sad. I wish she didn't hate me, but I can't blame her. I know she's going to miss her son, and if I were in her shoes, I'm not sure how I'd feel either," I say, my eyes tracing the scenes of painted angels and demons that seem to taunt each other, etched in gold.

"Do you think she'll be at the ceremony today?" Hollie asks as Chepi belly crawls between us to settle in.

"She better be. It would really hurt Colton if she wasn't there. He's visited her a few times this past month. He hasn't mentioned anything about her disapproving of the binding ceremony, but I don't think he would. He'd be too afraid of hurting my feelings," I explain, reaching out to scratch Chepi behind his ears.

"Did you ever tell him how she threatened you at your engagement party?" Hollie probes, her tone light.

I laugh, the memory feeling like it belongs to another lifetime. "No, and I won't. We both want what's best for him," I start, pausing as a recent doubt creeps in. I've been questioning if I truly am what's best for him, but Colton's assurances dispel my fears. He wants this life as long as we're together, and that thought alone brings a smile to my face.

Flora bursts into the room. "Time to wake up and get beautiful," she announces.

Hollie stands, arms crossed. "Lyra's been up for hours."

Flora gives me a sympathetic look. "Nerves getting the best of you?"

"Err, something like that," I reply, sliding off the bed.

"Okay, off you go! You can take a bath, or if you prefer, the bathing chamber down the hall has a shower. Stay on this floor. It's bad luck to see the groom before the ceremony, and Colton knows to stay on the third floor," Flora instructs, gesturing for me to hurry.

"Okay, I'll take the shower. I promise I won't leave this floor," I assure her, seeing her relax slightly.

"Great! I'll have some food brought up, and then we can start getting you ready!" she exclaims, and I head down the hall to the shower.

CHAPTER 30
LYRA

"So what time is the ceremony supposed to start?" Lili asks, expertly weaving a strand of my hair into a braid from behind me.

I'm so happy she's here. I wasn't sure she would come after everything that happened in the Sorcerer Realm. Things are much more stable there now though with Bim currently overseeing everything.

"Promptly at 3:30 p.m. That way, the sun will be setting during the reception," Flora explains, applying a touch of blush to my cheeks.

"That means you'll probably be completing the ceremony right around the time you were born. How poetic," Lili muses, securing another braid.

"What time was I born?" I ask, genuinely curious.

"At 4:03 p.m. I remember it like it was yesterday. Hard to believe it's been nineteen years," she reflects, and I can't help but agree. It feels like the first seventeen years dragged on, then the last two flew by, especially this past year.

"There. Now you're perfect," Lili announces, securing one last pin in my hair. I turn to the mirror to see her handiwork—my hair cascades in loose waves, crowned with braids interspersed with tiny white flowers. Flora's makeup enhances my features, giving me dark, dramatic eyes and soft, pink lips.

"I feel beautiful," I admit, turning to see their reactions.

"That's because you are beautiful! Now it's time for your dress!" Flora crow, and Hollie claps excitedly from where she and Chepi are perched on a throw pillow on the couch. I haven't seen the dress since my last fitting, and the anticipation of showing it to Lili and Hollie, who haven't yet seen it, fills me with excitement. Only Flora and I know what it looks like.

"Come, I'll help you get dressed in my room. Then you can come back and show everyone," Flora says, her excitement palpable as she tugs me out of the room and down the hall.

Once we reach her bedchamber, Flora begins to remove my robe, her hands quick and efficient as she helps me into the dress. Without magic, the process would be a nightmare of laces and ties. Instead, with a wave of her hand and a snap of her fingers, I'm perfectly fitted.

She nudges me toward the mirror and steps out, allowing me a moment alone to take in my reflection. Seraphina has outdone herself. The gown is beyond my wildest dreams, a true work of art. The bodice features a daring low V-neck, adorned with white crystals that catch the light with every movement, like stars against my skin.

The luxurious white lace flows from the crystal-studded bodice, expanding at my knees into a voluminous skirt that cascades to the floor. Silver stitching weaves through the lace, adding an enchanting shimmer and complexity to the design.

What truly sets this gown apart is the shadow magic within the stitches—dark wisps that flow through the fabric, making the dress pulse with life, mirroring the beat of my heart. I turn slightly to admire the long, translucent cape extending from my shoulders, trailing behind me like a veil of mystery, infused with shadowy black designs that move with me. The entire ensemble is breathtaking. I can hardly recognize myself.

My makeup is bold, perfectly complementing the dress, and the tiny white flowers woven into my hair add a touch of innocence to my otherwise commanding appearance. In this moment, I truly feel like the Queen of Night. Dark enchantress, indeed... I giggle softly, imagining Colton whispering those words to me.

"How do you feel? Is it perfect?" Flora asks as she reenters the room, her eyes sparkling with anticipation.

"It's perfect. I don't know how to thank you. I couldn't have done any of this without you. I'm going to miss you so much. I wish we could have met sooner—I really could have used a friend like you growing up," I confess, my voice tinged with a bittersweet longing. She pulls me into a tight hug, her warmth enveloping me.

"Don't talk like you're disappearing. Being queen of Cloudrum doesn't mean you can't still visit Nighthold. I'll visit you too. We'll still hang out," she assures me.

I force a smile, though my heart clenches with the weight of the truth. "Of course." Only I know the truth—well, Colton and I know the truth, and I don't think I'll be seeing much of anyone after today. Flora might understand, but it's better this way. Better no one knows until later. I wouldn't want to ruin today.

But there is one person I do need to tell, and I probably shouldn't have waited until the last minute to do it—Nyx. Life has been so busy, and if I had told him sooner, he would have tried to find a way out of it. This way, he has no chance to stop it.

I will make him understand because I cannot stand the

thought of hurting him again. We have both hurt each other enough already in this life.

"Do you know if Nyx is coming today? He said he wanted to stop by and talk to me before the ceremony," I say, trying to keep my voice casual, though my heart races with anxiety.

"I'm not sure he'll come. Don't hate me, Lyra, but I may have told him to stay away. Forgive me, but I don't want him ruining your day. He might still come—he rarely listens to me anyway—but if he does...be careful," she says, her voice filled with concern.

I smooth my hands down my gown. "I understand. Come on, let's not leave them in anticipation any longer," I say, leading the way back to my sitting room.

As soon as we enter, Hollie's eyes widen. "Oh my gods, Colton is going to lose it when he sees you!" she exclaims, bouncing on the couch before taking flight and circling around me in excitement.

"You look beautiful, Lyra," Lili says softly, her eyes shimmering with unshed tears.

"Don't cry," I plead gently, a smile tugging at my lips. "You're going to make me emotional, and I have a feeling if I ruin my makeup, Flora will kill me." My attempt at humor earns a watery laugh from Lili, who wipes away a stray tear.

"Okay, I need to go get myself ready now. I can't wait to see you out there," Lili assures me, giving my hand a quick squeeze before leaving the room.

There's a quick knock at the door, and we all turn our heads, my breath catching in my throat as I silently hope for Nyx to walk through next. Instead, Drew pokes her head around the door. "I heard this was the place to find the bride," she says.

I smile, relief washing over me. "Yes, come look at what a

beautiful bride she is," Flora says, holding the door open wider for Drew.

"Hey, guys, can I talk to Drew alone for a bit?" I ask, my voice steady despite the fluttering in my chest. Flora nods with a warm smile.

"Of course, dear. I'll come get you when it's time for the ceremony to start. Come find me if you need anything, and don't forget your shoes," she says, as if I'd walk down the aisle barefoot.

"Thank you," I reply, chuckling as she slips out of the room.

Hollie flits over to me, her tiny wings a blur. I extend my hand, and she lands gracefully. "You're going to do great. Don't be nervous," she assures me, her smile bright and encouraging before she zips out of the room.

Chepi hops onto the bed and settles in for a nap.

"A formidable queen indeed," Drew says, her red eyes full of admiration as she settles onto the couch.

"Thank you," I say, feeling a warm rush of gratitude as I move to sit across from her in one of the chairs.

"I came from Colton's chambers, and he had quite a lot to share," Drew says, her tone still cryptic.

"Oh yeah?" I reply, keeping my face stoic. I know Colton planned to tell Drew everything, but in case he backed out, I don't reveal anything.

"I've been waiting a long time for this, you know," she continues, her eyes distant with memories. I look down, unsure how to respond, wishing I had a drink in my hand to steady my nerves.

"I know you sought my guidance before, and I couldn't give it. I've always tried to provide you with the tools to reach your own conclusions," she pauses, her gaze drifting out the window as if lost in her own thoughts. "Eventually, you'll understand why I couldn't interfere, even when I desperately wanted to. But I believe you're making the right choice, and I'm so grateful for you," she says, her voice filled with genuine emotion.

It's my turn to look away, gathering my thoughts, unsure of how to respond. "Grateful for me? Why?" I ask, my voice barely a whisper, wondering if we're even discussing the same thing.

"I know the choice you made was not an easy one, and anyone who sacrifices the way you are will bring about great change. You will be a formidable queen, and I know you will use your dark magic to rule with compassion. Despite everything that has tried to harden your heart, you still thrive, you still remain kind, and that takes true strength," she says, her eyes locking onto mine with an intensity that leaves me breathless.

I've always felt like I was falling through life, barely getting by. Some days, I even wished I wasn't alive... If it weren't for Chepi, I might not be. Samael made my life a living hell for many years, and my parents only added to the misery. I've never truly felt like I belonged anywhere, and I wandered aimlessly, not knowing my purpose.

Despite all of this, I've always been empathetic. I try to show kindness, to give others the benefit of the doubt, even after all the wrong that's been done to me. Drew probably doesn't realize how much her words mean to me, but I feel it deeply. Although I don't need validation, it feels good to hear it. It's a rare balm for my soul, a reminder that my efforts to do what's right, even when it means my own suffering, have not gone unnoticed.

"I'm grateful for you too, more than you know. You were there for me when I needed someone, and I noticed the signs and the little pushes you gave me along the way. You gave me a place to stay when I had nowhere else to go, and I'm grateful to know you," I tell her, my voice thick with emotion. Her eyes soften, but before she can respond, we both sense it.

I smell him first, and a split second later, he appears. "King Onyx," Drew says, rising to her feet. She pauses to look down at me, winks, and then she's gone.

I clear my throat, standing up. "Nyx, I could have been naked or...gods know what, and you channel in here without knocking or anything. What the fuck?" I chide him, but inside I'm relieved and happy he's here.

"Maybe that's what I was hoping for," he says, his gaze raking over me. I realize I'm in my wedding dress, and he's seeing me for the first time in months.

Then I notice he's holding a stack of books, notebooks, and journals. "What is all of this?" I ask.

He places the stack on the table and steps directly in front of me. I don't step back, even when he raises his hand to gently lift my chin, coaxing me to meet his gaze. Those soft gray eyes, glowing with intensity, hold mine captive.

The weight of his presence, the mystery of the journals— everything feels charged with significance. The air between us hums with unspoken words and unresolved tension.

"We need to talk," he says, his voice a quiet command.

"Yes, we do," I say, glancing over at the table where the stack of journals sits. He cups my face again, his touch firm yet tender, until my eyes are drawn back to his.

"You can't marry Colton and can't go through with the bonding ceremony," he says, his eyes now like hardened steel.

A chill spreads through my body, freezing me in place. The room seems to shrink around us, and my heart starts to pound harder in my chest.

He shakes my shoulders, breaking me out of my temporary

stupor. "Lyra, did you hear me? You cannot complete the ceremony with Colton," he insists, his voice urgent and desperate.

"I know—"

CHAPTER 31

COLTON

"Lyra is going to love this," I tell Flora, glancing out at the terrace below from my bedchamber's balcony. The white marble terrace is impressive, with massive pillars and archways opening up to a sprawling seating area. Rows of chairs are set up, each adorned with simple yet elegant white flowers, flanked by an army of candles—seriously, there are candles everywhere. Floating orbs of flowers and candles add a touch of magic to the scene.

The aisle is covered in white petals, lined with candles that flicker like tiny beacons. Beyond the chairs, a few steps lead up to a stage, which is decked out with even more flowers and candles. Past the stage, the sea stretches out, high up on the cliffs, with low-lying clouds hovering above the water. The air smells fresh and salty. I take a deep breath, enjoying the scent.

It takes me back to summers spent here as a kid. My mother always loved this place. She used to say there was nothing like falling asleep to the sound of waves crashing below. I never got it back then, but now I see why it's so calming.

"I hope so. You're going to die when you see her. She looks

so beautiful," Flora says. I have no doubt. I wonder how Lyra's holding up today after I kept her up late last night.

People are starting to arrive and mingle below. I told my mother Lyra wanted a small, intimate ceremony. She narrowed down her guest list a lot, but there'll still be a decent crowd. Everyone important to Lyra will be here, and that's all that matters to me.

"Okay, well, I wanted to check on you and let you know it's almost time! I saw Drew earlier and went through everything with her to make sure it will all run smoothly. I think you guys made a good choice with her. She'll do great," Flora says, peering over the edge to look at the guests arriving below.

Usually, an elder officiates a bonding ceremony, but with Lyra and me, our unique history and heritage called for something more personal. Drew was an easy choice to officiate, and she was happy to do it when we asked her.

After my extensive talk with her this morning, she now knows everything. She handled it well, but that's no surprise. Drew always seems to know everything. She didn't outright say it, but I have a feeling she pulls more strings than she's given credit for.

"In case we don't get a chance to talk later, I really appreciate you doing this for us and for being kind to Lyra. I know we haven't been close ever since...well, ever since Z died and Nyx and I had our falling out, but I appreciate you being there for her even though things didn't work out with her and Nyx," I tell Flora, honestly.

"Aww, stop it. You're going to make me cry before the ceremony even starts. I'm happy to do it, and I love Lyra. I never stopped caring about you either. I'm glad we're all friends again. You know, I think Nyx is coming around more and more every day," she says.

I think he's coming around. I just peeked in on Lyra a few

minutes ago and had a chance to talk to him—I'm feeling optimistic about the future. I won't tell Flora though...she'd lose it if she knew I saw Lyra in her dress before the ceremony. She did yell at me not to look, so I tried to keep my eyes off her. As if that worked!

She continues, "I'd better head down. I left Twig in charge of greeting guests, and I'm not sure he was too keen on the idea. Come down soon. It's almost time." She squeezes my arm and gives me a genuine smile before hurrying off down the hall.

I let out a long, steadying breath. If I'm feeling anxious, Lyra must be a ball of nerves. It's not the ceremony itself that gets to me; it's everything that comes after. I take one last look in the mirror. Dressed in all black, I must say I look pretty damn sharp—definitely exuding those kingly vibes. I considered tying my hair back but settled for twisting a few pieces out of my face.

I head down the hall to the lower level, but before I reach the terrace, my mother intercepts me, linking her arm through mine and tugging me into a sitting room.

"Elspeth, you have such a beautiful home," a woman remarks as we pass.

"Thank you. The terrace is through those doors to the right," my mother replies with a polite smile. She ushers me inside and shuts the double doors. Once we're alone, her pleasant facade fades into a serious expression.

"Are you sure you want to go through with the bonding ceremony?" she asks, concerned.

I release a frustrated sigh. "We've been over this. I've accepted my fate—or rather I've chosen it," I reply, moving to open the door.

"Wait, come here," she says, pulling me into a hug, her eyes misty. I hug her back, trying to offer some reassurance.

"I'm not dying, Mom. This isn't a funeral," I tease lightly, and she gives my arm a gentle slap.

"You are my only child, and I wouldn't wish this fate on my worst enemy. That girl is poison, and I know what courses through her blood," she insists. Anger flares within me—I hate hearing her talk about Lyra like this—but now isn't the time for that fight. We've had too many already. Instead, I sigh, exasperated.

"Is there nothing I can do to change your mind?" she asks, desperation edging into her voice.

"Mother, I love her. She completes me, and my soul would be lost without her. Please, let me go through with the bonding ceremony with the woman I love. My destiny is mine to embrace, and I am happy. Be happy for me," I plead. Her eyes soften briefly, and she nods, gripping my arms tightly.

"I'll be in the front row," she promises, and before she can get more emotional, she releases me and hurries back down the hallway toward the terrace doors.

I wait a moment, letting some distance grow between us before making my way to the terrace. As soon as the double doors open, the scent of flowers mixed with the sea overwhelms my senses. So many flowers. Flora hands me a glass of water while she's standing with Twig, greeting guests. I take it and thank her. Rix and Rune hover behind them with a few of their family members. I wave and move to the stage.

Little groups are mingling all around. Some people have already taken their seats while others are sipping drinks and chatting. I spot my father with a couple of his friends. Even though things have been strained between us ever since I found out he's not my biological father, I'm still glad he's here. He doesn't approve of me being with Lyra either, but at least he's not as vocal about it as my mother. I walk over and shake his hand then continue greeting friends and family along the way.

I see Drew standing on the stage, her back to me as she leans over the railing, peering out at the ocean. Hollie is here too, and she's brought a couple of her friends. Lyra will be ecstatic to see more Pixies, I'm sure. I shake hands with a few more people and finally make it onto the stage.

"You ready for this?" Drew says without looking back.

I lean against the railing, angling my body toward her. "You have no idea," I chuckle, brushing the hair out of my face as the breeze picks up.

She turns to face me, her hip propped against the railing. "I bet you didn't think it would turn out like this when I asked you to come train Lyra in my realm," Drew says with a slight smile, one of her fangs catching the sunlight.

She had asked me to help Lyra with her Fae magic after Nyx had fucked everything up. It feels like a lifetime ago now and yet also not so long at the same time.

"Honestly? I thought you wanted an excuse to see me more often," I say with a wink. We both laugh, the sound mingling with the distant crash of the waves below.

"Will our dear King Onyx be in attendance today?" Drew asks, her tone light but her eyes sharp as she glances from me then back out to the horizon.

"Oh, he's here alright. He's with Lyra right now. Honestly, I wouldn't put it past him to be trying to talk her out of the ceremony. If she weren't so godsdamn powerful, I'd worry he'd try to capture her and hide her away just to stop this wedding," I say, half-joking but fully aware there's some truth to my words.

"You two have more in common than you realize. It's a wonder no one figured out you were half-brothers sooner," Drew remarks, a hint of amusement in her voice.

I shake my head, laughing. "Hey, I might be tolerating him lately, but that doesn't mean we have anything in common."

"Sure, you sacrificed your life to save his because you 'tolerate' him," Drew says, narrowing her eyes at me. I push off the railing, not wanting to admit I might have a small soft spot for him.

"There are a lot more people here than I anticipated," I say, shifting the focus as I look out at the crowd. More and more people are starting to take their seats.

"Don't pretend you're getting stage fright. We all know you love the attention," Drew teases, moving to stand at the center of the stage.

Flora makes an announcement, and everyone finds their places, ready for the ceremony to begin. I scan the crowd and spot my mother and father, seated as promised in the front row. Lili and Hollie have also secured spots up front.

I glance around, searching for Nyx, but he's nowhere to be seen. He never said if he was staying for the entire ceremony or not. I can't really blame him if it's hard for him to see.

A low hum of music begins to play on the wind, an ethereal melody that seems to come from the very air itself. The guests rise, a sea of anticipation, and then the double doors open. Lyra steps out, and I swear my heart stops in my chest.

Everything I thought I knew vanishes, and all I can do is drink in the sight of her. She is indescribably beautiful, and she's mine.

All mine.

Chepi hovers beside her, flying at shoulder height, a small white bow tied around his neck. Even he seems to understand the gravity of this moment.

Her dress sparkles and shifts, the shadows intertwining with the lace details like living fabric. It moves as if it's part of her, responding to her every breath. As she walks down the aisle, the path lights up, each candle bursting to life.

I know there's music playing, but I can't hear it over the pounding of my heart. My mind is filled with nothing but her.

Her eyes scan the crowd before locking onto mine, and they stay there, pulling me into her. Her hair catches the sunlight, sparkling almost as much as her dress.

I feel an overwhelming urge to go to her, to meet her halfway and claim her before everyone, to show them all that she belongs to me. She is striking, a vision of power and grace. I open the tether between us, reaching out to feel her presence, but her shields are up. Maybe she doesn't want me to feel her nerves.

Finally, she reaches the stairs leading to the stage. I step forward, extending my hand to her. The moment she takes it, the world narrows to the two of us. The magical connection between us ignites, and I feel her essence, her love, her power.

It's me and her.

Lyra and I stand facing each other, Drew to my right and our friends and family seated to my left. The atmosphere is charged with anticipation, streams of warm sunlight shooting across the terrace in long beams as the sun begins its descent from the sky, and candles flicker to life all around us.

Drew's voice breaks the silence, jolting me back to reality.

"Welcome, honored guests, to a ceremony unlike any other. Today we gather not merely to witness a union but to celebrate a convergence of destinies, a merging of souls forged in the fires of fate. Under the watchful eyes of our gods, we honor the love that binds Colton and Lyra. This is a ceremony of blood and spirit, where life forces entwine and two hearts beat as one. Through blood, we acknowledge the sacrifices made and the strength shared. Through the bonding of souls, we embrace the eternal bond that transcends the physical realm."

She pauses, her gaze moving from me to Lyra then back to the crowd. Her voice hangs in the air, a palpable magic surrounding us.

"As we begin, let us remember that love is the most potent

magic of all, capable of transforming darkness into light and despair into hope. Let us now complete the ceremony that will forever bind these two souls as one," she finishes, her voice carrying across the terrace.

"I understand the two of you would like to say a few words to each other with all of us as your witnesses before blood is shared," Drew says. Lyra and I nod in unison.

"Colton, please go first," Drew says.

I take a slow, steadying breath, stepping forward and taking both of Lyra's hands in mine. Her hands are warm and soft, grounding me in this surreal moment. I glance down at our joined hands then back up to her eyes. In this moment, it's me and her.

"Lyra," I begin, exhaling slowly, "standing here with you today, I am reminded of all the moments that brought us to this point. You are the most resilient person I have ever known. Through every trial, every shadow, and every obstacle, you have emerged stronger, refusing to let the darkness define you. Instead, you shape it, turning it into something beautiful and powerful.

"Your magic, though dark and mysterious, is a testament to your strength and will. But what makes you truly remarkable is your heart. No matter how dark the path, you always choose to do good. Your soul shines with a light that no shadow can dim. You are a beacon of hope, not only for me but for everyone who is fortunate enough to know you."

I pause, squeezing her hands slightly and watching her eyes glisten with fresh tears. I take a deep steadying breath and continue.

"We share a love for creatures, and I have seen your empathy and kindness extend to even the smallest beings. Your compassion is boundless, and your ability to see the beauty in everything, even in the darkest places, inspires me every day.

"You are incredibly beautiful, both inside and out. Your strength, your kindness, your unwavering spirit—these are the things that make you who you are. And it is these qualities that have captured my heart completely.

"Today, I vow to stand by your side through every storm, every dark day and every unseen challenge that lies ahead. I vow to support you, to protect you, and to love you with everything I am. Our bond is more than just a connection; it is a merging of souls. You make me better, and I promise to cherish you, to honor you, and to never take for granted the incredible gift that is your love.

"My shadow, my dark enchantress, my heart, my soul, my mate, my everything—I am yours, now and forever, in this life and the next."

A wave of emotion washes over me. I never thought I could feel so vulnerable yet so strong at the same time. Looking into Lyra's eyes, I see the same intensity and love mirrored back at me. It's like the entire world has faded away, leaving the two of us standing in this sacred space.

My heart races as I think about everything we've been through. Every challenge, every moment of doubt, every dark day has led us to this moment. She has been my anchor, my light in the darkness, and now I am hers.

"Now, Lyra, what would you like to say to Colton?" Drew asks, bringing our focus back.

Lyra takes a deep breath, her eyes locking onto mine. "Colton, before you came into my life, I was in a dark place, broken and unsure of how to piece myself back together. But you didn't just help me put those pieces back together—you showed me how to rebuild myself."

I watch as her lips part and her tongue flicks out to wet them before she inhales and continues. "No matter how much I pushed you away, you stuck by me. You healed my heart and made it whole again. Your strength and love made me stronger, and every good quality I have, I owe to you being by my side and believing in me. Your love has given me the courage to face my inner demons, not only to overcome them but to harness that darkness for good."

She pauses, pressing her lips together as a single tear streams down her face. Chepi swoops in and licks her cheek, nudging her with his nose, causing a sweet smile to spread across her face. My heart swells, seeing her strength and vulnerability combined.

"I was so afraid of prophecies and making the right choice, but then I realized it was never about who is the light and who is the dark, because to me, you will always be my light. I can't imagine a world or realm where you're not by my side. I would rather suffer an eternity of night with you than the most beautiful day in the sunshine alone."

She stops, and I squeeze her hands, letting her know it's okay. I want her to say everything she needs to say. Right now, we're in our own bubble.

"You are my person, and I vow to stand by your side and love you with my entire being for all of eternity because my heart belongs to you. There is no me without you. I am ready to bond our souls together because you are my soulmate and we are destined to be together. True fated mates, my soul recognizes your soul.

"Colton, my heart, my soul, my light in the darkness—I am yours, now and always. Let's start our forever today and follow each other into the darkness if that be our fate."

She finishes, her voice filled with unwavering love and conviction. I feel a profound sense of completeness wash over me. This is our moment, our eternity beginning now.

CHAPTER 32
NYX

"Now, each of you, give me your left hand," Drew says.

I try to refrain from pacing where I stand, shadowed at the back of the terrace, mostly out of sight. My heart pounds as I watch Drew take a small dagger and slice Colton's hand down the center. Then she slices Lyra's, and I see her visibly flinch as the blade pierces her skin. I have to clench my fists at my sides, calling upon all the strength I have not to intervene.

She places their hands together, and the moment their blood mingles, the bonding begins. A shimmering cloud emits from their joined hands, swirling with magic as blood drips between their fingers onto the pristine white flower petals covering the stage. The drops of blood seem to echo as they hit the marble floor, the crowd so silent, watching in equal parts awe and fear.

I glance at the clock through the window—4 p.m. How much longer is this ceremony going to last? I should leave, but a part of me needs to see it through. I can't bring myself to walk away yet.

"The bonding ceremony is complete. There is only one last

step," Drew announces. I shift my position, moving a few steps closer to the stage along the right side.

Drew's slight smile tells me what's coming next, and she says, "You may seal it with a kiss."

I internally cringe. Lyra steps forward on her tiptoes, and Colton cups her cheek. They stare into each other's eyes for a moment before he kisses her. It's no simple peck. He twists her around his body and dips her back, kissing her deeply.

My jaw clinches so tight I think I'm going to crack a tooth, but still I can't leave. He is my brother, and he saved my life. I want him to be happy, and I want her to be happy... It's just hard to stomach right now.

The sunbeams stretching across their bodies and into the crowd suddenly disappear. I tear my eyes away from them and look out across the sea for cloud coverage. But it's not clouds that cover the sun—it's something else.

I squint into the horizon, noting the dimming sunlight, but the crowd remains oblivious to the impending threat. My instincts scream that something's coming—no, something's here. Initially, it looks like a giant flock of birds, but as they draw closer, the ominous sound of flapping wings carries over the crashing waves. My eyes sharpen, and I see them clearly—Sarrols. Dozens of them, their dark, leathery wings slicing through the sky, heading straight for us.

A surge of adrenaline floods my veins. As I'm about to sound the alarm, a deep vibration begins under my feet, spreading rapidly. A collective gasp ripples through the crowd as the ground itself seems to roar in protest. The pillar I'm leaning against groans and splits, fissures racing down to the ground and snaking through the rows of seats. The crack yawns open, wide enough to swallow a leg, sending people stumbling back in terror.

My heart pounds as I snap my gaze back to the stage. Lyra

and Colton are no longer locked in a kiss. Their moment of intimacy shattered, Lyra's gaze is fixed on me. Panic grips me as I witness her transformation—her beautiful sapphire and emerald irises bleed into an abyssal black. The pure, raw power emanating from her is both mesmerizing and terrifying.

Time seems to slow as the Sarrols descend, their screeches filling the air. The crowd erupts into chaos, screams mingling with the monstrous cries. The sky darkens further, shadows creeping over the terrace. The anticipation of an impending battle electrifies the atmosphere. Every fiber of my being is on high alert, ready to defend, ready to fight.

This is it. The moment we've all feared. The darkness we've fought to keep at bay is here, and it's been here all along, waiting.

Waiting for this ceremony.

Waiting for this exact moment.

Shadows start to melt out of the cracks in the pillars, spilling across the white marble floor like liquid smoke. I'm stopped dead in my tracks as I look back at Lyra. Shadows burst from her chest, not forming into the ribbon-like wisps as they normally do. No, this time her darkness morphs into creatures—demons, giant birds, and snakes, all erupting from her. Dozens of beings made from pure liquid night pour out of the shadows emanating from her. I've never seen anything like it.

The creatures take to the sky, descending upon the Sarrols with ferocity. I watch as a giant eagle made of swirling night grabs onto a Sarrol. They tumble across the floor at the base of the stage steps, the Sarrol snarling and frothing, a black tar-like substance staining the ground in its wake. The shadow eagle captures it in its talons and drags it down into one of the cracks in the ground, forcing it back into the darkness it came from.

The scene is made of nightmares yet strangely mesmerizing. The Sarrols are fierce, but Lyra's shadow creatures are relentless. The air is thick with the sounds of battle—screeches, roars, and the sickening squelch of shadows clashing with flesh. I can feel the adrenaline coursing through me, my instincts screaming to join the fight, but I'm frozen in place watching it all play out before me.

The pillars continue to crack and crumble, the earth beneath us trembling. The crowd is in a frenzy, some trying to flee while others are stuck in place, captivated by the dark spectacle unfolding before them.

I think I hear my name and snap my attention back to Lyra. Yes, she definitely yelled for me. I want to rush to her, but I already know what she wants. Our eyes meet, and when hers narrow on me, I nod, forcing myself to move.

I start pushing people off the terrace and back into the palace. Drew is doing the same, grabbing people by the arms and tugging them toward safety with Flora. I don't see Twig, but I know he's well-equipped to handle situations like this.

Granger slips and falls back, tripping over one of the cracks in the ground as he tries to pull Elspeth away from the stage. Tears stain her face as she screams for Colton, but her cries go unnoticed. I dodge a tangle of monsters, barely missing the mess of claws and fangs. Grabbing Granger by the shoulders, I lift him back to his feet. He gives me a thankful look before successfully pulling Elspeth further toward the palace doors.

A new demon crawls up out of a gap in the ground. I recognize it instantly as the one Bim told me about—one of the creatures that attacked people in Nighthold and Cloudrum. It's humanoid, with a pale-gray body crawling across the floor and over the toppled chairs. Its gaunt rib cage protrudes grotesquely, and I wonder how it knows where it's going with its lack of ears or eyes, only a giant gaping mouth of teeth in the center of its head.

Colton steps down from the stage and kicks the demonic

creature in the head. Not exactly what I would have done, given its giant mouth starts chomping at his leg. He kicks it again, and one of Lyra's shadow creatures attacks. A serpent of night wraps around the creature's neck, slamming its pale, bald head against the stone floor. Another snake coils around its leg, dragging it back into the depths of the earth through one of the fissures.

Only minutes ago, it was a sunny afternoon. Now, lightning crackles overhead, and thunder rumbles so loudly I think it might knock the entire terrace off the cliff. One of the white pillars starts to sway then, almost in slow motion, falls behind the stage platform, breaking the railing and tumbling down the rockslide to the water below. It's after 4 p.m., but by the looks of it, you'd think it was midnight. Heavy dark clouds have rolled in from nowhere, forming a storm so fierce I can't tell if the darkness is coming from the sky, the fissures in the ground, or Lyra herself.

Colton fights off another Sarrol and finally makes eye contact with me for the first time since the ceremony started. "Get out of here. You don't need to be here for this," he yells over the bedlam.

"I have to see this through," I shout back. The moment of understanding in his eyes tells me he gets it.

A Sarrol whips past me, and I grab onto its leathery wing, ripping it out of the air. Grabbing ahold of it, I toss it to one of the shadow creatures, which drags it back into the ground.

The scene around us is utter madness. Lightning illuminates the terrace, casting shadows and bright flashes as the storm rages on. The air is thick with the scent of ozone and the metallic tang of blood. Lyra's power is a raw, untamed force, and she unleashes her fury upon the invaders in a way I could never have imagined.

I always knew Colton wasn't the one. I felt it in my godsdamn blood—he is not her beacon of light. Her darkness isn't going to destroy me, and I'll be damned if I let it consume her or anyone else. I think I know how this is supposed to end, but this is quickly spiraling out of control.

Fuck—I'm hit from behind and stumble forward, barely catching myself. A demon barrels into me from the front, knocking me flat on my back. Raging, I prepare to summon my magic and incinerate the bastard. Before I can act, Chepi leaps onto the creature's back, sinking his teeth into its neck. I seize the moment, waving my hand to turn the demon into ash.

Chepi looks up at me, panting, and I give him a quick pat on the head. "Good boy," I mutter, getting back on my feet.

He quickly spins back around, sprinting to Lyra's side. She has moved from the stage to the center of the terrace. I scan the area and see that all the innocent bystanders are gone. Everyone has been herded to safety inside. Besides Lyra and Colton, only Chepi and I remain among the demons and shadow creatures.

My heart pounds in my throat as I look back at Lyra. Colton reaches her side as she lets out a scream that echoes louder than the thunder above. The sheer force of her voice sends a shockwave through the air. It doesn't kill the monstrous things but stops them in their tracks, sending them fleeing back into the open crevices around us.

The shadow creatures morph back into clouds of smoke, and the darkness starts to seep back into the ground like slow-moving lava. Inky ribbons absorb back into Lyra's hands and chest. The tips of her hair are still dark, and her eyes are swirling black pools that vein out onto her face.

I step toward her, refusing to heed her shaking head. I won't back down, vowing to see this through. Colton wraps an arm around her lower back as Chepi nuzzles between them.

The cracks beneath their feet widen, the darkness trickling down until the earth rumbles violently.

The ground beneath my feet trembles, the vibrations escalating into a full-blown quake. The surface under our feet finally gives way, opening into a massive, gaping hole. They hover momentarily on a cloud of darkness, suspended above the abyss. I stop breathing as I watch the last of the shadows melt into the earth. In that instant, they fall, swallowed by the darkness.

"No!" I roar, sprinting to the edge of the chasm.

The terror and adrenaline surge through me, my mind racing with the fear of losing them. I peer into the black void, my heart hammering in my chest. The sound of the ground cracking and the echoes of the monstrous creatures fading into the distance fill my ears.

I'm on the edge of a precipice, not only physically but emotionally. This is not just the end but the beginning as well. Either way, I'm not going to let this be the last time I see her. I won't believe it until I see it with my own eyes.

I dive into the chasm.

I TUMBLE THROUGH THE CHASM, hot air whooshing past me, and then suddenly it's cold—freezing. My fall steadies, and I throw my arms out in front of me, bracing myself as I slow. It's pitch black, and I'm carried on an invisible wind until finally my feet hit the ground.

I blink into the darkness, taking a few steps as my eyes slowly adjust to the forest around me. I recognize it instantly. I've been here before. I know this place.

I start to run down the winding path ahead until I see it in the distance—the towering gates. I slow my steps as I approach, looking up at the massive structure.

The giant trunks and branches seem to move with life, tangling around the iron bars. The otherworldly moonlight of Zomea shines overhead, illuminating the faces of souls entangled around the gates as if they are part of the very structure.

Between me and the gates are Lyra, Colton, and Chepi, their backs to me.

I watch, unable to think or speak, as a crown of obsidian branches forms atop Colton's head, followed by one of shadow and gemstones on Lyra's. Colton looks back at me, giving me a single nod, his eyes content, then he turns back to the gates. Lyra's hand falls to her side, and he takes it in his. Chepi's wings materialize, and he hovers beside her shoulder.

Without anyone moving, without Lyra even touching them, the gates slowly creak open. My heart races inside my chest. I take a couple of steps forward, looking through the gates to what's beyond.

The scene before me is almost indescribable, a complete paradox. Giant mountains covered in snow and ice loom in the distance, their peaks piercing the sky. Blackened, twisted trees with leaves that appear to be on fire dot the landscape, the flames dancing without consuming the wood. The ice remains unmelted by the fiery vegetation, an impossible coexistence of fire and frost.

Finally, Lyra turns her head and looks back at me, a hint of blue and green peeking through the swirling shadows that have become her eyes. She broaches a beautiful, wide smile that sends warmth through my heart even down here. Then she turns back, and the three of them walk through the gates.

Once inside, Colton picks her up, and she wraps her legs around his waist and her arms around his neck. They kiss deeply, one that speaks of love and eternity. He pulls back and kisses her cheek and forehead, and she laughs—a natural, beautiful laugh that echoes past the gates and through the forest.

They're happy.

They're happy, and I think I can be okay with that.

I take a few steps closer to the gate, watching as he puts her down, and they walk hand in hand into the perpetual night. The dark landscape seems less foreboding with their presence, their love illuminating the path ahead.

I want to say something, but it's all already been said. Instead, I watch as my brother and dear friend embark on their happily ever after, imperfectly perfect in its own way.

As the gates slowly close, a bittersweet sense of peace washes over me.

CHAPTER 33
ONE HOUR EARLIER
LYRA

"SORRY, you know you can't marry Colton and complete the ceremony? Then what the fuck is going on here?" Nyx's voice is sharp and incredulous. I take a step back, wanting to deescalate the situation.

"What's with the stack of journals?" I ask instead of answering. Moving over to the table and picking one up, I recognize Callum's sloppy handwriting right away.

Nyx snatches it out of my hand. "Can you stop moving and sit down...please?" He takes a steadying breath, so I move over to the couch and take a seat. He follows and sits next to me, so close our knees touch.

"Why did you bring a stack of your father's journals here?" I ask again.

"Lyra, I don't know how to tell you what I found in here, because my father doesn't just mention the prophecy about his sons light saving you or the darkness destroying us all. He goes into detail about everything." He pauses, and I have a feeling we both need to discuss the same thing.

"Haven't you ever wondered why the evil creatures never attack you?" he asks, catching me off guard.

"I guess I never really thought about it before," I tell him. He runs a hand through his hair, exhaling.

"I noticed it first when the Sarrols attacked at Drew's. None of them seemed to be trying to hurt you. Instead, they were always trying to grab you. They even successfully snatched you at one point and carried you into the air." He looks over at the stack of journals, deep in thought. He isn't wrong. That was when I fell into Blood Lake.

"Darkness has been spreading in Eguina long before we ever knew about the hearts in Zomea or Euric's plans. Evil creatures have been multiplying, and attacks have been increasing. It all happened so slowly that we didn't notice it at first." He looks back at me, meeting my eyes. "This entire time, they have all been attracted to you. Even before your dark magic was awoken, they knew what you would become. They sensed it—drawn to your essence."

I start to gnaw on the inside of my cheek, unsure how to tell him that none of this matters, that I already know the truth.

"Nyx." I turn toward him, ready to explain, but he silences me again, jumping up off the couch and shuffling through the journals and loose pages.

"You don't understand. I also have proof that I am the light. I am the one you're meant to be with, not Colton. My father explicitly states he spoke to one of the gods in a dream, and I am the light. I am the one to save you from all of this, to make sure your darkness doesn't destroy you...destroy us all."

He frantically flips through the papers. I put my hand over his, stopping him.

"Nyx," I start, but he pulls his hand away, shaking his head and interrupting me again.

"I have it here somewhere. I brought it because I knew you would need proof. I didn't want to come here and break up the wedding ceremony, but Lyra, damn it, I have to. You and I are meant to be, and I finally found what I needed to prove it to you. Colton will be okay. He can survive this, so don't—"

I reach up and place my fingers to his lips, unable to hear more. I can't let him continue this rant. "Nyx, I need to talk, and this time I need you to sit down." He opens his mouth to protest, but I take his hands in mine, pulling him back to the couch.

"I believe everything you're saying. I don't need you to prove anything. I believe you, and before you say anything else, I need to tell you about the time I spent in Zomea." That finally captures his attention, and he settles down, eyes fixed on me, ready to listen.

"I finally traveled beyond the gates, and it wasn't what my father thought. Euric was wrong. It's not where all the gods live, and you don't ascend to being a god when you cross the threshold." I shift, crossing my legs. Nyx remains still, his anticipation evident in his intense gaze. "I did see some gods there. I spent time with Ryella, the Goddess of Darkness and Shadows. I also met Riddick, the God of Decay; Misha, the Goddess of Forgotten Memories; and Delfi, the God of Nightmares, to name a few."

I pull my bottom lip into my mouth, my chest tightening with unease over what I need to tell him. "You spoke to all of these gods? What did they say? What were they like?" Nyx asks, finally moving to face me more, propping an arm over the back of the couch.

"They were different. Some were kind, and some were not. But I learned a lot in the short time I spent with them. The most important thing I discovered is that my true destiny has always been a choice." I take a deep breath.

"The choice to be with me or Colton," Nyx says, his voice almost a whisper. I shake my head.

"I don't think I ever truly understood the difference between destiny and fate before. I now know fate is something that was always meant to happen, no matter my actions, while destiny is the path I am meant to follow but can be influenced by choices along the way. Destiny can always change, shaping how you reach your fated outcome," I explain, my voice steady. Nyx nods, urging me to continue.

"I saw a future with you, Nyx. We could rule over Egunia together, have children, and live a happy, fulfilling life. That is a choice I could make, but it wouldn't change my fate. It would only delay it," I tell him, my voice tinged with sorrow. Nyx sits up straighter, his eyes narrowing in concern.

"What is your fate then, if not to be with me?" he asks, his voice trembling slightly. I swallow hard, trying to rein in my emotions.

"You are right about one thing. You are the beacon of light your father spoke of, and I am the dark sorceress he predicted. But he didn't have the whole picture. If I chose to be with you and rule over Egunia, you would help me stay true to myself. I don't doubt that you would keep the darkness at bay. But my fate is to embrace it," I say. Nyx stands, starting to pace in front of me, making it harder to say the next part.

"My fated mate is Colton, and my fate is to be the ruler of the underworld. I am the Dark Sovereign, the Empress of Darkness—however you want to say it, they all mean the same thing. I am the queen of Hell, and that is my fate." Having finally spit it out, I get to my feet and standing in front of him so he sees me, hears me.

"The queen of Zomea..." he starts, but I cut him off.

"No, Zomea is a realm of second chances. It's a realm between life and the afterlife. What lies beyond the gates is the true underworld. What lies beyond the gates is where souls go in the end. What lies beyond the gates is hell," I tell him, my voice steady and resolute. He freezes in place, the weight of what I'm saying sinking in.

"That's why the darkness has been spreading? The demons multiplying but not attacking you outright?" Nyx asks, beginning to pace again, running his hands over his face.

"Yes, and the darkness would continue to spread if I stay here. The demons, the monsters, have all been after me all along—not to directly harm me but to drag me down to where I belong. Anyone getting in the way has been hurt or killed. Those deaths are all on me." I don't bother trying to stop his pacing. Instead, I move to the other side of him and sit on the edge of the bed.

"What about the other dark Sorcerers in history? Why you? Why is this your fate?" His voice starts to rise, frustration mounting.

"There hasn't been a proper ruler of the underworld in a very long time. Those before me with this fate didn't fulfill it for various reasons. I don't have all the answers, and I won't pretend that I do. But I know the souls are restless. Evil has been seeping into Zomea, Eguina, and beyond because there has been no ruler to keep it in check."

I take a deep breath, trying to steady myself. "I need to accept my fate and embrace it now so I can bring about change. I will embrace my dark power, but I will rule from a place of wanting to do good. I will keep the evil at bay, protect the souls, punish those who deserve it, and bring peace to those who have suffered."

I pause, taking a deep breath. "I've always had a deep empathy for all creatures, something I didn't fully understand until now. There are dark parts of me, and with this immense power, I sometimes feel a pull to use it for harm. But it's about balance. I was chosen for this because of my empathy and my ability to balance light and dark. I can embrace the darkness without becoming evil."

I look at Nyx, willing him to understand. "This is my fate, Nyx. I have to embrace it to prevent more suffering. I hope you can see why this is the only way."

His eyes furrow.

"I know you love me. I have felt it and still feel it now. There is a connection between us you cannot deny. Why not stay here and be with me? Let's have a family together, and together we can fight the darkness and find a way to change fate," Nyx says, tears welling in his eyes as he stops to stand in front of me, facing me. He reaches out and grasps my chin, coaxing me to meet his eyes.

"I love you, and I came here ready to fight for you and prove to you I am the one you are meant to be with. Don't tell me it's not possible—I can't accept it," he says. For the first time ever, I see tears stream down his face. My heart breaks in my chest, and I fight to maintain control over my own emotions.

"Nyx, of course I love you. A piece of me will always love you. You came into my life when I needed you most, and I learned so much from our time together. You shaped my destiny, helping me grow into who I am today." He lowers to his knees in front of me, and I gently wipe his tears away.

"Trust me, the thought of staying in Eguina and starting a family is tempting. I know we could be happy, but that would be selfish of me. As hard as it is for you to hear, I do love Colton. He is fated to be my king, and together we can bring great change and peace to the underworld. I will not postpone this fate—I cannot. My heart will not allow it." He starts to shake his head, not wanting to accept it, but I see the look of defeat on his face.

"Nyx, when I was beyond the gates, don't think you weren't

heavily on my mind. I spoke with the gods and saw your fate. It's partly why I can leave Eguina in peace." He moves to sit next to me on the bed, finally meeting my gaze again. "You will rule as the sole king of Eguina."

He interrupts, "A fae cannot be the ruler of Cloudrum."

I shake my head, taking his hand in mine. "Why not? Just because it hasn't happened before? You dealt the final blow to Samael and killed the King of Cloudrum. You saved the people and earned their respect by placing your people in charge and rebuilding the Sorcerer Realm. You already earned Rhett's respect, or he wouldn't have joined the battle, and I know Drew cares for you. You are the best person for the job, and I have seen it. You will be the king of Eguina and unite the realms."

He pulls his hand away, glancing out the window. "It means nothing to rule if I have a life of solitude. I already lost the one I loved once. I thought I would never recover after Z. I told myself I never loved her, and I forbid anyone from ever speaking about her because it was too much. I wanted her memory to be lost. Then you came along and made me feel things I thought were gone. You made me love again and healed my heart in ways I never told you."

My chest squeezes as my emotions swell. "That's because I was also a part of your destiny. I was put in your life to help you learn and heal, but I am not your fate. I've seen your fate, Nyx, and I promise you will not be ruling as king alone. You will have love and have a queen by your side. I promise that this is your fate."

His features soften as he takes in everything I'm saying but then his eyes harden again. "Why can't I rule below with you? If this is your purpose, your fate, then let me be a part of it instead of him," he says. I hate having to tell it to him like this, but I know he needs me to be clear. He needs to hear me.

"Nyx, I love you, and I want you to be happy, but don't

misinterpret my love for you as a lack of it for him. I am in love with Colton. I chose him long before it was ever revealed that he is my fated mate, which makes it all the more true. I connect with him on a level I can't explain, and I don't expect you to understand. My soul recognizes his soul, and my heart is already his. He makes me happy, and I want to be a better person every day because I love him that much."

His eyes start to glisten again, but no tears fall as he clears his throat and sits up straighter. "I understand the love you speak of, and I have felt it before. You two are lucky to have each other. As much as I was ready to fight to the end, I see that this is your fate. I can accept it because it's what you need from me right now."

"Thank you. Now, I know I don't deserve it, but I have to ask you one last favor," I say, swallowing uncomfortably. Nyx is still in shock, his body a bit rigid, understandably so, but I don't have time to let this information sink in. The ceremony is set to start soon, and I still have a few loose ends to wrap up.

"What do you need? You know I'll do anything for you, even when you choose my brother over me and tear my heart out of my chest. I'm still here," he says, his lips quirking up on one side.

"Oh, in a funny mood now, huh?" I giggle, the mood in here is anything but funny, but I'm glad he's at least smiling now.

"I don't know exactly what is going to happen when we complete the ceremony, but I do know we will be pulled back to the gates to start our roles in the underworld. The gods told me this can be a bit chaotic, and I don't want anyone getting hurt. I will try to rid Eguina of whatever evil I can on my way out. Please look out for everyone. When the ceremony is over, get everyone inside to safety if needed," I tell him, and he gets to his feet.

"You know I'll always look out for my people. I'll make sure no one gets hurt," he says, and I let out a breath of relief.

There's a knock at the door, and I jump to my feet, ready to answer, when Colton peeks his head in. He studies us for a moment before fully entering and closing the door behind him.

I squeal, "Stop looking at me! You're not supposed to see me in my dress before the ceremony."

He laughs, "Okay, okay, I'll focus on your face. I wanted to check on you and make sure you're not getting cold feet."

I roll my eyes.

"You can look at me, you know," Nyx says, and I'm surprised he's still trying to make jokes given he was in tears moments ago.

"Yeah, that'll be the day," Colton mutters, his gaze still fixed on me with a smirk on his face and big emerald eyes so full of love it makes my heart swoon.

"It's a good thing you came in now, because you should be here for this," Nyx says, turning to face me.

"I want to say something to you, Lyra," Nyx begins, his voice steady and warm. "You brought us back together. From friends to enemies and now to brothers." He gives Colton a playful nudge before continuing. "Sure, we may clash, and yes, part of me may always envy him for winning your heart. But I love you both. He's incredibly lucky to have you, and so am I. You've enriched our lives simply by being part of them. Thank you for being who you are—kind, generous, empathetic, and even stubborn as hell. It's because of you that I not only gained a brother in Colton but also found a best friend in you." As Nyx's sincere words sink in, tears begin to well up in my eyes.

"Oh, look at you, turning us both into saps," Colton says, his smile broadening as he watches a tear slide down my cheek. "Come on, bring it in," he urges, draping an arm around me and beckoning Nyx with the other. We come together in a tight embrace, the three of us. Forever bound not only by the love and heartache we've shared but because we truly are family—and honestly I wouldn't have it any other way.

EPILOGUE

DREW

"It's nice to see you're all healed up from the battle now," I say to Soren as I approach him from behind. He stands on the edge of the forest, taking his shift guarding the bridge.

"Yeah, I'm feeling back to normal. Did you get back from Nighthold?" he asks.

"Yes, I decided to stay for a couple of weeks after the ceremony. I promised Colton I would check in on the Dream Forest and make sure things were settling alright without him," I tell him, stepping around the gaping hole in the ground that is the bridge to Zomea and over to the cliffside.

It's a blue moon tonight, full and magical. I look out across the sea at the reflection and think about him. I don't bring it up to Soren—I know the boy has feelings for me, so it's not something I can discuss with him. But knowing Lyra is where she belongs now means my mate might finally be released and find his way back to me.

All these years of waiting...all these years of meddling without actually meddling, careful to push but not interfere enough to alter destiny.

"How did the ceremony go?" Soren asks, coming to stand beside me.

"It went as well as one could imagine for the queen of Hell," I tell him, and he laughs.

"Hard to believe that innocent, heartbroken girl—lost and unable to properly use magic—is now the queen of the underworld," he says, and I glance over at him.

"Lyra is a very young queen. She had to face many tribulations in a short amount of time. It was the gods' way of preparing her for her final role," I tell him. He nods, kicking a rock off the cliff and watching as it hits the pristinely calm waters below.

So unusual for the water to be so calm on a night like tonight. High tide and a blue moon—I can feel it in the air, almost a static, a light magical hum that something is coming.

"Yeah, Lyra went through a lot for a young girl. No matter what the gods think, I think it was a bit excessive," he says. I wonder, *Who are we to question fate or the gods?*

"I imagine Lyra now has a special place in Hell for the ones who did her wrong...and I imagine Colton probably visits those souls often, if you know what I mean." I give Soren a wicked smile, and we both laugh.

"You're right. I think Aidan is probably getting everything he deserves and more right about now. Samael too, and Euric, the whole lot of them," he says, and I couldn't agree more.

"So after the bonding ceremony, what happened? Did they really vanish into hell?" Soren asks. I think the boy already knows too much for his own good, but I humor him.

"It wasn't as clean-cut as them just vanishing. They left with a bang, one might say." I glance over my shoulder and walk back to the bridge.

"A bang, huh? Well, it was certainly felt all over Eguina. I can't really explain it, but it was like a wave of energy hit us all," he says, bending to look down the hole in front of us. "Things did change rather quickly. After they left this realm, the weather changed, and the destruction that happened during the ceremony magically rebuilt itself." I think back to how wrecked the terrace was after that scene of chaos.

"How did King Onyx take it?" he asks.

I shrug. "He is doing surprisingly well. In fact, I saw him earlier. He's here in Cloudrum, overseeing things in the Sorcerer Realm to make sure the people are happy. He may not have been my favorite brother of the two, but he still has a good heart. He makes some poor choices, like us all," I tell him.

Soren nods. "Yeah, us men, always with the poor decisions, especially when it comes to the women we care about." He laughs and kneels down lower, like he's going to see something in the dark hole before us.

"You know, I don't think you need to guard the bridge anymore. I have a feeling our king and queen of the underworld will have things under control. I'm not worried about anything evil coming out of there," I say as a small hum starts to emanate from the bridge.

"Do you hear that, or am I losing it from being out here for too long?" he asks, and I shake my head.

"You're not losing it."

The ground starts to vibrate, and we both take a step back. A shadow wisp, like one of Lyra's shadowy ribbons, pops out of the hole and hovers right in front of us like a snake eyeballing its prey. It's almost as if she can see us through that shadow, but no, that would be crazy. Then again, I've seen crazier things.

Another wisp pops out, and another, until an entire cloud of inky blackness oozes out of the bridge. A person materializes, her feet hitting the ground right in front of us.

"Who the hell are you?" Soren says, taking a step back.

I recognize her instantly, her features so similar to Lyra's, except her hair falls in a mess of strawberry-blonde waves, and her eyes are a deep brown with golden flecks. Otherwise they could pass for sisters— same full lips and small nose dusted in freckles. I never realized it before but how peculiar it is that they would look so similar to one another.

"Z," I say, studying her for a moment.

"I need to know where to find Nyx," she says. My smile grows as I tell her exactly where I left him earlier tonight. She disappears in an instant, channeling without another word.

"Who the fuck is Z? What happened?" Soren says beside me, bewildered.

I turn to face him, a knowing smile playing on my lips. "What kind of queen would Lyra be if she didn't make sure both her kings got their happily ever afters?" I revel in the miraculousness of it all then add with a wink, "After all, every story deserves a perfect ending."

IN LOVING MEMORY OF MISCHKA

Ashley R. O'Donovan is an author of fantasy romance born and raised in Monterey, California, Ashley loves spending time with her friends and family, and when she's not writing, you can almost always find her cuddled up with one of her dogs reading a book, or catching the latest horror movie with her husband.

If you enjoyed this book, please consider leaving a review on Amazon and keeping in touch with Ashley on social media. She loves hearing from readers and is exciting to share more of her stories with the world.

***

For more books and updates:
www.AuthorARO.com

Printed in Dunstable, United Kingdom